The item should be returned or renewed by the last date stamped below.

Dylid dychwelyd neu adnewyddu'r eitem erbyn y dyddiad olaf sydd wedi'i stampio isod

CENTRAL

1 9 MAR 2022

To renew visit / Adnewyddwch ar
www.newport.gov.uk/libraries

Perfume Paradiso

'What a beautifully written book. You are transported ~ ~ ~ time capsule of scents, that are carefully described ~ ~ ~ ge. I ~ ~ Charlotte trying to research and create her ideal exquisite fragrances. As a perfumer, I found some similarities between myself and the main character . . . It's not always an easy path but it's always amplified by the fantasy world of scents one creates on the journey to success. I recommend this exciting and romantic story to everyone who wants to dive into the world of artistic creations of perfumes. The question is – will you follow the notes your head loves or the ones that your heart prefers?'   – AZZI GLASSER, *Perfume Designer*

'A beautiful, fast-paced summer romance that makes you laugh and warms your heart . . . Allow Janey Jones to whip you up and whisk you away to Italy for one week, enjoy the sun and enjoy the happy moments.'   – @THE.BOOKREADER

'A lovely summer romance set in Italy, complete with lavender fields and infuriating but handsome men . . . this slice of escapism is delightful.'   – RAMBLING MADS

'The captivating backdrop of the Italian countryside makes *Perfume Paradiso* a summer vacation you never want to end!'   – @MRSHIBLEREADS

'I absolutely adored this book! I could just picture myself sat beside the pool at the Rossini Hotel sipping frizzante.'   – @A_GIRL_WHO_LOVES_TO_READ

The Secret Life of Lucy Lovecake

'Like a perfect glass of Buck's Fizz: bubbly, effervescent with a cool, sharp tang. I loved it.'   – SHAZ'S BOOK BLOG

'I have NEVER read a book as quirky, fun, mischievous and darn right fabulous.'   – THE WRITING GARNET

'That delicious cover is just the icing on the cake for the incredible feel-good vibe that fizzes throughout. Its flirtatious charm tells the tale of the highs, lows and romantic woes of a budding debut author – what a little cracker of a book this is! 5/5.'

– LITTLE BOOKNESS LANE

'The perfect read for fiction fans everywhere. With scrumptious cakes, sexy lingerie, and characters that feel like your best friends, I completely fell in love with this story! 5/5.'   – BOOKS OF ALL KINDS

'Oozes charm and appeal . . . best of all it's full of optimism and the idea that you can take hold of the reins of life, give them a good pull and decide where you want to go.'   – THE QUIET KNITTER

'If you like cakes, books, and romance, you should definitely give this book a read!'   – A DAYDREAMER'S THOUGHTS

'I can't remember the last time a book left me with such a good feeling.'   – WRITER IN A WHEELCHAIR

'I truly adored this novel, and for me, who doesn't usually "do" romance and chick-lit, it was a fabulous day's read. It left me with a feel-good feeling and a big smile.'   – TRACY SHEPHARD BOOKS

Perfume
Paradiso

JANEY JONES

BLACK & WHITE PUBLISHING

First published 2020
by Black & White Publishing Ltd
Nautical House, 104 Commercial Street
Edinburgh, EH6 6NF

1 3 5 7 9 10 8 6 4 2   20 21 22 23

ISBN: 978 1 78530 249 7

A CIP catalogue record for this book is available from the British Library.

Typeset by Iolaire, Newtonmore
Printed and bound by CPI Group (UK) Ltd, Croydon, CR0 4YY

In loving memory of
Natalie Horsburgh

1

New York in April

Sipping frizzante from an ice-frosted flute, looking out over the Manhattan skyline, I drank in the perfect moment. The deal I'd just struck was life-changing. Triumphant, I considered my situation. Executives from global cosmetics giant, Florinda, were buying my successful artisan perfume brand, Damselle. My personal wealth would soar. The Damselle brand would grow from its humble London roots into a worldwide name. An evergreen classic, they said. And I would get to live and work in New York City for at least two years while the brand transition took place. I did cartwheels in my head. Life had never felt better. My years of workaholic loneliness and sadness, and yes, my weirdness, wouldn't be in vain. If only my parents were alive to see how well I'd done. I knew they'd worried about their strange little girl, who preferred to draw wildflowers and make perfumed potions in old scent bottles rather than play with toys. I swallowed back a sob. It seemed inconceivable they would never know about this moment of fulfilment.

But, swiftly, I dismissed my nostalgic thoughts. They were futile. Once I was living in New York, my new life would begin. I would do yoga, start barre classes, sail off Cape Cod in a cute wooden yacht in summer, walk through Central Park in fur-lined boots in the snow. I would meet friends for deli brunches, eat plant-based lunches in Benito's roof garden, cook exotic suppers in my loft kitchen with its herb-filled balcony. Maybe, just maybe, I'd even fall in love. This was the defining moment of my life. I'd had it with eighteen-hour days, and with finding those last ounces of patience and energy to seal deals and negotiate terms with incompetent suppliers. I wanted to be happy. To live a bit. I wanted to be alive, and peaceful and excited and free.

Towards the end of that New York meeting, the Florinda acquisitions manager, immaculate Bryony Forbes, had brought up the subject of lavender, explaining that I had to make a choice before signing.

'A choice?' I said, a little alarmed. It'd seemed like everything was already agreed.

'Don't look so worried,' she assured me. 'It's just that we don't like the lavender running costs in the current business model, Charlotte,' she said. 'Who would? Skews our plans, lowers our profit considerably. So, the long and the short, two options for you to consider. We can either use synthetic lavender oil – which many of our rivals do. And we don't see it as cheating – it does take pressure off Mother Earth, no?'

My face contorted in disapproval. Fake oils? Yes, it saves on intensive flower farming, but who knows how harmful they might be?

'Or,' she continued. 'You could source a lavender farm so

we can produce the essential oil "in-house" from our own harvests.'

My heart leapt. A lavender farm! Ideal! But Bryony was still speaking.

'We think a smallholding could be a neat way of having a very on-brand and ethical production system. A talking point. The accountants have studied a similar model at Bonnie Elridge Cosmetics, who started growing their own flowers for their Peony range. Our marketing team are all over the idea; seriously, they love it! Our own lavender farm! So cute. We would buy a smallholding as part of the overall deal. Capped at $350,000. What do you say?'

I was *breathless* with excitement. 'I love this!' I said. 'But how would it work? Where would it be?'

'You would have to find the perfect place within that budget, ideally in mainland Europe, so we can have this fragrance made at our plant near Grasse. You'd secure the purchase through your Damselle company, then we would step in with the cash and the contract on the day of transfer. But there's no time to waste. Thoughts?'

I didn't hesitate for a second.

'I'll find us a lavender farm,' I said. Synthetic oil was unthinkable for my Damselle brand ideals. I was determined to prove natural oils could work in a commercial marketplace. 'I'll fix it by August. You have my word. I'll get right on it.'

It was a big promise, but I'd done tougher things along the way. I wasn't too stressed about it. I wasn't even paying for it. Hell, it would be fun to check out lavender farms across Europe. I couldn't wait.

'I like your style,' said Bryony. 'We figured you'd go for

that option. Can you give me a fortnightly progress update? We'd need the paperwork completed in July for a September deal. We can't let this slip away from us. Our schedules are pretty much unmovable once they're in place.'

'I don't want to miss this chance.'

'Who would?'

'Thank you for giving me the choice,' I said, meaning every word. 'I'll stay in touch about the lavender farm. I'll ask my assistant, Lara, to get onto it straight away. We'll check out Provence first of all. And, there are some lavender fields in the UK...'

'No, sorry, we want mainland Europe. The UK perfume scene isn't as strong.'

'Okay, got it.'

'Excellent.' Bryony nodded. 'We will produce Damselle in the south of France then air-freight to our global distribution points.'

'Wouldn't shipping be more environmentally sound?' I asked.

She smiled. 'We've got it under control.'

I'd struggled with the carbon footprint of Damselle, but I wasn't about to get into the small details of their environmental policy. I was relinquishing control. I had to accept that.

'And, Charlotte,' said Bryony. 'If you'd like help in finding a house in Manhattan, we can have our relocations manager call you.'

'Wow, thank you. That would be helpful. I wouldn't know where to start.'

'It's not an issue. I'll message Naomi right now. Her fees are very modest.'

She tapped on her laptop. 'That's that done.' She stood up. 'The lawyers and accountants can deal with the rest.'

We faced one another and shook hands. I admired her style. Smart business dress, invisible make-up, an immaculate blow-dry.

'I can't wait to move to New York,' I said. 'I've always wanted to live here.'

She nodded absently as she got back to her emails. 'Yeah, great, stay in touch.' She was gone. Onto the next issue. The next takeover.

As I was leaving the ninth floor Florinda office, the broad-shouldered finance director, Cooper Dean, a very easy-on-the-eye cross between James Bond and James Dean, waved me towards him. I tried not to bound over like a puppy.

'Charlotte,' he said, leaning forward enough for his citrusy John Varvatos scent to lap over me tantalisingly, 'congratulations on the deal. Impressive. We must do a celebratory dinner as soon as you get here in September? What do you say?'

'Oh, I think my diary is already full up to Christmas,' I said. 'Sorry.'

He looked at me, askance.

'Kidding!' I said. 'That would be great.'

He didn't even smile. Cooper Dean. For some reason, he got into my head.

*

As I strode along Park Avenue, dizzy with frizzante, elated by success, buzzing with Cooper Dean's offer of dinner – was it dinner with him or the wider company? – I wondered if I would ever again feel so jubilant. A perfect day. The result of spending my mid-twenties having no fun at all. Surely I deserved a perfect moment after all that omission of joy.

And yet I knew the one nagging thing about perfection is this: it's always short-lived.

2

Montecastello

I didn't want to spend more than a week or two in the north of Italy. I arrived there in early July and, much as I loved Italy, it seemed like a distraction from my main goal. My head was filled with thoughts of the new life which awaited me in the Upper West Side house I'd just signed a lease on. The place where Cooper Dean would come for dinner. Maybe stay the night, who knew? But I'd have to stay in Italy until the lavender farm deal was sorted, using a Venetian lawyer called Ariana Pisani, recommended by my usual London firm. We had located the perfect lavender smallholding – Lavandula – about an hour from Venice. Lara and I had found it by accident, just when we were getting worried about the prices in Provence, which all seemed to be beyond our budget. And, after negotiating a complex perfume deal with a Milanese designer a couple of years before, my spoken Italian was better than my French.

Following a smooth flight into Marco Polo from London, I travelled by water taxi into the city, on a wide ribbon of rippling blue-green water, edged with ochre and terracotta buildings, their firmly closed Venetian shutters guarding a thousand secrets from Casanova to Canaletto. I was transfixed! It was fiendishly hot as I boarded a train, bound for the countryside. The journey was uneventful, until the last ten minutes. A tall, glamorous young woman approached me. Striking, with glossy curls and berry-red lips.

'Do you mind if I sit here?' she asked. She leaned in to whisper. 'I've had enough of the chauvinistic bragging of the guys I'm stuck with.' She threw her glance down the carriage where a group of businessmen were braying among each other.

'Not at all.' I moved my handbag.

'I'm Allegra Capaldi,' she said.

'Charlotte Alexander.'

'How nice to meet you. You sound British?'

'That's because I am.' I smiled at her.

'I love London. Do you live in London? You look like you do.'

'Yes. I'm not London's biggest fan, I must say. But it's essential for my business.'

'I'm originally from Rome,' she said. 'Another big bad city. Where everybody gathers to do deals, right?'

I saw that the next stop was Montecastello, so I excused myself, got my case and wished her all the best with the rest of her journey.

'I hope you enjoy your stay in Italy,' she said.

*

Getting off at the romantic little station in Montecastello, I was instantly charmed by its old-fashioned appeal – the polished wooden booths and vintage tiles made it seem like I'd stepped back in time. Even so, small rural towns were not for me. I already knew this. But the farm I wanted to buy was on the edge of this town, and we'd picked a grand-looking hotel, the Rossini, on the adjoining vineyard estate. Lara had thought of everything. 'You can walk on pathways from the Rossini to Lavandula,' she said. 'And the hotel looks gorgeous. It's a villa which was the home of the famous Rossini family until the First World War – they still own it, as a hotel. And Bryony is happy with the room rates – she's paying!'

I was blessed with Lara. She'd been at my side since year two of the business, and saw to all the detail. The small details and the big details. In fact, everything. I'd never have succeeded without her. She was the only person I'd take criticism from . . .

It was *riposo* time in Montecastello that Wednesday afternoon when I emerged from the station. All was quiet. How was I going to get to the hotel? There wasn't a cab in sight. My phone told me it was just a seven-minute walk, so I decided to go on foot. My case on wheels posed no problem, although my wedge sandals were another matter. I was pretty pleased with my choice of a white shift dress, as the early afternoon sun was blisteringly hot.

As I walked along the almost deserted main street, a sleepy silence surrounded me. Montecastello dozed, but it did look like a very charming town, with shops boasting flowers, cheeses, honey and antique books. The quaint town hall with its clock-tower stood behind a town square. An ice cream parlour called Gloria's teased with its promise of twenty-five flavours. A wine shop had one word above its window: Rossini. I admit, I was

9

mildly excited about being in the town where this most delicious fizz is made. I imagined Montecastello bustled in the mornings and late afternoons, but for now, there was not a whisper.

Until, that is, I heard the sound of a truck trundling noisily over the cobbles. I glanced over my shoulder to see a green tractor and trailer bouncing towards me like a giant grass-hopper. It certainly was rural here, no doubt about it. Cute enough, but very countrified, and I'd finished with country places as soon as I got out of my tiny childhood village of Ambler when we'd moved to London for Dad's job. I'd missed the horses, and my stable buddy, Jonny Kent, but that was all.

The tractor got closer. I looked back again, and although the glinting sun blocked my view of the driver's face, I saw the strong, tanned forearm of a farmer, as he rested his elbow on the door. As he drove by, the tractor bumped over a raised block in the cobbled road and the contents of one of the barrels in the trailer splattered over the side, spraying through the air and HELP! spotting my white dress with a thousand little pink dots. Baptism by rosé wine. No!

You'd think the farmer would be apologetic, but, no. He just raised a hand by way of a surly, 'Oops, sorry,' his heavily bearded face unmoved, and then he carried on, leaving me furiously messed up on the pavement. I was completely blind-sided. And now my dress looked like a total disaster! I took my rage out on the pavement, pounding along the cobbled surface crossly, planning what I'd change into at the hotel, and then... Goddammit! OW!

Caught between two cobbles, I lost my footing and, in painful slow-motion, twisted my left ankle as I went over on it. The damned wedge heels. It was e-x-c-r-u-c-i-a-t-ing.

Nauseous with pain, I had to stop, telling myself it would soon pass. I took deep breaths as I rested by the doorway of a bakery. Sadly, the pain only intensified. I tried to walk, but my ankle collapsed under me. I couldn't believe the agony. I took my shoes off, but still couldn't walk, and the burning heat of the pavement cobbles didn't help. The world really was against me!

It was one of those moments when I wished my mother was still alive so I could call her. She always advised taking tiny steps forward. I couldn't even do that! I was trying to decide what to do when, confusingly, I heard the tractor getting closer again – making its way back to me from the opposite direction. *Great*, the return of the rude farmer. I was embarrassed by my foolishness and the last thing I wanted was his pity. I tried to make some progress along the pavement as he approached, but barefoot and in agony, it was hopeless.

He rolled the tractor – gently – to a stop by the kerb. His face was clear to see now; handsome perhaps, under a beard, brow smeared by a morning's work, framed by unkempt dark hair. He looked irritated, so why he'd turned back to assist was beyond me.

'Do you need help?' he asked, in Italian. Impatient voice. Glum expression. Inexplicably annoying demeanour.

'No, thank you. I'll manage,' I replied, curtly, in Italian. I then muttered under my breath, in English, 'Stupid country bumpkin.'

'I came back to give you a lift.' This time he used near perfect English and glowered furiously. I guessed he'd heard my childishly rude comment.

'I'd rather not,' I said, eyeing the one seat in the tractor.

'Okay. I watch you walk, then I go,' he said. This sounded like an order. God, he was bossy, too.

I gathered all my strength, trying to take a step forward, but as my left foot hit the ground, I couldn't stop an agonised cry as my ankle gave way. I felt like such a fool, but I knew I wasn't going to make it on foot.

'I will lift you,' he said, jumping down and striding towards me.

First, he promptly lifted my case onto the trailer.

'My good case,' I protested. 'It will get all sticky.'

'Sticky or stay here?' he said.

I was in an impossible fix. 'Sticky,' I conceded.

Next, he gathered me up and hoisted me across his shoulder. I was mortified. My dress was not the longest. I could tell that my thighs were on show. How had my arrival in Montecastello deteriorated to this situation of deeply chaotic shame so quickly?

'Where to?' he asked.

'The Rossini,' I mumbled into his shoulder, engulfed by the smell of manual labour, Italian cigarettes and spiced soap.

Not a flicker from him.

'You know it?' I asked.

'Yes, I know it.'

He lifted me onto the trailer, offering me a sack to sit on.

I gathered all the dignity I could as I slumped into a pile of grapes while sitting on the sack.

He looked at me with what might have been amusement. I pulled my dress down over my thighs.

'Those legs are too white for a white dress,' he observed.

I was speechless.

3

The Rossini

I lay back in the trailer, designer dress splattered with rosé wine, ankle swelling like a ripe peach, white thighs on view, a few salty tears tumbling down my hot rosy cheeks. We bumped along the old cobbled street, every bump underscoring my self-pity. I couldn't help but steal a glance at the farmer's powerful shoulders as he drove, and his wild dark hair, skimming the collar of his cotton shirt. I didn't meet men like that in London. Men in London know how to treat women, I decided. Even though I'd never met one who treated me in a way I liked. At one point I locked gaze with his dark brown eyes in his side mirror, and I shot him a death look then glanced away. I thought he laughed but I couldn't be sure.

It was all his fault. If he hadn't messed up my dress with his careless driving, none of this would have happened. For him to then act all heroic! And comment on the colour of my skin! And laugh at me!

Thankfully, it wasn't far to the Rossini. After the main street, we turned right onto a private road, lined with cypress trees, and followed it for about half a mile, and there it was. Wow. An elegant stone villa with ornate pillars, balconies and a striped awning protecting an all-round terrace. We drove onto a road in front of the hotel, encircling a cherubic fountain. At the entrance to the hotel, the farmer stopped the tractor dead, causing me to lurch forward.

'Add whiplash to my woes,' I mumbled. 'Why don't you?'

'You speaking to me?' he said.

'No, to myself,' I clarified.

He jumped down and motioned with his hand that I should stay put, acting like a policeman stopping traffic.

'Okay, Supercop,' I muttered, 'I'm going nowhere.'

I gritted my teeth, unsure if anger or indignity would destroy me first.

As he was away for a few minutes, I surveyed my ankle. It had now exceeded ripe peach and was more cantaloupe melon. I poked it. Vile! It had a swollen, jelly-ish feel to it. I distracted myself by admiring the tidy scented gardens around the hotel, and noticed a gardener with a wheelbarrow, hard at work trimming a box hedge, sweat pouring from his brow. He smiled at me, giving a mini-salute. God knows what he thought of me arriving at this smart hotel by farm trailer. But he looked kind so I smiled and waved back.

My tractor driver, whose attitudes seemed to herald from circa 1954, was now coming back, chatting to an older man, whose thatch of white hair framed a careworn but tender face. This turned out to be Umberto, the hotelier. He was distinguished but not haughty. My heart leapt for a moment; he was so like Grandpa Alexander.

'Hello, hello!' cried Umberto warmly. 'We were expecting

you, Miss Alexander. What's this I am hearing about your injury? Alessio here says your ankle is the size of a pumpkin!'

A pumpkin, is it?

'It's a little inflamed,' I admitted, unable to stop myself shooting this Alessio the side eye from hell.

Umberto came to the back of the trailer, putting on a pair of half-moon spectacles taken from his waistcoat pocket.

'Oh no!' he said, coming up close. 'That's *horrible*.'

I gulped. I had always rated my ankles; this was a devastating turn of events.

'Alessio will carry you inside. He's stronger than I am these days.'

No, please not another lift from Farm Boy. It was too much to bear. I let out a sob of despair.

'Unless you want to ride in my wheelbarrow?' called the gardener good-naturedly, from the box hedge.

I blushed, but laughed.

'I think,' said the farmer, 'there is a wheelchair in one of the sheds, left over from the war ...'

Impossible! I reluctantly accepted the farmer's lift, longing for my ordeal to come to an end.

Inside, Alessio deposited me at Reception, on a white sofa, like a delivery of rather bashed grapes. Even when he'd gone, I could smell his scent. From where I lay, I could see out to the impossibly beautiful pool terrace to the rear of the hotel. This place was a slice of paradise. At least it would have been, had I been mobile. Umberto then organised an icepack which felt *heavenly*. A boy took my bags to my room, the Botticelli. I knew from Lara that all the rooms were named after famous artists. Meanwhile, my check-in was completed by fountain pen. Things were done in the old way at the Rossini. Umberto and Alessio chatted companionably at the desk, talking in fast, hushed Italian so I hardly picked it up. But I did hear the word 'Lavandula' whispered, which piqued my interest. It was clear they knew each other well. No doubt Alessio worked on the vineyard estate and was well known to the Rossinis.

I admired the hotel's interior. An elegant, pillared entrance hall, decorated with fine *objets d'art*, and a square antique desk in the centre. It all looked more like the home of a low-key count than a hotel, with trompe l'oeil panels on the walls and woven silk rugs on the marble floor. There was no signage anywhere, which added to the impression of a private home.

Before he left, Alessio offered a curt goodbye.

'Thank you for helping me,' I said.

He shrugged. 'It's nothing.'

No, really, this whole thing is *not* nothing, I thought, but I bit my lip. It's all your fault.

I could only hope that all the locals were not as gruff and arrogant as this man.

4

The Fight

Indeed, Umberto Rossini, by contrast, was a delightful, courteous man. He asked if I was hungry.

'Yes, a little, actually,' I said, suddenly ravenous now that I'd reached a place of safety and comfort.

'We serve on the pool terrace all day. Salads, cold meats, olives, peaches, cheeses, breads. Cakes and pastries. A light pasta. Once you settle in, we can bring you a selection. How does that sound?'

'Sounds perfect, thank you. I'll just get myself organised first, if that's okay?'

'Sure. And, of course, the family frizzante is always available,' he said. 'Breakfast runs from seven to eleven. Dinner is served between eight and ten. But we're relaxed. We want you to relax.'

'Lovely, thank you! This is such a beautiful place.'

A quick internet search as I reclined on the white sofa had revealed the Rossini family owned vineyards on every patch of land in the region. Beyond the pool terrace, I could see the endless rows of vines and medieval turrets of the main Rossini vineyard building in the middle distance. According to my search, it had originally been a monastery.

There was a lot more I wanted to know about this place, but I longed to wash, change and rest before eating, so began to make my way to the stairs, taking tiny steps. The ice pack had helped a lot. However, I needed to rest halfway up, and as I turned to look at the view from a side alcove window on the broad stairway, I saw that a line of pointed cypress trees edged a path leading to an ornamental lake. I knew that the smaller estate of Lavandula was adjacent to the Rossini estate and, as I idly wondered which way it was to Lavandula, I caught sight of an unfolding scene which made my jaw drop.

What's happening out there? I thought, not quite believing my eyes.

Two men were arguing, almost fighting, behind one of the trees, their backs to me. I winced. I hadn't expected to see this in such an idyllic spot. They both raised their fists as if about to box. It was when they began to circle each other that I recognised one of them. Could it be true? It was the tractor man, Alessio.

'I can't believe he's in a fight!' I exclaimed to myself, shuffling right over to the window for a better look. What had the other man done to anger him? The guy looked about thirty, but with a high forehead and receding hairline, and a dark, swirling sleeve tattoo on his right arm. As the two men began to throw punches, the unknown man stumbled, but regained his footing and lunged forward towards Alessio.

I bet you think no one can see you, I thought, so horrified by the unfolding scene that I forgot I had a sore ankle, and almost fell over. The other man swung a serious blow and even though it wasn't accurate enough for the full force to hit Alessio, he did tumble to the ground momentarily, giving the other man just enough time to run. By the time Alessio regained his footing and started to chase him, he'd got away, heading for the woods.

'Don't you ever come here again!' Alessio hollered after him. 'You'll be sorry if you do.'

What a pair of thugs, I thought, wondering if kindly Umberto realised Alessio could be such a brawler. Right here in the grounds of this charming hotel!

I rarely took an instant dislike to people, but this Alessio was an exception. I hoped he wasn't going to be a regular face round the hotel. His very presence made me want to press on with concluding the sale of Lavandula. But thank goodness I'd soon be far away in New York. The prospect of a civilised, intelligent dinner in the company of Cooper Dean floated into my mind. Now there was a fine man. I couldn't wait.

5

Diana

My room was gorgeously airy and bright, with a high ceiling from which a vintage chandelier shone. Glass doors led out to a large stone balcony, almost like a roof garden, overlooking the terrace and pool, and the estate beyond, all scented by pots of jasmine, geranium and bougainvillea.

I slept soundly on the queen-sized bed for an hour or so. For a moment, when I woke, I didn't know where I was. Then the pain kicked in. And everything came flooding back to me. I actually let out a little scream when I saw the state of my ankle. Hobbling to the marble bathroom, I took a couple of painkillers, bathed in a cold bath, mainly to extinguish the heat of my embarrassment, and changed into a fresh sundress. Convincing myself the ankle was going down a bit, I was distressed when a backless sandal refused to fit on my monstrous elephantine foot. All because of that idiot guy! My lower half was a horrible state, but I made a special effort with my hair, piling it into an interestingly messy updo.

I made my way down to the back terrace in flipping flipflops

– a definite style faux-pas in a country house hotel – choosing a table by the pillared balustrade. Surrounded by perfumed gardens, the turquoise swimming pool rippled invitingly. Sunbeds, tables and chairs were dotted around the pool, between pink scented roses and box shrubs. The outbuildings near the pool were painted in faded yellow ochre, giving a look of ageing elegance.

On the terrace, only one other table was taken that early Wednesday evening, by a red-haired woman, reading peacefully under a parasol. She looked up when she heard me, smiling kindly.

I smiled back.

'Hello!' she said.

'Hi! Isn't this gorgeous?'

'Yes, I love it,' she agreed. 'Are you the girl with the injury?'

'Yes! Word travels fast. Or was it the footwear?'

She glanced down and smiled, then claimed her shoes were not much better – but they clearly were, being chic gladiator sandals over delicate fine-boned feet and slender ankles.

A lot like my old ankles. How I missed them!

'Umberto was worried about you, that's all,' she said. 'He wondered if you might need medical help? He knows a doctor who lives nearby.'

'That's good to know,' I said. 'But I'm going to be okay. Umberto has been so helpful. I think the swelling will go down if I rest it.'

She got up and, lifting her stuff, came over.

'He's a darling, Umberto. May I join you?' she asked.

'Of course, please do. I'd like that.'

'I will organise some food for you. I'm Diana. Diana Roache.'

'And I'm Charlotte Alexander.'

Her calm voice, her softness, her kindness. I was instantly entranced. She was a goddess, so like my mother, and her twin, Aunt Belinda. At the thought of Aunt Belinda, guilt flashed through me. I didn't see as much of her as I should.

'Relax and let me look after you,' she said. 'I'll find Rosa. You must always find Rosa if you want something round here.'

'Rosa. I'll remember that name. I'm famished, actually. Thank you for looking after me.'

'It's our pleasure,' she said.

I noted the 'our', with interest.

'But no wonder you're feeling hungry, poor girl. It's tea time! You'll love the food. And the wine. Wait here.'

She went off, calling, 'Rosa, Rosa? Where are you?'

I sat looking at the gentle hills in the far distance, beyond the vines, outlined so softly they seemed to have been painted against the cobalt sky in smudged watercolour. Perfect place for running, I thought. If you could run. I was starting to panic. Would I ever recover?

The goddess glided back to the table, walking so *smoothly*.

'All sorted,' said Diana, taking her seat, and thoughtfully repositioning the parasol to shade me. 'Shouldn't be long. Rosa is preparing a lovely selection. And Silvana will bring a glass of chilled frizzante.'

'Oh, wonderful. I'm very grateful.'

'It's a friendly estate.' She offered me another chair to put my feet up on, which I did, only too happy to remove the flipflops.

'Poor lamb,' she said. 'It's nice to have you here,' she added. 'Some female company.'

We were quiet for a few moments.

22

'Are you on holiday?' I asked.

'In a manner of speaking. It's more of an extended stay.'

'And is it a good place for that?' I asked.

'Very. Better still, not too many people know about it. But the reason I come is that my son works on the estate. I stay here for a while and see as much of him and his partner, Antonio, as possible.'

'I see. What does he do?'

'He's a scientist in the wine industry.'

'You mean he works for the Rossini group?'

'He does, yes. They're the biggest producers of frizzante in the area,' she explained. 'It's a great job, and he loves the life here.'

'How could you not,' I agreed.

'That's the headquarters of Rossini Frizzante,' she said, pointing beyond the pool. 'And nearby, on the horizon, can you see that castle on the hilltop?'

I followed her hand. 'Yes, I see it.'

'That was the home of the Rossini family before they made this hotel their home.'

I looked back to the rooftops of the turreted frizzante kingdom in the middle distance.

'Looks amazing,' I said. 'As if there might be monks gliding around making mead in there.'

She laughed. 'The Rossinis bought it from monks. But there's not a monastic vibe to the management team these days, I must admit!'

'I'd love to tour that place,' I said.

'And so, what do you do?' she asked, ignoring my comment.

'I make perfume, and I find the chemistry of winemaking interesting too. Both very transformative processes.'

'Perfume! What a lovely career.'

'Yes. I've always loved fragrance. My mother used to spray her blouse with scent and give it to me as a comfort if she had to go away. When I was little, I mean. I grew to love it. That was Mademoiselle.'

'How cute. What's your perfume called? Tell me all about it! The notes, everything!'

'Damselle. Mostly plum and lavender, notes of ylang-ylang and basil. It's been a lot of work. But sales are growing every year. I'm lucky. It's a crowded market.'

'Damselle. Damselle...' She said it over and over. 'How pretty. I love that. Wonderful. I will look out for it.'

'It's quite special – we use natural elements. Unusual these days.'

'Really?'

'Yes, most perfumes contain synthetic oils. There's an argument that it's better for the environment, to use chemicals instead of intensive flower farming –'

'But you are not convinced?'

'Well, I believe I've succeeded because of my commitment to natural oils. If I can develop a sustainable farming model, then I will have a profitable plus planet-friendly brand.'

'Good for you! Where do you sell Damselle?'

'There's a website, and concessions in most stores. You can get it in the larger airports, too.'

'Wow! Congratulations. That's really something to achieve, and at such a young age – you look like you're not yet twenty-one.'

'I wish!'

'I can't wait to try it. I wonder if somewhere in Venice would stock it...?'

'I have some in my bag,' I said, fishing my handbag from under the table.

I passed her the bottle, which in itself was a work of art, like a sweet little plum, with a leaf stopper and lavender design etched on the glass. She exclaimed about its beauty. I was so proud of that bottle. It took months to get it right.

She sprayed Damselle at her pulse points.

I waited for her reaction, holding my breath.

'Charlotte, this is divine! I adore it. I will buy it, for sure. All the notes are there. Of course, the lavender is lovely.'

I knew she was sincere in her response to the perfume. And, while most people did like it, I was always thrilled when someone admired it, because it was so much an extension of my own character.

'Please,' I said. 'Keep that bottle. I brought another.'

'If you're sure? I'd love to,' said Diana. 'What a treat.' She placed it carefully in her bag. 'I will buy something nice for you in return.'

I smiled. She was that sort of person who would take nothing for granted.

'Do you think I *could* take a look at the Rossini place where your son works? I want to make the best of my short stay here.'

But at this, Diana shifted on her seat. 'I'll certainly ask him.' She looked up. 'Ah, Rosa's here with your food. And Silvana has the wine.'

A delicious plate of freshly baked bread, hard and soft cheeses, olives, succulent peaches, grapes and cold-cut meats arrived, along with a chilled bottle of the famous Rossini.

Rosa was very jolly, with a round face and owl-like brown eyes. Everything about her was rounded, in a lovely way.

'Rosa,' said Diana. 'This is Charlotte. She's going to be staying with us for few days. Charlotte, Rosa has worked here for fifteen years. She practically runs the place!'

We exchanged hellos. I saw her eyes linger on my foot, raised on the chair.

'I heard you arrived by tractor,' she said, with a giggle.

'Yes! That's me. After drinking from a barrel of rosé, I was so drunk I couldn't walk!'

'That's what Alessio told us too,' said Rosa with another giggle.

'Him!' I said, a bit too crossly.

'He's wonderful,' said Rosa, clearly admonishing me. 'Time for me to set up for dinner. I look forward to seeing you again soon.'

The food was delicious and Diana chatted as I ate.

'You must love Provence as well, if you are a perfumier?' said Diana.

'I do, that's true. I trained in Grasse.'

'I love Grasse! But I, for one, am delighted you came here for a . . . break?' she said, pouring the wine into two glasses.

I wanted to tell her that I was here to close a deal on Lavandula. But I didn't. Mostly because I sensed she already knew, and the fact she did not say so made me cautious.

6

Market Day

I called the lawyer early on Thursday, expecting to confirm our Friday morning meeting with the vendor. To my disappointment and frustration, her assistant said that the owner of Lavandula, a countess called Gabriella Vinci, wouldn't be available until the following Tuesday, as she was suffering from heatstroke. How odd, I thought. And then I felt defeated, complaining to myself that I'd arrived almost a week sooner than I needed to, and if I hadn't come on that fateful Wednesday, I might never have been splashed by wine and twisted my foot . . . and that I might not have known of the existence of the intolerable Alessio, who had undoubtedly blighted my trip with all his audacity . . .

I called Lara immediately.

'Tuesday?' she said. 'Acht.'

'Yes. Do you think I should fly back to London, then come back again?' I asked, uncharacteristically indecisive.

'I don't know. Seems a bit of a schlep,' she said. 'Why not just work from your hotel, and have a quiet weekend? You could do with a break.'

'We'd have to see if Bryony accepts additional costs. This hotel is top-end.'

'Okay, sure, I'll check that with her. I think she was expecting anything up to three weeks.'

'Three weeks! I'm not sure I can live in the middle of nowhere for three weeks.'

'Don't you like it?'

'It's totally rural,' I said. 'And there's a very annoying vine-yard worker –'

'*What*?'

'Don't ask.'

'You're forever saying you're going to write a book. Make a start?'

'Good idea.'

'So, will you stay?'

'Yes, if Bryony agrees.'

'I'll check for you. And you're not too far from Venice. You could explore –'

'True,' I said, deciding not to go into the boring story of my ankle. It was already becoming too much of a defining feature of the trip. I felt so unathletic compared to Lara – she being an ace tennis player, hockey star and agile gymnast. Me, unable to connect a racquet with a ball or, seemingly, my feet with a cobbled pavement.

'Speak soon, Charlotte.'

Eventually, later on the Thursday, Lara confirmed that I could stay for as long as it took. Bryony thought it was a small price to pay for a sure deal. I was grateful for her generosity, though frustrated by the pointlessness of the next few days. It was too peaceful. I replied to every email in my inbox, scrolled endlessly through Instagram and doodled some sketches for a new fragrance I had in mind, to replace Damselle in my daily preoccupations, after the takeover. I knew I would be side-lined, no matter what they said about it being great that I'd be living in New York. I wanted to make sure my life didn't feel empty after the takeover. I was only twenty-seven. I pushed away thoughts that I was selling out too soon. I would have the capital and resources to do something else. The new fragrance I planned was lighter and fresher than Damselle. Something meadow-fresh, with a fairy feel. I hardly dared to say it, but maybe something more girlish. I hadn't thought of a name yet.

It was noon when boredom struck. I asked myself what I did all day in London. Mostly, I realised, I was taken up with meetings. Without the structure of my office, I didn't amount to much. I was a great big blah. Lara was the one in charge, really.

I decided I might as well try to make the best of it, and enjoy being here. I went out onto the balcony and looked across the estate, seeing that bit of the Rossini empire which had started to fascinate me, and I wondered why Diana had been so cagey about a tour. Odd. I was looking out, contemplating the whole empty day ahead, frustrated that my ankle prevented me from properly exploring, when I decided to take a swim.

I got together my kit and went down to the pool.

There were a couple of guests enjoying the sun. A woman and a man, deep in conversation. I took a nearby sunbed, nested there, then got into the pool. The cool water felt lovely, and I swam for an easy twenty minutes before returning to my sunbed.

As I was combing my hair, I overheard the man talking.

'I love it here, Marthe,' he said. 'I've been coming to the Rossini for twenty years.'

'That's quite a recommendation, Michael!' said Marthe, rubbing sun cream into her arms.

'The hotel is superb, of course,' said Michael. 'And the people. Umberto is a perfect host. And when I think what he's been through in recent times. Remarkable.'

'He's had a hard time?' said Marthe. Idly, I tried to place her accent. Dutch seemed most likely.

'Yes.' At this point, Michael began to whisper. Annoyingly, I could no longer hear what he was saying.

'Poor man!' exclaimed Marthe. 'How he carries on with such worries, I don't know. I don't think I've ever been treated with such kindness in a hotel.'

'Exactly. His professionalism is legendary.'

'And his nephew . . . Who runs the frizzante company?' said Marthe.

'Yes. He's a tower of strength to Umberto. Some have said that he's trying to, you know, "fix the situation".'

'I see,' said Marthe, knowingly, now in on a secret I could only guess at.

'All the money in the world can't fix some *situations*, of course,' said Michael.

'So true.'

They fell silent for a few minutes, Marthe applying more sun cream, and Michael reading a newspaper. Then Michael spoke again.

'Have you been to the Rossini castle, up there on the hill?' he asked.

'No.'

'It's fantastic. I longed to write a medieval novel for weeks after I saw it. Just a shame I'm far too rich and lazy to be bothered with writing anything.'

Marthe didn't laugh, but I did.

They both turned to me.

'Sorry, I couldn't help overhearing,' I said. 'Forgive me.'

'How do you do?' said Michael. 'I'm Michael Goddard, executive sunbed adviser and chief holiday rep for the Rossini.'

We all laughed and introduced ourselves.

'Maybe you can give me some non-sunbed-related advice?' I said.

'I'll try,' said Michael.

'I've got a bit of a wait here in Montecastello. For a few days. I'd like to do something tomorrow,' I said. 'But not over the hills until the swelling on my ankle goes down . . .'

'Oh, okay,' said Michael. 'What day are we on now?'

'Thursday.'

'Ah! Easy. Friday Market! In the town all day tomorrow,' he said. 'Perfect!'

'Market day? Is that worth a trip?' I asked, imagining lace tablecloths, beaded purses, hand-painted tiles and olive oil.

'Yes! It's superb, I assure you. The local honey from the Rossini estate! Spread it on your ankle, and I promise you'll be up that hill by Saturday. I use it for gout. I'm thinking of marketing it as a cure. But I do love to see my friends suffer, so I haven't shared it yet. Those old buggers can come up with a cure of their own.'

He laughed out loud and I thought how I was starting to quite like Michael, cringing though he was.

'Right, I'm up for the market. How do we get there?' I asked.

'They usually lay on cars from here,' said Michael. 'Rosa will know.'

He and Marthe went for a swim as I relaxed back on the sunbed. *Bliss.*

When Rosa came by a bit later with a tray of mojitos for a glamorous group now sitting by the summerhouse, I sat up to say hello.

'Hello,' she said. 'How are you, Miss Alexander?'

'Very well, thanks. Please call me Charlotte. Staying a bit longer than I first thought.'

'Everyone's the same. See the gentleman in the pool over there, Michael Goddard?' She looked his way, raising her voice. 'We've been trying to get rid of him for years.'

'I can hear you,' shouted Michael, chuckling. 'But it's perfectly true, I must admit.'

'Michael said something about a market in town?' I told Rosa.

'Yes, tomorrow in the town square,' she said. 'It's very good.'

At least that was my Friday planned.

I spent the rest of the day getting in and out of the pool, listening to birdsong, dreaming of the novel I might one day write, and eventually chatting more to Michael and Marthe. Such a slow day, but oddly enjoyable.

I did sleep soundly that night, and I woke feeling excited about going to the market and picking up some honey. God, Charlotte, you're thinking like a county bumpkin already, I thought, as I got ready for breakfast, looking forward to seeing Diana.

Over breakfast, Diana told me that a few people were going down to the market at ten o'clock, and that I could easily get a lift in one of the hotel cars.

'Are you coming?' I asked.

'No, not today,' she said. 'I'm going to Venice.'

*

A gang of us met in the car park at ten o'clock. There were three convertible cars, with staff at the wheels, part of the hotel's extraordinary service. I recognised the gardener, now a smart driver! Within seconds we were playfully squabbling and laughing noisily, like an exuberant family on a rare day out. I was the youngest, except for a toddler, Willow, who was a delight. There were endless discussions along the lines of: 'Why doesn't Charlotte sit in the front? Let Elise travel in the biggest car, as it has air-con and she's feeling off-colour. Michael can have a car to himself, as he's so annoying . . .'

It was a miracle that we ever set off in our three-car convoy, tooting and hooting goodbyes to Umberto, Diana and Rosa. The journey into town didn't take long, but I overheard another interesting conversation, this time between the gardener-driver and inquisitive Marthe.

'Have you worked at the Rossini for a while?' she asked.

'Yes. For years.'

'As a driver?'

'I do all sorts of jobs as well as driving,' he replied. 'Gardening. Fencing. I used to look after the stables. But we got rid of the horses when, well, a couple of years ago.'

'The gardens are beautiful,' said Marthe. 'However, I heard there was some sort of fight there the other day?'

'Something like that, yes,' said the driver, hesitant, clearly not wishing to be drawn.

'I wouldn't have expected *fighting* here!'

I completely agree, Marthe, I thought, but said nothing.

'It's a long story,' said the driver. 'But I can't say more.'

'Of course,' said Marthe. 'But I heard it was about *drugs*.' She said the word 'drugs' in a shocked stage whisper.

There was an awkward silence.

'What are you looking to buy at the market?' I asked Marthe.

'I have no idea. I'm just here for the ride,' she said. She then turned her face to mine and whispered: 'Definitely *drugs*.'

We went our own ways at the town square, agreeing to meet for lunch later. The market was just as good as everyone said. The smells! Fresh bread, cakes, herbs, beeswax candles. And the Rossini honey stall! There was a chart explaining how well vineyards and hives co-exist. I bought a small jar, and being the impatient – and regretfully unthinking – sort, I stopped on a step and smeared some on my ankle. Immediately, I was surrounded by wasps. I desperately needed a wash basin to clean my sticky hands and ankle.

As I looked for a café with a washroom, I walked past the Rossini wine stall. It was the largest in the marketplace, with chilled cabinets, almost like a proper shop. There was a bustle around it; queues, people jostling, locals taking away six bottles in a carrier. Almost immediately, I saw the dark-haired Alessio, bossing everyone around behind the stall, but I was glad he didn't spot me. He seemed as self-important and bossy as when I last saw him. And he was unkempt. Wild hair and beard, scruffy jeans and T-shirt as before. Why would anyone put *him* on the stall? I wondered.

7

The Secret Meeting

I was definitely curious about the Rossini family firm. Maybe because I enjoyed the wine so much. If they had once lived in the Rossini hotel as a private home, and had a castle before that, they were obviously quite something. And their frizzante was superb.

I bought a cappuccino in a café on the square, as a courtesy for use of their washroom, where I washed the honey from my hands and ankle, and tidied up my face and hair.

Incredibly, my ankle did feel much better. It was as I left the café, that I saw the back of Alessio heading down a cobbled alleyway, just off the market square. I was sure it was him. He turned to the side and I saw him in profile. Yes, it definitely was him, striding fast, clearly on a mission. Even the way he walked irked me, as if he owned the whole town. I glanced at my watch. An hour until the group lunch at the trattoria. I don't know what I was thinking of, or what possessed me, but I followed him down the alleyway. It was a bit crazy, because if he turned around, he'd have seen me straight away, and then what would I have done? But I wanted confirmation that he really was the kind of man who gets involved in a brawl in the garden of a villa, of all places.

I hung back a little, but saw that he turned left at the end of the alley. I walked down to the end quietly and did the same. I found myself on a narrow back street now, which smelled of baking bread and rich tomato sauce. It was lined with traditional houses, with high-up washing lines strung across the street, various garments dancing in the breeze. There were quite a few people about and, at first, I thought I'd lost sight of Alessio. I picked up speed, as much as my ankle would allow, and spotted him ahead. He was slowing down, so I did the same. He came to a halt in front of a neat, whitewashed church.

'Perhaps he's going to confess his sins,' I thought wryly, as I sidled into a recessed doorway near to where he stood, praying he wouldn't see me.

He moved from foot to foot, then checked his watch. Clearly, he was meeting someone.

He got out his phone and paced around, making calls. I looked down at my phone for a moment, to read a message from Lara, and when I looked back up, he was vanishing into the church, with a long-haired girl just in front of him. Damn. I didn't get a chance to see her properly. But I got the impression she was glamorous or, at least, very svelte. I went for coffee nearby, taking a table by the window. I was sending a reply to Lara when Alessio and the girl came down the street. He had his arm around her, while she rested her head on his shoulder. She was Bambi-limbed with honeyed skin – unlike my too-white skin – and flowing hair. So much for my absurd imagining that I was about to uncover a local crime boss. He was just meeting his girlfriend at lunchtime on market day. But why in a church? For secrecy? Or maybe they were going to get married there. Reluctantly, I had to concede this detail didn't help build up my imaginary gang-boss profile.

I decided to head back to the market. We'd planned our group lunch before the *riposo*. Out on the street, I could see Alessio saying goodbye to the young woman as she got on a scooter. For some reason, I felt an atmosphere of secrecy between them. She whizzed off, and he headed back to the alley. He didn't look joyful. In fact, he looked concerned. I decided to find a different way back up to the square and, after taking the long route, was quite tired when I met my new friends. Luckily, there was no need to talk during lunch. Listening was the thing.

8

The Man on the Terrace

That evening in the bar, I was delighted to report to Michael that the honey definitely had magical properties!

'Told you,' he said. 'It's amazing stuff.'

Michael and Marthe introduced me to some new guests, from California, and I went to bed after midnight, after chatting over frizzante on the terrace.

I passed my weekend lazily at the Rossini: making small talk, reading back copies of Italian *Vogue* and ancient romantic novels on the sunbeds, dipping in the pool, and eating antipasto, washed down with the fizz. I even made some notes for a possible novel. I decided not to explore the Lavandula farm until my ankle had recovered completely, as I wanted to be able to walk around it. But I was longing to see the haze of lavender fields and the clutch of historic buildings shown on the sale brochure, and I thought I'd be up to it very soon. Certainly before the rescheduled meeting the following Tuesday.

And chatting to Diana and Umberto was the best of it. They always stopped short of asking exactly why I was in town.

Discretion suited me well. I was just passing through and it was best that I didn't go into detail about a big American corporate taking over the sweet lavender farm on the edge of the Rossini estate. It did cross my mind that it was slightly odd that the Rossinis owned everything for miles around, besides that one little farm.

But nothing really troubled me. I'd even started sleeping in a way that was new to me. I realised I hadn't slept so soundly since childhood. In London, over the previous six years, I rarely got to bed before midnight, then I'd re-check all social media, sometimes becoming enraged by a certain comment about Damselle, or some other minor slight. Then I'd wind down by listening to a business podcast, or watching something about the beauty industry on my tablet. I'd enter a fitful sleep, often waking to write things on a pad at the side of my bed. The name of a flower, a contact in Mumbai, a marketing idea... then I'd usually get up at six o'clock, and rely on coffee and beauty products to bring me back to looking more human. I never felt refreshed. But those first few days in Montecastello, my sleep was deep and nourishing. I would read a few pages of a novel, put out the light about half past eleven, and before I knew it, I heard breakfast being laid on the terrace below my window at seven.

On the Sunday morning, I came down for my first swim of the day, feeling elated that my ankle had gone all the way down to resemble a large tomato. To celebrate, I was wearing a red bikini with some espadrilles tied in bows at the ankles. Yes, I had two ankles! And, yes, I appeared to be the favourite new flavour of the local mosquitoes, too.

I'd expected an easy-as-a-Sunday morning atmosphere in

the Rossini but, instead, the hotel was caught up in a frenzy of activity. Deliveries arriving, flowers being arranged, silver being polished, men on ladders hanging fairy lights and speakers on the terrace, vintage chandeliers being tickled with feather dusters. It was all go.

Apparently, they were having a party.

'Oh, fun,' I said, looking into the lavish private dining room off Reception, crammed with antiques and portraits, decorated with streamers and flowers. 'Family gathering?'

'Yes,' said Umberto, dashing off towards his garage with his car keys. 'A birthday. Sorry, Charlotte, catch up later, I must collect my crazy sister from the station. Back soon.'

But, this dining room! I gazed in, admiring every detail.

Glittering glassware, dazzling white tablecloths, glinting silver – the room appeared so inviting like this, instead of its usual hushed darkness. Diana arrived at Reception, looking lovely in a pink swimsuit, covered with a little wrap, and joined me as I peeped in.

'Umberto does these things so well,' she said. 'Doesn't he?'

'He's very impressive.'

'Oh, he is. A perfectionist, but not a control freak.'

'Have you known him long?'

'I've been coming every summer for four years,' she explained. 'Well, summer plus autumn, and sometimes spring.'

I felt like she was only really telling me half of her story – and the unsaid words hung between us as we headed out to the terrace for breakfast.

*

Diana told me more about the area, chatting about how remarkable it was, how two major families still controlled the region, as they had done for centuries.

'Medieval dynasties!' she said.

'I bet they hate each other?'

'They do! They still don't get along at all!' she said. Then, lowering her voice, 'It's the Rossinis versus the Morettis.'

'What do they argue about?' I asked.

'Everything and anything. Land. Money. Power,' said Diana. 'Ownership. The Rossini family is more industrious, and goes back further, but the Moretti family thinks itself superior. Classier. From aristocracy. Educated abroad. They feel entitled.'

'Wow. I can imagine things get complicated where land is concerned.'

'Yes. Like in all countries, large or small, the land, the territory, is what matters most. Feuds about ownership, boundaries, title deeds. Who would have thought that a little pocket of land would matter so much?'

She let that comment hover, as if I was meant to seize it, while she poured coffee from a silver cafetière into two white breakfast cups. Did the 'little pocket' refer to Lavandula?

She looked up and smiled. My instincts were to trust Diana, even though I felt she was talking in loaded sentences at times.

'Is Umberto involved in any of these land feuds?' I asked, recalling that he and Alessio briefly mentioned Lavandula in their conversation at Reception the day I arrived.

'In a way, yes.' She hesitated. 'Indirectly,' she added. 'But it's too long to go into just now,' she said, as she spread primrose-yellow butter onto slices of bread. 'Here, you have this piece.'

I thought she meant she didn't know me well enough yet to go into it, or that she had been asked not to, so I accepted that, asking her instead about places of interest to visit locally. It was a fascinating conversation, centring on the Rossini castle on the hills ahead of us, which dated back to the eleventh century. I wanted to know more. How had they first established power? Through bad deeds or good? But Diana had to go and help Umberto with his sister, Maria, who seemed to be making a fuss on the terrace, dressed in a full-length ballgown and tiara, while Umberto carried a vintage gramophone to the gazebo at the end of the terrace.

'Let's chat later,' said Diana. 'Maria is a little ... disconnected from reality.'

I watched her manage the elderly lady expertly, encouraging her to sit down in the shade of a parasol, and have some tea and fresh fruit. I caught sight of Umberto looking lovingly towards Diana, unnoticed by her. But perhaps she sensed it. Umberto put a record on the gramophone. Some kind of jazz song of heartache and desire, playing very low.

I decided I would find out more about the Rossini castle during my stay. I finished breakfast, then lazed about by the pool before going in for a swim. I noticed that I hadn't checked social media once this weekend, and any messages from Lara were met with one-word replies. She had sent a searching response: 'Is this definitely you, Charlotte?' My London messages were usually tensely tortuous constructions.

Worryingly, I was even bird-spotting, something I had learned from my mother's father, Grandpa Alexander. Plovers, lapwings, gallinules mostly. I borrowed a set of binoculars from Reception. It was when I was peering through these, following the progress of a lapwing over many acres of lush Rossini vineyards, that I first caught sight of the swathe of purple lavender to the far west.

'Oh, my goodness, Lavandula!'

I hovered the binoculars over it. I saw about six fields, maybe more, all shades of purple, blue and mauve. There was a lovely farmhouse at the centre; I recalled it from the brochure. Modest but very attractive with stables and other outbuildings, one with a tiny clock tower.

It was every bit as delightful as I hoped.

I remembered the purpose of my trip and, feeling renewed enthusiasm, couldn't wait for the moment when I could tell Bryony that Lavandula was ours. The New York high life was just around the corner and I got excited all over again.

Meanwhile, unknown to me, Umberto had come down to the poolside, to attach party bunting to the trees.

'Looking at something interesting?' he asked.

'Hmm? Oh, hello. Yes, the lavender fields,' I said.

'Ah, so pretty at this time of year.'

I dreamily watched him attaching the cord of the bunting for a few minutes, then remembered my manners. 'Is there anything I can do to help?' I said, getting up from the sunbed. 'I could take the other end.'

'No, I won't hear of it. You need to recover. You are a guest! Diana is, well, family, practically. She tells me she gets bored if I don't let her help. I hope that is true.'

'I'm sure it is. I must say this is a perfect place. I could get used to it. I'm starting to relax. It's quite worrying.'

'You are welcome to stay for as long as you like. Don't be worried. You need to relax at times,' he said.

'I suppose. But I love to work. You seem to enjoy your work?' I said.

'I enjoy work because it occupies my mind,' he replied.

'I'm the same. A diversion from the demons.'

'Indeed.' He looked wistful, and a bit heartbroken.

I settled back on the sunbed. Poor Umberto, there was obviously something on his mind.

On the other hand, I didn't seem to have much on my mind at all. I hadn't expected to enjoy doing nothing quite so much. I dozed on and off, feeling relaxation seep deep into my bones.

In the late afternoon, I sat reading a novel at a table by the pool, sipping occasionally on a tall drink of lemon on crushed ice. Umberto was right, I decided, about needing to relax. I was starting to enjoy life at the Rossini. Zooming about London for the last six years, stressed to the max, I had no idea that this level of quiet pleasure even existed. When I thought about it, I hadn't been able to engage with a novel for years, let alone think of writing one. I was always reading business manuals, share prices or the life stories of perfumiers and designers. Coco Chanel, Nina Ricci, Yves Saint Laurent, Jo Malone – I enjoyed learning about their business acumen and strategies. But stress had shot my concentration for fiction to pieces. Until now.

I hadn't given my appearance much thought that day; the red bikini was quite boring, or let's say classic, tousled hair caught up in a very messy knot, shades on, no make-up. The ankle wasn't so bad. Who cared? Maybe even my tummy was more rounded from all the eating and lazing, but that didn't bother me either. I wasn't posing, I was just being. I was absorbed in the regency romance I'd found in the hotel lounge. Every word of it evoked a time when men and women occupied different roles, but I was gripped.

Little swims cooled me down, little snacks kept me going, little chats with other guests – Michael, Marthe and their Californian friends – prevented loneliness. I was in that blissed out, otherworldly state that relaxing in intense sunshine often brings.

At about four o'clock, voices on the terrace shattered my immersion in the novel. The chattering voices persisted on the terrace. I heard Diana. I looked up to see her, now immaculate in a floral tea dress, embracing her son, Ed, and then his partner, Antonio. She'd shown me photos of them on her phone, but they were even more handsome in life.

Behind them, lingered a striking but uncomfortable-looking man, hands in pockets, shifting from one foot to another. A well-tailored shirt, classic chinos, loafers and expensive sunshades; he was a like a cut-out from the *Gentleman's Journal*. There was something familiar about him. His dark hair was quite long, worn off his face. Clean shaven. Maybe he was a movie star? Or one of those gorgeous, moody Italian footballers Lara had been besotted with in the office. She'd advised me to look out for one of those guys, ideally one for each of us. I looked again. I did know him, for sure. Was he on a billboard advert for underpants? It was bugging me... Such a handsome face. Such a sexy presence. But who was he?

As I stared at the pages of my book, thinking about that face, it came to me in a slow, incredible, alarming realisation.

I knew him!

9

The Red Bikini

Alessio! The ill-humoured farmer, from the grape trailer on Wednesday? The one who had thrown me over his shoulder twice? The one who I watched fighting in the garden from the alcove window? It *was* him! Incredible. Clean-shaven. All dressed up. I gulped. Why was he here? What was he doing at a Rossini party? Was he really that close to the family? They obviously didn't know what he was really like! And why was he always right in the middle of everything?

I glanced at him. He looked over towards me for a nanosecond. I looked down at my book. I looked back and he had his back to me now. Thank goodness. This was a very unsettling development; that he was here was bad enough, that he looked as sexy as Paul Newman on that boat in Venice was an additional challenge to overcome. That I was feeling like an ugly mess just added to my anxiety.

I re-read one line of the novel over and over again:

'He kissed her deeply, abrupt but tender, and held her so close that she could hear his heartbeat . . .'

I listened in to the terrace chatter as I fake-read.

There were so many voices, so much laughter and cross-chatter. I was getting used to the local dialect and could understand some of what was said. It was someone's thirty-fifth birthday. They were all part of the Rossini family, catching up with news, mostly about family, and work. One cousin had a new baby. Another was engaged. Somebody had built an eco-house across the valley, yet another had a new job. I could hear people saying 'Happy Birthday' over and over, but I didn't like to look up and see who they were addressing. But the voice saying 'thank you' each time had a familiar tone. At first, I couldn't believe it. But I pieced together that it was *his* thirty-fifth birthday. No way. This made no sense.

Umberto had definitely said it was a family party. I don't know why I was so shocked to find Alessio was part of the Rossini family, and so reluctant to believe it. I should have realised, perhaps, from the way that he and Umberto chatted with such ... equality. But, to give myself some excuse, maybe I would not have expected a classy Rossini to scrap in the garden? All of a sudden, questions were swirling in my head. What did he do in the family firm? Besides driving grapes in a tractor? Why was he always looking so furious? And what was the unseemly brawl in the cypress trees all about?

More family members arrived, all dressed beautifully in the Italian way, women in trouser suits and elegant dresses, the men in classic chinos and jackets, though none turned out as fancily as Aunt Maria, all greeting each other affectionately. They seemed like a warm, loving family, all delighted to see each other. Even Alessio was warmly affectionate to his aunts and uncles and cousins. And especially to the little nieces and nephews who demanded of him: 'Do the Dinosaur!' Which involved him roaring and chasing them as they shrieked and whooped.

But maybe they were different when it came to other families. Maybe the fight I'd witnessed had been with a member of the rival family. What had Diana said, the Moretti dynasty? The nemesis of the Rossini clan. Business life had taught me to read into things, to imagine I always knew only half of the truth, so that I was ahead of my opponents. Sometimes I analysed too much. Lara had pointed this out on occasion. Was there any point in overthinking any of this? It was none of my business. I was nothing more than a passing guest in their hotel.

As the clock ticked on, I began to dread getting past everyone to get to my room, but I couldn't sit by the pool much longer. I tried to wait it out, hoping they would all go inside soon enough. But they seemed settled on the terrace, drinks in hand, the buzz of chat unabating. Umberto started playing records again from the gazebo gramophone, mostly old American and Italian love songs this time, as well as Gregory Porter, while more frizzante flowed. I considered various routes back to my room, maybe through a side door? But I'd still have to pass them. I decided they'd never notice me, that I was investing too much importance in myself. I noted that Alessio was no longer on the terrace and this emboldened me to make my move.

Finally, I stood up casually, gathered my belongings and my courage, tied my espadrille ribbons round my ankles and walked nonchalantly to the terrace. Everyone turned to look at me. Oh God. I hadn't meant to cause such a scene. It was, after all, quite a small bikini and I felt naked in comparison to the elegant party-goers. Diana waved and called, 'Hi, Charlotte. Please join us for pre-dinner drinks in a couple of hours or so, if that suits?'

I nodded. 'That sounds good. I'll go and get changed.'

'Such a lovely girl,' I heard her say. 'From London ...'

As I walked through Reception, something stopped me in my tracks. Alessio Rossini stood alone by a pillar, scowling darkly, staring at his phone. I struggled to think of him as part of the dynasty I'd arrived among. I felt so fond of Umberto; I couldn't compute that Alessio was his nephew. I walked towards him, recognising the fresh cedar notes of Acqua di Parma from a foot away. It suited him well.

He glanced up as I walked by. It was as if he couldn't place me. I wasn't the one who'd shaved off a beard!

I decided not to stop, but when I was on the third step of the stairway to my room, he called:

'Ankle looks better.' So, he'd taken note of me.

I didn't look back, but said, 'It is. Thanks.'

He'd said so little and bugged me so much.

The next aim was to get through the evening without crossing paths with him again.

'The sooner you conclude on Lavandula, the better,' I told myself. 'That man's trouble.'

Back in my room, I saw that Lara had messaged to ask how things were.

'Nothing much to report,' I replied, economically.

Just the ankle injury, the 'farmer' who twice gave me a fire-man's lift, who turns out to be central to the Rossini family – and the nagging feeling that Lavandula has a complicated backstory involving local feuding dynasties ...

And the fact that I just might have discovered that I've been working too hard these last six years, and that I *can* relax given the right circumstances. I flopped on my bed feeling completely, deliciously shattered, and slept for a solid hour.

10

The Party

Honestly, I was thrilled to be getting ready for another evening in the Rossini. Maybe I related to the rural element of my Italian stay more than I knew. Country life meant it was worth getting to know people and their stories because faces stayed the same day after day; there wasn't the city's transient feel. I felt as if I was being drawn slowly into an entirely delightful world. There was only one thing – only one person – with the potential to spoil it.

After a cool shower, I applied every smoothing hair product I had, then dried my hair carefully on a big round brush, trying to mimic Marc, my hair guru back in London. While it was setting on big mesh rollers, I put on some low-key make-up, just eyeliner and mascara, peach blush and some gloss. I dressed up a little, in white palazzo pants with a silky black vest. Chandelier earrings? Why not? I managed to fit into some sandals which were no more than a criss-cross of fine silver spaghetti strands on kitten heels. I brushed out my hair. Not too bad. Clutch bag. Spray of Damselle. Ready.

I found that I was shaking when I went downstairs. You expect to feel anonymous in the first few days in a foreign hotel, don't you? But the Rossini was different. From the very first moment, I felt connected to the place and the people. But with Alessio in the house, well, anything could happen. I couldn't say if I was anxious or excited. Let's just say I could easily have ordered dinner in my room, but I didn't.

Umberto and Diana caught sight of me as I arrived at Reception.

'Charlotte!' Diana said. 'You look *absolutely* beautiful.'

'Thank you. And so do you.'

'Oh, this old thing...' The emerald chiffon dress she'd changed into, edged with delicate ivory beading, worked perfectly with her pale freckled skin, glorious red hair and frosted pink lips. Two perfect oyster pearls on her earlobes completed her look.

Diana nudged Umberto, nodding encouragingly at him.

He cleared his throat. 'Charlotte, I've had a thought.'

'Oh?' My eyes darted between him and Diana. They were definitely a couple, I realised.

'Why don't you join us for dinner? Come to the party,' he suggested. 'We've had a cancellation on the guest list. Spare place at the table. That never looks good. You'd be doing us a favour.'

'That's kind, very sweet, but I couldn't do that!' I said, totally surprised. 'It's a family event.'

This was nuts. I was almost dumbstruck. How could I turn up at Alessio's private birthday party? What would he think? Was I being fast-tracked into the inner circle? I mean, had any other hotel guests been asked?

'But Diana would love your company, wouldn't you, my dear?' he pressed, charmingly, as he turned to her.

'Absolutely. My Italian is shaky to say the least. And I get to feeling a little lonely when Umberto is on duty. Ed and Antonio speak such brilliant Italian. Well, Antonio *is* Italian! Please, come and sit next to me, Charlotte. Aunt Maria is going to be to my left! I would be so grateful.'

'Well, I suppose . . ' I said. They did seem sincere and without an agenda and I *was* all dressed up with nowhere to go. That dining room looked so sumptuous, too. 'If you are sure. Thank you. I would love to come.'

'Excellent! It's settled then,' said Umberto, leaving us, when he saw someone with an empty glass.

We both watched him fill the glass from a bottle of chilled Rossini frizzante rosé.

'This is a lovely event,' I said. 'I'm very touched to be included.'

'They're all such nice people,' said Diana. 'Look, sitting by the oval window? That's Nonna! Alessio's grandmother on his mother's side. Everyone adores her.'

'She looks delightful!' I said, admiring the elderly lady, dressed in a white lace blouse with a black skirt, with lustrous waves of white hair styled perfectly on her shoulders.

'She is. It's very sad, about Alessio's parents.'

'Oh?'

'Yes, they both passed away. Poor Nonna, losing her daughter.'

'Oh no, how awful! What happened?' I suddenly realised I'd asked a very personal question and tried to deflect it, 'I mean – I really can relate. My parents are dead, too.'

'I'm so sorry. How incredibly upsetting. A tragedy like that –'

'I know,' I said, wanting to draw our talk of death to a close. 'But, please, tell me more about this tribe. Who's who,' I said, trying to take in the cast of glamorous characters milling around us.

'Umberto's parents had six children, so there are a lot of cousins,' said Diana. 'The next generation. Over there is Alfredo. He's a very successful actor, based in Rome. So handsome, as you can see. Tempted by Hollywood but preferring the European scene. Oh, look, there's Lily. She's written a book on the Rossinis and their history... It's a celebration of the women in the family. Very inspiring. I love the story of Maria Rossini, the opera singer who saved so many Jewish lives in the war. Complicated situation with Lily, though.'

'Really? She sounds delightful. Why complicated?'

'Her mother is a Moretti!'

'Wow! I get it. And next to Lily?' I asked.

'Next to her is Leonardo. He's the same age at Alessio and they squabble for supremacy all the time... They are both sharp businessmen, horsemen, custodians of the family name.'

'Rivals, but loyal as well?'

'Yes, exactly. It's lovely to see them all getting together. It's just a pity that...'

'Yes?' I tilted my head to her.

'Oh nothing. Sorry, I was just thinking aloud.'

She looked sad, but had clearly decided against telling me what was on her mind. I was itching to find out more about Alessio. How could I square the thuggish man in the garden with this seemingly idyllic and esteemed family group?

'What does Alessio do?' I said. 'Apart from driving grapes around. Is he a big part of the family firm?' I asked.

She threw her head back, laughing, showing her beautiful teeth, as if made from exquisite ivory pearls.

'What's so funny?' I said.

'He's the boss!'

I was speechless. '*The* boss?' I stuttered.

'Yes, the head of the Rossini empire. He's grown the frizzante business tenfold in recent years. He's been running it since he was twenty-one. His father was the senior brother, Alessandro, who died tragically, as I mentioned. Alessio's mother died many years before.'

I gulped. 'I didn't realise he was *in charge*.'

'I know. He acts like one of the team. And that's how he likes it. He can do any of the tasks he asks others to do. He gets a lot of respect that way. My Ed thinks the world of him.'

'Does he?'

'Yes. He takes a while to trust. But he's very honourable.'

'It must just be that he doesn't like me,' I murmured.

'But he rescued you, did he not?' said Diana.

'That's true,' I admitted, realising it would be petty at best to mention his appalling bad manners and the horrible fight.

'But please, back to this fascinating family group,' I said, wanting to be reeled in further.

'Let's be glad the Countess has cancelled,' said Diana, in a low voice.

My ears pricked up at this. I knew that Lavandula was owned by Gabriella Vinci, Countess of Veneto; it said so on the brochure. Lara and I had googled her and, my goodness, she was stunning.

'Which Countess?'

'Of Veneto. Gabriella.'

I gulped. 'She was supposed to come?'

'Yes, but . . . she has heatstroke apparently. Acht! She's a pain.'

That was her! The Countess of Veneto, owner of the lavender farm I wanted so badly. She had been invited? Why? What was her connection to Alessio Rossini? I just *knew* that Lavandula had a complicated story. I'd sensed it from the start.

'I've heard of her before,' I said.

'Have you? She can be tricky. But Umberto won't give up on her. He's faithful like that.'

'He's such a lovely man. '

'He is. Here's a story for you.' She winked and lowered her voice, like we were playground gossips. 'She's Lily's mother. A Moretti. She was married to Dante Rossini for a decade or so. A very controversial match. But he was the pilot in a plane crash that killed him. After he died, she quarrelled with the family over a Titian painting she wanted. Umberto insisted she got the painting. He said Dante would have wanted her to have it. Then she married the Count of Veneto a few years ago and now everyone thinks she has more Titians than she could ever enjoy. She's so wealthy, but so vengeful. Still, she's very fond of Umberto. Everyone is. He's always trying to encourage the others get along with her, for Lily's sake. He's patriarchal, I guess. It's not easy, though.'

'I can imagine.' I wanted to ask how the Countess came to own Lavandula, but I didn't think I should. Luckily Diana helped me out.

'Family comes first with Umberto and he can overlook slights and arguments. But some of the others are more – entrenched, shall we say. There's a feud at the moment and I did think it might be awkward if she came.'

'A feud...?'

She paused, as if wondering whether to tell me more. 'Ah well, everyone in these parts knows about it. It's complicated. There's a disagreement about land. Land she *claims* she was left by her husband.' She hesitated. 'I don't want to say too much... I'd love to, Charlotte, but... I'm sorry –'

At that moment, it was apparent Diana knew why I was there. Did they *all* know I was here to buy Lavandula? And was there some reason I shouldn't or couldn't buy it?

The more I heard, the less I understood. I felt a bit uneasy.

'Thank you for being so discreet,' I said. 'And helpful.'

I was now slightly unsettled, but I had committed to the party. Maybe it would be an opportunity to find out more. I found myself being ushered into the private dining room, glass in hand, wondering how on earth I'd ended up at Alessio Rossini's birthday celebrations. I was mortified in case he found it odd that I was there. He might be annoyed. He might think I was a gate-crasher. God, he might throw me out. I saw him in a corner, glowering under a portrait of a man who looked a lot like him, except in fifteenth-century clothing. I braced myself and went over to explain that I'd only come as I'd had my arm twisted.

'First your ankle. Now your arm,' he said, with only the trace of a smile. 'You are very unlucky.'

'Next thing,' I tried to laugh, 'this place is going to twist my mind.'

'It's possible. You should leave as soon as you can.'

'Why, thank you for the warm welcome.'

He shrugged. Why did he dislike me so much when he didn't even know me? Well, the feeling was mutual!

'Anyway,' I continued. 'I'm sorry to be at your party. It was Umberto and Diana's idea. I can easily leave –'

'My uncle does the invitations,' he said, casually.

His tone irked me, but it seemed as if he was saying it was okay to stay – or that he didn't really care either way. It all seemed a bit stupid, as it wasn't as if I wanted to be there anyway. I considered leaving, but thought that would be rude – and baffling – to Umberto and Diana, and awkward as I had to stay at the Rossini for a few more days.

The meal began. I wasn't seated near Alessio, which was something, and we could avoid looking directly at each other. The food was delicious and the first two courses passed without much to report. But as people relaxed, the banter heated up.

Leonardo, the cousin, teased Alessio across the table.

'Why the bad mood?' Leonardo challenged. 'Your girlfriend dumped you?'

Alessio smirked. 'At least I had one to be dumped by.'

Much whooping.

'Hey, so true. My problem is trying to find a girl in the area whose heart you haven't already broken.'

There was wild laughter around the table; even Alessio seemed amused.

I glanced at Diana, who said, 'Alessio has a reputation.'

'I see.'

'A commitment-phobe,' she explained, 'rather than a cad.'

Aunt Maria, seated on the other side of Diana, woke from a little snooze at this moment. 'He's an objectionable boy,' she said, looking at Alessio. 'Handsome, but so surly. He was such a moaner when he was in his pram. When he was a baby, we used him to scare the Morettis.'

This made everyone laugh again and turned the conversation to the Morettis.

'Hey, Lily, I thought your mother was coming?' said Leonardo.

'She has heatstroke,' said Lily, groaning.

'Nothing to do with Lavandula?' pressed Leonardo.

Lily blushed. 'I don't know what you mean.'

And it was clear she really didn't. I was intrigued by this, but Umberto, obviously thinking the conversation was getting too risky, stood up, chinking his glass with an antique butter knife.

'The cake and the toast! Let's celebrate Alessio's birthday with a cake! And raise your glasses!'

A feeling of curiosity whipped up about the cake.

'What kind of cake this time?'

'How many tiers?'

'Let's see the cake!'

'Cake! Yes!'

'Umberto always provides the most splendid cakes,' said Diana, taking the subject change from Umberto and running with it. 'The chef here, Marissa de Luca, makes them. She's quite wonderful.'

'Excellent! I can't wait to taste it.'

A beautiful cake was brought in by Marissa herself, three tiers, decorated with fresh cream and red berries. '*Buon Compleanno, Alessio!*' was piped in dark chocolate and there were shards of bitter chocolate on top. As we sang to Alessio, he raised a flicker of a smile, but it was brief.

Such a miserable, selfish man. Probably a narcissist, I decided. True, the undoubted devotion of his family didn't fit my analysis. However, I mentally glossed over this by telling myself that, of course, everyone pretended to like him. He held the power, didn't he, and the purse?

After the toast and some brief speeches, which were more like in-house jokes between the family, it was time to sample the cake, which was simply scrumptious. I tucked in without a care. So much for counting my ribs as I did in London. As darkness fell, we were informed by Umberto that it was:

'Time for dancing!'

11

A Work of Art

We straggled out to the rear terrace gradually, some people taking a moment to indulge in a cigarette at the front of the hotel first, some of us touching up lipstick in the sumptuous pink powder room. When I got out to the terrace, the sky was dark blue, twinkling with stars. The coloured fairy lights shone along the edge of the terrace. Waiters topped up our champagne flutes with the nectar-like Rossini frizzante. The first song to play on Uncle Umberto's record-player was: the Macarena!

'AlessiO. AlessiO. AlessiO!' The family chanted and clapped.

He looked sheepish as he took a sip of his own frizzante. A smile played on his lips. His aunts took to the dance floor, pulling him with them, then started to move their hips with him! The cousins joined in too, and Lily, I noticed, was a great dancer. She'd obviously perfected the routine. She had a lovely figure, quite curvy, with dewy skin, and lots of dark hair in a shoulder-length bob. She wore vibrant red lipstick which looked incredible with her bright yellow halter-neck dress and red shoes. And she had a joyful, exuberant attitude to match. They were a supremely good-looking family, the Rossinis. And of course, Lily was half Moretti, and although I hadn't seen her mother in real life, I knew from the images Lara and I had found online, that she was also very beautiful.

Alessio took his jacket off and threw it high in the air. It landed in the pool. SPLASH! But he didn't seem to care. Grooving with his aunts at parties was obviously his thing.

After a few more songs and an increasingly entertaining dance display with his aunties and cousin, we all joined in, then Alessio announced, 'I need to fish out my jacket.'

Clearly, he'd decided it was time for a dip in the pool. Before any of us knew what was happening, he'd stripped down to his underwear and was executing a perfect dive into the pool. I heard Umberto sigh lightly as he arranged for a pile of fresh towels to be delivered to the poolside.

'You see, he *can* be good fun,' said Diana.

I couldn't recall saying he wasn't. Diana and I continued to chat on the terrace as a few people bathed in the moonlight.

'Charlotte!' It was Alessio's voice from the pool. 'Are you not swimming?'

'No!' I called back.

'Coward!'

It must have been the frizzante, but I immediately excused myself from Diana and charged down to the pool's edge, where I removed the palazzo pants and slid as elegantly as I could into the water.

Of course, once I was in there, he ignored me completely. 'Who's the coward now?' I said to myself, seething.

To save face, I splashed around with some of the cousins,

who were plotting to hide Alessio's clothes around the garden while he wasn't looking.

I got out of the water before that particular joke kicked in, and as I enveloped myself in a huge fluffy towel, Diana came to chat.

'Fun?' she said while I dried off.

'Yes. I don't know what came over me. Perhaps "coward" is my trigger word.'

'You are certainly no coward,' she said.

'Well, this has proved to be quite an eventful evening,' I said, my skin tingling from the chill of the water.

'Even more fun than usual,' said Diana. 'I think you have a good effect on Alessio.'

I tried not to gawp at her. 'Are you kidding?'

'Not at all, he often leaves much earlier than this,' she said.

'Well, I'm positive I've played no part in him staying. But it's his birthday and I hope he's enjoyed it.'

The younger members of the family were now getting out of the pool, laughing and goading Alessio.

'I bet I know what will happen next,' I said.

When Alessio came out of the pool, I had to avert my eyes from the sight of him in his underwear. Meanwhile, he looked around for towels and his clothes. All had disappeared. The group of cousins giggled as they teased him, 'Go on, Alessio, get dressed. You don't want a chill on your birthday, old man!'

He soon caught on to the joke and started to chase them, calling out, 'I'll get you for this, you little devils!'

There was a lot of shrieking and laughter, and he caught up with Lily and another cousin; while they screamed for mercy he insisted he would tickle them to death, then fling them in the pool.

When he finally found a towel, he came over to where Diana and I were standing.

'Good birthday?' said Diana.

'Yes, I'm enjoying it this year,' he said, turning to me as she glided off to get a drink. 'What about you, Charlotte?' His tone sounded mocking – I got the impression, again, that he didn't really care about my response.

'Yes, thank you. I shouldn't really have been here, but it was very kind of everyone to have me.' I knew I sounded absurdly prissy, but his tousled hair and muscular chest were almost too close for comfort.

'You like what you see?' he said, either smoulderingly or menacingly, I couldn't decide which.

'Sorry?' I gulped.

'Of the area?'

Oh. The *area*.

'Yes.' I tried to gather my wits. 'It's beautiful. I only wish –'

'How long are you staying for?'

'I'm not sure. I might fly home on Friday.'

'I see. And if you don't achieve your objective in a week?'

He knew I had an objective. Obviously. They all did.

'Oh, I will.'

A heaviness hung in the air between us as he stared moodily into the middle distance, in the direction of Lavandula.

'I must go to bed. Thank you, Alessio. And happy birthday.'

With that I decided to leave the party. But as I swung away, he placed a hand on my shoulder and asked to borrow my phone for a moment.

Presuming he'd lost his in the pool antics, I hesitantly handed it over. 'If you want to take photos, it's hopeless . . . I forgot my good camera.'

But he didn't take any photos. A moment later, he passed it back. 'I've saved my number for you,' he said. 'In case you twist the other ankle – or anything else.'

'Thank you.'

I carried on my way, feeling a bit giddy about having his number. But. The first lesson I'd learned in business was: never get too close to your opponents or your partners. And, somehow, I already knew that he was my rival for Lavandula. The details were scarce, but the rivalry was established. Something told me he could block the sale. He evidently had so much power in the area.

I found Diana before I went upstairs.

'Goodnight,' I told her. 'It's time for me to retire – not so gracefully now!'

'Okay.' She smiled warmly at me. 'Hope you had a nice time?'

'I did, thank you. I love it here.'

Just as I was heading inside, Lily came to speak to me, wet hair brushed back, revealing perfectly arched brows.

'Hi,' she said. 'Can I have a chat with you?'

'Yes, of course.'

She looked a bit sheepish. There was a pause.

'I hear you wrote a book,' I said, filling the gap.

'That's right. One published, one on the desk,' she said.

'Congratulations. It's a great achievement to get a book published. I'm in awe! It's something I'd love to do eventually. I'd love to read it.'

'Yes, I'll get you a copy. I'm pretty proud of it. I wanted to write about the amazing women in my family,' she said. 'But I heard you design fragrance. That's even cooler.'

'Ah, thank you. Yes. It was something I always wanted to do.'

'Massive congrats.' She paused again. 'But, you know, I just wanted to say, hi, and that it's nice to meet you.'

'I'm glad you did. I'm having such a lovely time here. I feel so welcome.'

'The Rossinis are a good bunch. But I have so many family gatherings, with the Morettis as well! Awkward!'

'Even so, you're lucky to have such a lot of family members in your life.'

'True.' She moved a bit closer, shifting from foot to foot, pulling at a ring on her fourth finger.

'Is there something on your mind?' I asked.

She nodded, twisting the ring in her slender fingers.

'I'm listening,' I said, as warmly as I could.

She cleared her throat. 'My friend and I are thinking of moving to London for a while. She's looking for a change of scene. And I can work anywhere. Could you give us some tips on where to look for flats? Do you have good contacts? She wants to get a job working with designing wedding flowers, something like that...'

'Sure. I can tell you the best places to live. And I know a few florists. I'll ask my assistant to see what she can find out.'

'Would you really do that? Cool,' she said. 'We'd be so grateful.'

'Okay, well, I'm sure I have one of my cards in my purse.' I fished one out. 'Here. My number's on that. Please, stay in touch and I'll see what I can do.'

'Amazing! See you around.'

*

When I got up to my room, I went out onto my balcony to think things through. What a Sunday it had been. As I looked down to the garden, Alessio Rossini was standing by the pool with a glass of frizzante in his hand. I couldn't help but think he looked like a work of classical art as he stood against the moonlight, deep in thought. As sculpted as a statue by Michelangelo. As I turned to go back inside, I could tell that he had looked up. I swung back towards the garden, and caught his gaze for a fleeting second. Our eyes locked, maybe for the count of three, maybe less. It was impossible to read the expression on his face. I hoped he couldn't see my features clearly.

He was handsome, successful, maybe kind, maybe devious, who knew? I was pretty sure that he knew I had come here on a mission and, for reasons I didn't fully understand, I knew he didn't want me to proceed.

No matter how much I liked life at the Rossini, I sensed trouble ahead with this man. I was determined that nobody was going to stand in the way of me and Lavandula. I had to close that deal so that my new life in New York could begin. Sure, the Rossinis were a good bunch and their parties were fun, but they would never get in the way of my ambitions for my business.

12

The Photograph

Next morning after breakfast, I received the following email from Bryony, which she must have sent Sunday evening her time:

Dear Charlotte

How are you? I hope you are making progress in Montecastello?

I have some news for you. Our team met last week about Damselle and made some good progress. I know you'll love our ideas.

My heart lurched at this point, and then I read on.

Fourteen of us sat round the table and drilled down into the future of the Damselle brand. And we realised that we ADORE the essence of the brand.

But we will, naturally, have to make some small changes to suit our wider development plans and our company profile, which is more international than artisan.

Of course, everything will be done with your approval.
Looking forward to sharing our ideas with you!

Regards
Bryony

At first, I brushed away my feelings of indignation and concern. That all sounded fine. Didn't it?

But moments later, I couldn't help but ask myself if these would be actually *small* changes?

I told myself it was the price to pay for such a lucrative deal. I mean, nothing mattered more than the money, not really. Surely. Maybe. The sooner I got to New York, the sooner I could be better involved in these sorts of things.

I called the Italian lawyer's office to confirm our meeting the next day. I had to get myself back to New York. Urgently.

I was put through to Ariana Pisani's assistant.

'There are some details here about the meeting,' she told me. 'Do you have a pen? You are going to meet tomorrow, Tuesday, at the Villa Veneto, on Casa Doges in central Venice, at noon.'

'Got that. Thank you. I'll be there.'

'Miss Alexander?'

'Yes?'

'It's the residence of the vendor.'

'Right. The Countess will be present then?'

'Of course. Ariana Pisani will meet you just outside.'

'Perfect. Thank you.'

I exhaled slowly. This was a good turn of events for me. If I could agree terms with the Countess directly the next day, who knew, perhaps I could be home by Thursday. Although I felt badly about it, I decided not to tell Diana. I'd only known her for a few days. Discretion seemed the best option. I wanted to keep Alessio in the dark so I could have a deal done before he knew it.

I dashed off an email to Bryony. I didn't respond to the proposed changes to the brand, but simply said that I had an important meeting with the vendor the next day. Another email informed me that Bryony had arranged for an interior designer to contact me regarding the Manhattan house.

'She's very reasonable and I'd say the house needs a little bit of attention. Just a new kitchen, shower room, some rugs and key pieces,' wrote Bryony.

The designer was called Minerva Forbes. Her sister. It was quite unlike me, but I didn't reply to that message from Bryony, or one from Minerva. In fact, I ignored 127 new emails. Something I had never done before, even during my appendicitis, bird flu and carpel tunnel episodes.

Come on, I said to myself, Charlotte, do you want to do this deal and get to New York, or not? And I did. But something had happened to my concentration. I had released the long-suppressed pleasure chemicals in my brain, and I was finding it hard to focus on business.

I had all of Monday ahead of me now. As evidenced by recent dancing and swimming activities, my ankle was pretty much back to normal, perhaps thanks to the honey. What should I do? I could read by the pool, but, no, I wanted to explore. Taking my binoculars out to the terrace, I surveyed the estate. The hills looked manageable, with the outline of the castle emerging at the top. I desperately wanted to see the castle, but maybe it was too far on foot. The castellated Rossini offices fascinated me too, except for the prospect of meeting Alessio Rossini there. But, of course, what I really wanted to do most of all, was walk to Lavandula. The brochure made it look delightful, and it looked lovely through the lens of the binoculars, but would it be the same in reality? I told myself it would be a real plus for the meeting tomorrow if I could talk knowledgeably about the place.

I changed into shorts, a vest-top and trainers, packed a small rucksack with water and sun cream, and went downstairs.

There was nobody around, and I felt I should tell someone my route, just in case the ankle packed in. I looked for Diana on the terrace and by the pool, then in the drawing room, but she wasn't in any of those places.

'If you're looking for Diana, she has gone into town for her Monday book club,' said Rosa.

'Ah, thank you, Rosa. Do you know where Umberto is?'

'Usually he's in his office at this time, doing the delivery invoices. Check there?' she said. 'He won't mind.'

Umberto's office was on a hallway to the left of Reception. I had never been there before. I tiptoed along, in case he was in a meeting or on a call. The door was slightly ajar. At first, I thought I could hear laughing. But as I got closer, I realised it wasn't laughing, but weeping.

I thought perhaps I should turn back, but I was concerned. Who was in there and why were they sobbing?

I took a few hushed steps backwards, then made a fresh, noisier approach, calling, 'Umberto? Hello? Hi! Are you there?'

After a moment, he called back, his voice thick. 'Is that you, Charlotte? Yes, I'm here. Do come in.'

I didn't want him to know I'd heard the sobs, so I kept things breezy as I entered.

'Good morning, Umberto. I just wanted to let you know I'm going for a walk to Lavandula. Can you tell me the best route to take?'

'Ah, that's a lovely walk. You have to go past the lake, on the path to the Rossini Towers, then go right. That path takes you straight into Lavandula. It's less than two kilometres.'

'Brilliant, thank you.' I nodded down at my ankle. 'Can you send out a search party if I'm not back by dark? I think I'll spend a bit of time over there...'

'I will come looking myself. Let me organise a lunch bag for you if you're out for the day.'

'No, really... you're too kind.'

But he was already on the phone to the kitchen.

While he was talking, I noticed a framed photograph lying on his desk. It was of a woman and child, both smiling. It seemed as if the photo was a few years old, but I didn't want to stare, so turned to look instead at a huge map of the entire Rossini estate on the office wall. The Rossini hotel, the Rossini Towers, endless vineyards, woodlands, lakes, a river through the centre, stables, and to the western edge, Lavandula. The size of a postage stamp in comparison to the big parcel of Rossini land, but it still struck me as odd that they didn't own it. Maybe it had been their land in the past...

'Please, have a morning coffee on the terrace and Rosa will bring a nice lunch bag for you,' said Umberto when he came off the phone.

'Thank you. I don't know how I can repay your kindness.'

He smiled. 'It's our pleasure to have you.'

72

I sipped on a glass of iced water on the terrace as I waited for Rosa. I thought about Umberto. I didn't know what had happened to his wife and child. Perhaps he was still mourning? Diana hadn't mentioned it in her stories of the family ... But, with reflection, I realised she had almost mentioned it.

As I looked over at the pool, I remembered Alessio standing by it the night before. Alessio Rossini. The head of the whole Rossini empire. I still struggled to take it in. No wonder he had an air of self-importance around him. I considered the connection with Lavandula. Leonardo had asked Lily if her mother's absence from the party was connected to Lavandula. Which had spooked Umberto. If the Rossinis wanted to buy it, why didn't they? As for how much they knew of my interest, I guessed Lara might have asked how close the hotel was to Lavandula when she booked. It was obvious I wasn't a holiday-maker.

Rosa's arrival with my lunch interrupted my musings, and I set off through the beautiful grounds towards the lavender fields. The heady scent in the air reminded me of how I'd first created Damselle in the last year of my biology degree. I'd always known that plum and ylang-ylang would be in it, but the lavender and basil surprised me, counterbalancing the sweetness with their headier notes. I had worried there were already enough perfumes in the world, and that mine would sink without trace. But I persisted and believed, and hoped and dreamed. Novelty always has its place, even in a saturated market, I discovered. And I'd allowed myself the vanity of thinking that the packaging and design elements are what got Damselle noticed. It was too awful to imagine Florinda changing all of that. But I pushed away those unpleasant thoughts until another day.

I soon realised that to get to Lavandula, I'd need to go literally right past the front of the Rossini building, and the looming spires of the frizzante industry got ever closer. He'll be busy in his office, I told myself, you'll never see him. I walked along a wildflower path and it opened onto a complex of buildings, some medieval, and some modern. I started to see beehives along the way, and I noticed meadow clover flowers around the fields of grapes. This fascinated me as I loved the honey, which had healed my injury, and I'd read about how vineyards often keep bees for increased yield, and produce honey as a by-product. I was still interested in touring the winery, but only if I could be sure that Alessio wasn't there. My heartbeat quickened as I approached the building. I spirited myself past the main door, hoping Alessio wouldn't see me.

13

Allegra's Ankle

As I walked past the parking area, quite a few cars drove up. I realised there was something happening; that not all of these people worked there. I overheard some people chatting as they got out their vehicles, and worked out that a press and media Tasting and Biodiversity Awareness day was being held at the Rossini empire. By the sounds of the chatter, the tasting element was the main attraction.

There was a lot going on. People milled around, wearing name badges. There was a banner saying: 'Biodiversity: Vineyards and the Ecosystem.' Another exhorted us to: 'Bee Smart.' A very efficient-looking woman, dressed immaculately in a navy-blue dress and chic red shoes, called everyone over to where she stood by the pillars near the entrance.

'Hello, all,' she called. 'I'm Nina. Thank you for coming to our event on the importance of bees in vineyards,' she said. 'Here at Rossini, we pride ourselves on respecting the natural world and helping the ecosystem to flourish by growing wildflowers among our grapes. Our honey is legendary, along with our wine …'

I stopped and listened intently, finding myself agreeing with everything she said. I couldn't fault Alessio's commitment, even if it would be so much easier if I could just continue to dislike him.

As I began to walk back to the path for Lavandula, I turned to see what Nina was up to, and promptly bumped into a young woman, with curly hair pinned up, and pouty crimson lips, tottering in high heels, looking flustered.

'Sorry!' she apologised. 'I'm all over the place today.'

'Don't worry. It's totally my fault. I wasn't looking.'

'I'm late and disorganised,' she said. 'You are too kind.'

'I don't think you're late if you're going to the Rossini event. They're just assembling.'

'Ah! That's the first bit of good news today. My car broke down and I had to get the train then walk. Guess I didn't wear the right shoes,' she said. 'My ankle's killing me.'

'Tell me about it,' I said. 'The same happened to me the other day, and I managed to twist my ankle, too.'

'No way!' she said, laughing.

I grinned back at her. 'By the way, I'm Charlotte Alexander.'

'And I am Allegra Capaldi. How do you do?'

'Wait a minute,' I said. *Allegra Capaldi.* The name sounded familiar. 'Didn't we meet before, very briefly?'

'Your face is familiar. Remind me?'

'I'm sure it was on the train, when I arrived at Montecastello last Wednesday. Do you remember? You came to sit with me to escape some obnoxious guys further down the carriage?'

'Oh, yes! How amazing that you remembered. Wow. How is your trip?'

'Fine. A bit slow, but I'm making the best of exploring the area,' I said.

'Yes, it is beautiful.' She peered over to the gathering. 'Just checking I'm not going to be late for this damn thing,' she said.

There was still a general melee there, and in the carpark, with people arriving and jostling for spots.

'Glad to see it's still mayhem over there. Gives me a moment to catch my breath,' she said. 'So, you like it here?'

'Yes. Maybe it's fate that I'm getting time to see it. There's been a delay.'

'Ah, things never go quite smoothly here,' she said. 'It's a miracle we get anything done at all.'

'Life here is certainly ... eventful. A lot has happened in a short space of time,' I said. 'Just not the things I was expecting to happen.'

'Sounds like life around the Rossinis. Do you know them?'

'Not well. But I'm staying at the Rossini hotel.'

'Nice! Fancy!'

'Yes, it's beautiful. I'm not sure I could holiday anywhere else now.'

'Ha. Are you in the wine business yourself?' she asked, with one eye on the hotel entrance, minding her time.

'No. But it interests me. And with rising temperatures in the UK, the wine industry is really taking off.'

'That's interesting. I write about wine for one of the big newspapers here. *Il Giornale*. And, just so you know, people really do still read the papers here.'

'Nice job!'

'It is. I love it. There is so much intrigue between all the big

77

wine producers. Price wars. Taste wars. Marketing wars. They try to get us onside with these "event days" and who can resist an afternoon of free frizzante?'

'Can't blame them. Every business has to get noticed somehow.'

'Spoken like a true businesswoman. What is it you do, if you don't mind me asking? I'm guessing you're an entrepreneur?'

I nodded. 'I make perfume.' I glanced round to the front of the building, concerned the tour might start without her. But it seemed they were serving drinks outside and everyone was still there.

'Wow, perfume,' said Allegra. 'But there isn't much perfume-making in this area?'

'True.'

'So, what brings you? Oh, I know! Is it the lavender?'

'Very good deduction.' I smiled.

'You know there is a lavender farm for sale, right here? And I for one would love it if Alessio Rossini didn't get it back.'

'Oh? Was it his before?' I asked, wondering what she meant by 'get it back'.

'Yes. He thinks it belongs to him by right, but he already has enough land and power.' Then she grinned. 'Anyway, I don't like him!'

'Really? But you're here today?'

'I know. My paper sent me. I don't have to like the people I write about.'

'That's true,' I conceded, then a little wickedly, 'What don't you like about him?'

'Where do I start? The way he treated his aunt, the Countess of Veneto, for one thing –'

'I heard something about a Titian painting?'

'Yes. The Titian. And this crazy feud about Lavandula. Ridiculous. He wants EVERYTHING! All because she's a Moretti. Full stop.'

'Do you think there is a dark side to him?' I asked.

'Why do you say that?' she said, suddenly switching from gossip into journalist mode.

'I don't know –' I paused. 'Forget it.'

But Allegra's eyes lit up. 'Can I give you my card? I'm working on a big story about Alessio Rossini, have been for ages. Maybe we could meet for coffee before you leave the region?'

I hesitated for a second, feeling a bit uneasy about the turn the conversation had taken. But, fuelled by the thought that he might be a real villain hiding in plain sight, I said, 'I'd be happy to do that. But there's not much I know as yet.'

'Keep your eyes and ears open,' said Allegra, reaching into her bag. 'Here's my card,' she added. 'I really should be going. Do you have a card?'

I went into my purse and gave her one of mine as I took hers.

At that exact moment, I looked across to the gathering on the lawn at the front of the building. Stood in the centre of his guests was Alessio Rossini. For a fleeting moment, it seemed he was looking at us. Or, more accurately, *scowling* at us.

Oh, who cares? I thought. It was about time someone found out what he was up to.

'Hope your ankle heals soon,' I told Allegra. 'Really, it feels like fate for us to meet for the second time in less than a week!'

14

Lavandula

I joined the path and within minutes, purple plumes emerged to my left, and right. I took some photos on my phone, frustrated that I didn't have my good camera with me. I messaged them to Lara and Bryony, captioned: Our Lavandula.

The Lavandula lands were more extensive than I imagined, and even more enchanting. I was starting to feel hot and bothered though, my ankle a little weakened by walking, when I finally reached the courtyard of the farmhouse and outbuildings twenty minutes later.

My heart skipped as I stopped to survey the view. It was just as lovely as the brochure! The house was a three-storey traditional stone-built property, a couple of hundred years old according to the Lavandula brochure, surrounded by informal gardens and a belt of tall trees. And stables! In a wave of nostalgia, I was reminded of Rose Hall Stables, where I had ridden a palomino, Zebedee, for many years under the instruction of Miss Crystal. My constant companion, Jonny Kent, and I spent all our time at the stables. Happy times. The smell of leather saddles and horse dander in my nostrils brought it all back to me.

There was a parasol and table and chairs to the front, rather worn, but all the better for it. The outbuildings, around a cobbled courtyard, comprised the stables – loose boxes, it seemed – and a multitude of sheds and barns. All was quiet, but I could hear snuffles from the stables.

Despite being quite tired, I hurried over. Whinnying came from inside. I let myself in through a main door which led onto a little corridor of mostly empty loose boxes. Only one of eight or so was occupied, by a fine black mare, who came to the stable door to say hello. She looked elegant and haughty from a distance, nostrils in the air, silky mane falling over one eye, like an equine supermodel. I went over to greet her and she nuzzled in cosily as I scratched her nose. Up close, she was a sweetheart, lonely and dying for gossip, I could tell.

'You're adorable, aren't you?'

A whinny of agreement.

'I'll be back in a moment,' I told her.

I looked around the stable block. To one end, was a tack room with a couple of saddles and bridles, as well as halters and lead ropes. An old-fashioned dresser was crammed with dandy brushes and curry combs, plus saddle wax and bandages. On low shelves, were some tan jodhpur boots, as well as hats and even jodhpurs. I was, again, transported back to my childhood, cantering on a beach, and even jumping over poles with Zebedee. I was tempted to take some grooming things and brush down the black mare. But I couldn't without permission. I went back to see her and said goodbye, noting that she was quite recently shod.

'Somebody's looking after you,' I said.

Back outside, I saw clusters of wildflowers; cornflowers, jasmine, geraniums. It was bewitching and I was smitten.

I turned my attention back to the farmhouse. There was a vintage convertible car in the courtyard, plus a quad bike, a trailer for two horses, and a pile of tools. There were some signs of love for the garden and the front door was slightly ajar. Clearly, the house was occupied.

I was nervous about drawing attention to myself. If Allegra's interest was anything to go by, it seemed as if the sale of Lavandula was a hot topic locally, maybe even across the region. I considered sloping away quietly. But I felt I had a lot to gain by understanding all that I could about Lavandula. Why was it still on the market? Why had super-rich Alessio Rossini not snapped it up? It had to be because of the feud with his aunt, the Countess, surely, rather than price?

I approached the house, then stopped, nervous of making a wrong move. But, I reasoned, there was no harm in ringing the bell, just to find out who lived there and what they were like.

My curiosity got the better of me. I summoned up courage and rang on the old-fashioned bell. At first, nobody came. I looked around the pretty cobbled courtyard, thinking perhaps I should leave and head back to the hotel. Then I heard noises inside the house. Eventually, the interior wooden door opened.

And that was how I met Cosimo.

15

Cosimo Moretti

We looked at each other for a few moments. I took off my sunshades and held out my hand. He spoke first, saying:

'Cosimo Moretti, how do you do?'

Moretti. The arch enemy. What was he doing living in the main house at Lavandula?

'Hello, please forgive me for dropping in like this. I am Charlotte Alexander –'

'Ah! Yes, I have heard all about you,' he said. 'From my aunt.'

'Your aunt?' I said, liking his refreshing honesty.

'Yes, Gabriella Vinci. Countess of Veneto.'

Of course, Diana had said she was originally a Moretti. 'Ah! what have you heard?' I asked.

'Would you like to come in and I'll tell you . . .?'

I looked at the fit young man on the steps, his jeans and vest splattered with paint, hair unkempt, cigarette in hand, small spectacles over enquiring eyes. He wasn't tall, but he looked strong. Intriguing.

Should I go in? Diana had said there was still enmity between the Rossinis and Morettis. But I wasn't part of that feud, was I? I argued with myself briefly, one half of me feeling it was risky, the other side saying it was good to be informed. And in the end I said, 'Thank you. That's very kind.' I was clearly going to find out more from Cosimo.

I went inside and he led me through a traditionally tiled hallway, littered with chicken feed, boots, brooms, painting things, leading to a big kitchen – flooded with light – at the back of the house. There was an antique table, with mismatched chairs. Open patio doors revealed a gorgeous secluded garden to the back of the property. It was a tangle of plants and white flowers, but a few statues made it seem somehow grand. The whole place looked disorganised, but welcoming, even enchanting. And maybe not as chaotic as it first seemed.

'Sit by the window and rest your ankle,' said Cosimo. 'I see it's a little swollen.'

What? I had thought it was back to normal!

'I will bring you some ice for it.'

'That's very kind, thank you.' I gave him a grateful smile.

As I waited, I could see through to an adjoining room, obviously his studio. Paintings hung on the walls there, some rested on easels, others were laid against the walls, yet more on chairs. They looked like works of fine art. He was no amateur. I wondered how he might fit in with the purchase of Lavandula. What kind of rent agreement did he have with his aunt? How long had he lived there? I didn't want to ask everything straight away. Actually, I did want to, but I didn't dare.

He made a lot of noise, as ice cubes banged across the work-tops, but he eventually returned with a bag full of ice.

He took charge, fetching a stool for my foot. He undid

my laces and removed the shoe, insisting that he would do everything. He placed the soothing ice on the ankle, quite masterfully.

'That's lovely, thank you,' I said. 'It was beginning to hurt.'

'It's no trouble at all.'

He then sat opposite me, looking at me in such a way that I cast my eyes downwards.

'It's charming, the way you blush,' he said. 'You are beautiful. Innocent, I would say. Quite refreshing.'

'Erm, you're too kind,' I said. 'I would say I'm not innocent at all.'

'Ah, but I can tell these things. In the important ways, you are. I study people for my art.'

'So perhaps that is why you take in a lot of details that other people don't notice?' I said, thinking of my ankle.

'Yes,' he said. 'Precisely.' He continued to stare at me. 'A very nice neck. Features well balanced. Yes, I would like to paint you. As Ceres, Goddess of Abundance.'

I never claimed to be petite, but I wasn't sure if 'abundant' was quite the compliment I would have hoped for ...

I blushed all over. 'I'm not staying in the area for long, unfortunately,' I said.

'Why not? Stay for the summer. Don't worry about your commitments. Just relax in the lavender.'

I laughed. Tempting, and yet ...

'I'm not patient enough to sit for you,' I told him. 'I'm here to work, in fact.' I briefly considered how dull the life of a muse must be. Sitting still all day long for a paint-splattered artist was like my idea of hell.

I tried to divert our chat away from posing as the Goddess of

Abundance for a complete stranger, even if he was the nephew of the Countess who owned the farm I wanted to buy. And the arch enemy of a man I distrusted.

Why had I ever thought a week in rural Italy was going to be dull?

He went to get a chilled beer from his fridge, offering me one, which I declined. I accepted a glass of white wine, however.

'How long have you lived here?' I asked as I took a sip.

'About ten years.'

I raised an eyebrow.

'I know. You're thinking the place looks like I just moved in, right?'

'No. On the contrary, it's very homely.'

'Thank you. It's a bit lonely, especially in winter, and I can't be bothered with the big annual lavender festival which has everything except Mickey Mouse going on, but I do love this place. People think it's odd that I live so near the Rossinis.'

'Odd?'

'Yes. Because of our family history.'

'Isn't that just pretend?'

'No, we do actually loathe each other,' he said. 'But of course I prefer it to the city. I lived in Venice for years. There is too much noise and distraction. Too many girls. I can't paint them all!'

I couldn't help but smile at the thought. 'But you tried?' I asked.

'Yes, but it wasn't just the girls that held me back. The gambling, the drugs, the alcohol, the dancing. God, it was fun! But I hardly finished any paintings. My aunt took me in hand. She said, "Cosimo, I have just the place for you to get on with your work. In the country. You can have the farmhouse at Lavandula on one condition." '

'And the condition was?'

'Oh, come on,' he teased. 'You must know that's a secret.'

'Ah. I feel there are a lot of secrets in Montecastello.'

'A few, that's true,' he said.

'I shouldn't pry.'

He hesitated for a moment. 'We've only just met.'

'I know. It doesn't matter.'

He reflected. 'I may as well be honest with you,' he said. 'My aunt wanted to make sure that the place was occupied so the Rossinis didn't muscle back in here, saying it was disused or whatever, trying to use old laws to take over a derelict place. The very sort of thing Alessio might do.'

That seemed as good a place as any to stop my probing.

'Even so, it looks like you're very productive here,' I said, glancing at the studio next door.

'Yes. Do you want to see at my work?' he said. 'So, you can imagine how I will paint you. As Ceres?'

I laughed and we went through to the studio. He explained that he'd trained in an atelier in Florence, in the classically academic tradition.

'I am part of the new Renaissance movement,' he explained. 'Perhaps you could say, the Re-renaissance. We want to show our skills like Titian and Raphael. But with a fresh eye. Something more modern as well. The mystical luminosity, but the photo-realism too.'

'Your style is lovely,' I said, honestly. He was exactly right; it was modern but with a reverence for tradition as well.

'Thank you. Moving here was the best thing I ever did,' he said.

We both looked at each for a moment. I was reluctant to say more, wondering what it was he might have heard about me.

'You know . . .' I began.

'Yes,' he said. 'I know you plan to buy the place. To tell you the truth, I'm relieved. An incomer. Hurrah! Alessio Rossini is so vulgar. Such a moody bastard! I'm glad he's not getting to buy it.'

I wasn't surprised by the venom in his voice. 'Why is he not getting to buy it?' I ventured.

He shrugged eloquently. 'The Countess thinks he does not deserve it.'

'He has wronged her?'

'Yes. He tells people she has no right to say it is her property! But if it's his, he should prove it! And, you'll have heard about the Titian his mother loved, which Gabriella now has. Her husband left it to her. But, oh no, Alessio wanted to snatch it from her.'

'And did the Titian belong to her husband?'

'He's such a vile person,' said Cosimo, choosing not to answer the question. 'He only wants Lavandula so badly because he's so greedy, justifying it with this new craze of his. So tedious.'

'Craze? What's that?'

'Says he's into biodiversity.' He shook his head, scathingly. 'That the lavender attracts bees and insects, which enhance his crops. He wants to integrate Lavandula into his estate. What a great guy, eh? Doing his bit for the environment. He's got some sort of conference on today. Lots of journalists are over at his place, talking about nature and the great connection between grapes and bees. Truly, he makes me sick. Everything is for show, for business. He's obsessed with money –'

'But maybe he really does want to conserve the environment, support biodiversity?' I suggested.

'He wants to conserve *money*. That is all you need to know about Alessio Rossini.'

Clearly, he wasn't going to elaborate. I mulled his words over and, piecing them together with what Allegra had said, my impression of Alessio wasn't exactly improving.

'How do you feel about the sale?' I asked, thinking how is it possible I'm already on my third glass of wine? 'What if you have to move?'

He considered this question – and me. 'I would like to stay. But I don't know if that's possible. Over to you?'

'I don't think we need the farmhouse as such, and maybe a rent would be attractive to the company –'

'Ah,' he said, squirming a bit. 'Oh dear.'

I gave him an inquisitive look.

'The Countess lets me live here rent-free. She likes my work, believes in me. She doesn't need the money.'

'That's very kind of her –'

'Yes, she is so kind to those in trouble. I don't know what I'd do without her.'

'I don't think an American corporate giant will be quite so kind, but I can mention that you come with the deal. I could say you provide on-site security. But they might want a manager to have this house, who knows? I'm just securing it, then I'm starting my life in New York.'

'New York?' He smiled beguilingly. 'When you could live

here and be my model? And ride out every morning on Calandra?'

Calandra? Oh, the black mare!

'Ah, so that's her name. She is very beautiful. I already met her. And it is delightful here –'

'See, you simply can't resist. Quite right. It makes no sense to live in New York with my offer on the table.'

I couldn't help but laugh at his charm and his cheek.

'You're staying at the Rossini, aren't you?' he asked. 'Are you sure I could not paint you before you go?'

'I have a lot of meetings ... but if I have time, I will come back, I promise.'

As if to prove my point, to myself as much as to him, I stood up to leave, only then realising I was a bit tipsy. Quite a bit.

'What about a painting lesson?' He'd thought of a new angle. 'We can go out into the lavender fields and I can teach you some techniques. Do you like to paint?'

I giggled. This already had overtones of the 'tennis coach' about it, but I was inclined to accept. The trouble was, I had nothing else to do.

'I *would* like that,' I admitted. 'I love the idea of painting in the open air.'

'It's wonderful. As are so many other things in the open air,' he said, fulfilling his role beautifully.

'You are determined,' I said, laughing. 'But so am I.'

'I am teasing. That's all. Let's get organised before you change your mind. This is going to be fun.'

'I have some lunch I could share with you,' I said, warming to the idea of painting out in the open.

'Give me five minutes. Let me pack some paints and some

wine. Wait there.' He then whispered: 'Oh, yes, and the Ceres head-dress.'

I could hardly wait to get out to the field. I knew my phone had buzzed a few times, but messages could wait. I was enjoying myself.

16

Lavender and Peaches

Cosimo packed two easels and chairs, and lots of painting stuff.

'We'll put this on the quad bike and go to a good spot I know,' he said. 'Shaded.'

Out in the courtyard, I went into the stables and had another rather one-sided chat with Calandra, then I kissed her goodbye and jumped on the bike behind Cosimo. We zoomed off to the 'top field'. He stopped near a wildflower hedgerow which more or less surrounded the meadow.

'Can you manage some of this painting stuff?' he asked, getting off the bike.

'Yes, of course.'

We loaded ourselves up with the equipment, and I followed him silently along the pathway, fringed by a row of olive trees. Finally, we set up under a pair of peach trees, looking out over the field of vivid purple, the vista also taking in a stone bridge over a small river and a few grazing ponies. Cosimo put up the two easels and folding chairs, I got out the lunch of cheese, cold meats, tomatoes, bread. More wine. He lay a small blanket on the ground and we sat on it, side by side, taking in the scenery, plus generous gulps of the delicious wine.

'You must feel lonely sometimes?' I asked him, as he poured two glasses of wine and handed me one.

'No, not really. Perhaps for a few days when a friend from Venice leaves after a visit, but no, I crave the solitude. You are never alone in nature, only in cities.'

'I understand. I'm starting to love it here. The peacefulness allows your thoughts to be heard.'

'Exactly. I think we use noise to blot out painful thoughts. A city is like a fairground for the soul. Maybe if we keep going on the fast rides, we won't notice we are no longer thrilled by the fairground.'

'Hm. Profound.'

'Are you teasing me now?'

'Yes, of course.'

He smiled and seemed perfectly happy about that.

We ate lunch in the shade of the peach trees and I then lay back, intoxicated by the scent of the lavender and perhaps now more than tipsy from the wine.

'I feel as if I am rediscovering my five senses,' I said. 'Or something.'

'Profound.' He smiled down at me, obviously echoing my previous statement. 'But really, have you been unhappy? Suppressing feelings?'

'Yes, suppressing feelings for a while. And, before that, totally bereft.'

'I am so sorry ... tell me about the bereavement. If you wish.'

I didn't open my eyes, but I found myself talking about

93

things I'd never talked about before. Definitely not with the therapist my GP had sent me to. I just couldn't share my thoughts in a clinical room in north London. But this was different. Talking to a complete stranger I'd never see again was strangely appealing and easy. I found myself making automatic responses.

'They died within six months of each other,' I said.

'Your parents?'

'Yes. It was surreal. First my father. He went to work one day, and never came back. It was horrific. My mother couldn't cope without him. She, she ... I don't like to say, I can't – it's too hard ...'

'Then don't say it,' he said, tenderly.

But I wanted to. For the first time. 'She took her own life.'

He was lying back now too. We both had our eyes shut, saying little sentences almost dreamily, which seemed to fall through the air before reaching the other's ear.

He touched my arm. 'It's brave of you to say it. She must have been so stricken by her grief.'

'Yes, they adored each other,' I said.

'You are lucky to have parents who were so in love. They would be proud of you,' he murmured. 'You are the product of their love.'

'I have been driven by the need to please them. And by diverting my thoughts away from them,' I said, speaking more to myself now than Cosimo.

'It's all we can do when we are overwhelmed,' he said.

'You have been overwhelmed? By grief?'

'A broken heart.'

'Poor you. And are you healed now?'

'Yes, but I am afraid. I feel so wounded. Terrified of those excruciating feelings of rejection, loss, betrayal, loneliness. And humiliation.'

'And so it's easier not to feel deeply.'

'Precisely. If I bury the feeling of loneliness, then it can never get the better of me. Do you see what I mean?'

'Yes, I see. I am so sorry you have suffered. But we can make something of our suffering, can't we? We can build a stronger self, with resilience, and then use our pain in creative ways.'

'That's true. But we must also find peace. We must, as humans, be able to stop and do nothing and feel well in that nothingness.'

I didn't move but I could hear that he had rolled towards me and I could sense he was looking at me. Still, I didn't open my eyes. It was the most unlikely therapy session I'd had. It felt exposing but he truly seemed to understand me.

I felt his hand over mine and I didn't mind. I was almost drugged by the lavender, intoxicated by the wine, fatigued by the heat. The heady perfume in the air, of wild lavender and sweet jasmine, had lulled me into a dream-like state.

Cosimo fluttered what I could smell was a broken-off stalk of lavender over my nose.

'That tickles!' I protested.

'Charlotte,' he said. 'I would like to kiss you.'

I'd met men like this before, so direct, apparently mannerly, and it usually didn't work for me. But there was something bewitching about the whole afternoon which made me lower my guard.

'Would you?' I said, my eyes still shut. 'Do you want to kiss all the women you meet?'

He paused. 'Pretty much.'

'Truly?'

'No. Only the perfect ones.'

He leaned in towards me, his face hovering over mine. He brushed his lips against mine, and I liked it, or at least I didn't dislike it. He waited for an objection which never came. Then he kissed me harder, holding my face firmly, as if he couldn't get enough. We became engrossed in that kissing and touching, under the peach trees of Lavandula. So engrossed that by the time we heard the thundering horse's hooves approaching, the rider was already very close by.

I pulled away from Cosimo. There was someone watching us. I could tell.

I opened my eyes but couldn't focus at first. When my vision sharpened up, I saw a strong chestnut horse, a few metres away. The rider was a blur.

'Cosimo. There is someone watching – on a horse.'

He jumped up, annoyed by the interruption.

I stood up as well, and that was when I realised who it was.

He was brandishing a camera with one hand, holding the reins with the other.

'Have you been photographing us, you fucking pervert?' said Cosimo.

'No, you idiot.' Alessio looked enraged. 'The camera is a gift for Charlotte. But I can see she prefers to explore the country-side in different ways.'

There was an awkward silence. Very awkward.

'Alessio Rossini bringing you gifts?' said Cosimo. 'You better go and get the camera.'

I went over towards Alessio, stumbling, embarrassed.

'Unsteady on your feet, I see,' he said. 'Again.'

'Only when you're around,' I said, then immediately hoped that didn't sound like I was flirting.

I giggled nervously, sensing that my hair was a mess and my lips bee-stung from the kissing. He looked away.

Nobody spoke.

Then, as his horse became restless: 'Whoa, Bruno.'

'It's very kind of you to bring the camera,' I said, rubbing Bruno's nose as I attempted to gather my composure. 'There are so many things I'd like to photograph.'

'Take it,' he said, handing it down towards me. 'You mentioned you'd forgotten yours.'

'Thank you. It looks great. Um. How did you find me?'

'Umberto said you'd gone to Lavandula,' he explained.

'It was kind of you to take the time,' I said.

'More like he wanted to see what you were up to,' said Cosimo, grumbling in the background, now munching on a chunk of bread.

Alessio shook his head, barely containing his anger. I thought it was just as well he was up high on the mighty Bruno.

After another moment of awkward silence, Alessio made to leave.

I thought he tutted as he left, which somehow made me giggle. As when you get a telling-off at school, and your only response is to laugh inappropriately. Moments later, I reflected that he'd probably simply clicked his horse to walk on.

God, I was behaving like an idiotic schoolgirl, not Business Woman of the Year, which was one of my claims to fame. Or was that some other Charlotte Alexander, from another parallel universe?

Either way, it wasn't my finest hour.

'You're pretty close with him already?' Cosimo said, a hint of challenge in his voice.

'No. Umberto and Diana invited me to his party yesterday. But I barely know him.'

'You need to watch him,' Cosimo warned.

*

Cosimo and I fell asleep in the sun, which seemed the best way to settle our differences, and when I woke up, I didn't feel much like a painting lesson. Cosimo laughed and said we could do it another day and that the Ceres offer was still on the table.

'You want me in a head-dress on a table?'

We giggled stupidly, but then I thought of something that I actually really wanted.

'Cosimo?' I asked. 'Calandra. Is she your horse?'

'In a way.'

'Do you ride her?'

'Not as often as I should. But I do look after her well.' He looked at me, reading my mind. 'Ah, I think you would you like to ride her, Charlotte?'

'Yes, I would love to.'

'I would recommend early evenings,' he said. 'It's not as hot for her then.'

'So, if I have the time, I can come over and take her out?'

He shrugged. 'Yes, definitely.'

'Thank you.' I couldn't resist hugging him. 'I will do that.'

'So, are you coming back to Lavandula with me now?'

'No, I need to catch up on my email, so I'll go back to the hotel.'

'Right. Well, any time. See you again, I hope – and not just for Calandra?'

I helped Cosimo load up the quad bike with all the equipment and we kissed each other chastely goodbye, those intense moments under the peach trees fading with the sun.

As I ambled home to the Rossini, the camera safely in my backpack, I smiled to myself. It had been quite some afternoon and I couldn't wait to ride out on Calandra and pamper her. There was another thing making me smile, too.

Had that been a look of jealousy on Alessio Rossini's arrogant face?

17

Sober

The next morning, I woke early. Could it really just be Tuesday? So much had happened since I arrived. Enough of the unsteady ankle, the indulgent behaviour, the parties. I had to do the property deal today and then I could get out of this rural drama, where every single person I met had some unexpected connection to all the others. I was a temporary extra to the main cast of this Italian soap opera. But I had a life beyond it. The world was waiting for me. New York and Cooper Dean were just a flight away.

My brain started to function. Slowly. Ouch. Intermittently.

Oh my God, had I really lain drunk under a peach tree, kissing (snogging, let's face it) a Venetian artist, a Moretti, enemy to the Rossinis, I'd only met an hour earlier? Had the boss of the Rossini frizzante empire actually brought a camera as a gift for me, on horseback, only to ride off, tutting in disgust?

What was this nonsense in my fuzzy morning head? Maybe it was a crazy dream, the sort that carries on even when you're awake?

I let out a little scream as I saw the Nikon camera lying on my dressing table. It had not been a drunken dream. It must be true. Was I unravelling? What if I really was an ill-disciplined good-for-nothing slattern underneath my veneer of enforced self-discipline and supreme organisation? I lambasted myself for a few brief moments.

But, try as I might, I couldn't properly tell myself off. Instead, I collapsed in a fit of giggles so intense I had to lie back in my bed.

The heat was clearly melting my inner steel. I needed a cold wind in my face and a bracing British seven degrees to return me to my senses. It's not as if I'd lived in a vacuum of perfection before now, but I had always remained in charge. I'd never let mindless fun overtake reason before.

My business life had not been without its explosive moments. Moments when I thought it was all over. Nights of sobbing into pillows. Such as when my bottle design for Damselle was stolen by Gorgeous Girl Cosmetics and I had to defend myself in court over intellectual property. That had been beyond stressful. Or, when the bank withdrew my overdraft and I literally ran out of cash, despite a good order book. There had also been a spate of cancelled orders, customers going bankrupt, marketing plans blowing up in my face. But if there was ever going to be an explosion, it would be a controlled one, because I remained in complete control of every situation. I was good at that. Staying laser-focused and finding a way out, striding into the future, immaculate in heels and lipstick, as buildings turned into fireballs behind me.

But now, in this idyllic corner of northern Italy, I could feel that focus draining away... inexplicably, deliciously, rebelliously.

Diana and Umberto had made no comment at dinner about Alessio and the camera incident, nor did they ask how I'd got on at Lavandula. Which made me think he'd already told them all about my escapades. Never mind, I hadn't said I was a saint, had I? I was a grown-up; I could kiss whomever I liked. I decided to take the initiative. I told them I was thrilled with the camera that Alessio had brought for me while I was out walking, and they said, Oh, that was very sweet of him, wasn't it, and I said, yes, it was and I was very grateful. We left it there.

I decided I would swim before breakfast. At seven o'clock, I put on a white swimsuit and robe, gathered my hair into a fearful pineapple topknot creation and facepalmed into my shades. It's amazing how the right sunglasses can rescue the direst of looks. Or so I told myself.

The swim was wonderful. I was the only person in the pool. Gliding through that cool water, I felt ... alive. This was a big day for me. Meeting my lawyer for the first time. Meeting the Countess for the first time. I hoped I could email Bryony by five o'clock, saying: 'Signed, sealed, delivered.'

Come on, I told myself as I swam up and down the pool, you took yourself from a penniless orphan to an award-winning entrepreneur in six years, you've got this!

I got out of the pool, tingling with energy. My head was buzzing with thoughts about how to harvest the lavender at Lavandula. Where would we make the essential oil? Would we build a unit? How quickly would we need to convert the picked lavender to oil after harvesting? I allowed myself to dream of doing it all at Lavandula, making a headquarters there, like a mini version of Rossini Towers. Yes, what if I could make the perfume there too? That would save on costs, wouldn't it? I could have a small local team. I could ride out on Calandra every day. Get a dog. Go to Venice once a week for business meetings, travelling the canals in style by *vaporetto*.

But these were mere dreams. I was bonkers to indulge them. The Florinda team was going to be making Damselle now. I had to let go. Which reminded me, uncomfortably, about all the changes they proposed. They would most likely truck the lavender to France. Bryony said they had a production place in mind there, near Grasse. It wasn't going to be my creation now. I was entering a phase where I didn't have to worry about the details. More accurately, I wouldn't be *allowed* to worry about the details. All the more reason to create my next fragrance and leave Damselle behind.

'Morning, Charlotte, dear,' said Diana, as I approached our favourite breakfast table, where we could smell the wild jasmine which grew beneath the terrace.

'Good morning, Diana. How are you?'

'Very well, thank you. I have something for you. In return for the perfume. Here . . .'

'Really, there was no need. But thank you.'

I took a small box from the gift bag she'd handed me. When I took the lid off, I found an antique compact mirror. Silver, engraved.

'Oh, I love it! Thank you so much.'

Diana was super excited to tell me all about it. 'I found it in a curiosity shop in town. They said it belonged to Maria Rossini, the opera singer. See her initials: *MR*?'

'That's so kind of you. I will treasure it always.'

We were quiet for a while, both thinking.

'I'm going to Pilates later,' Diana said. 'How about you?'

'I thought I'd go into Venice and do a bit of sight-seeing,' I said, which was partly true. It was as if we had both agreed not to discuss Lavandula, in case it ruined our rapport.

'Lovely. It will be hot. Take a hat.'

She smiled as she poured freshly squeezed orange juice into two squat tumblers. I buttered the bread and sliced the ripe velvet peaches.

'A few people have mentioned the Lavender Festival at the end of August,' I said. 'It's a pity I'm going to miss it.'

'It really is such a shame. It's a gorgeous event. You would love it. Local bands, games, delicious food, wine, dancing...'

'It sounds such fun. You must send me photos.'

'Will you be in New York by then?'

'Yes, with any luck.'

'I wish you could be here,' she said. 'Is there anything I could say to persuade you to come?'

I paused, a slice of peach in my hand. I could tell Diana wanted to say more. She looked a bit anxious, a bit excited. 'What's on your mind?' I asked. 'Spill!'

'I really can't...' She laughed. 'I just want you to be at the festival for a certain reason. Can we leave it at that?'

Now my curiosity really was piqued.

'What's going to happen? What's so important?'

She blushed. 'You won't be disappointed if you come.'

'Okay. I won't press you any further. I'll try my best to be there.'

'That's wonderful.' She jumped up, delighted. 'Umberto will be so pleased as well.'

We sat quietly for a few moments. Lavender scent travelled across the estate on a warm breeze. Birds wheeled overhead.

The breakfast juice and peaches tasted like the most exquisite nectar.

'You know, this place has healed me. I never would have believed it,' said Diana.

'Healed you?'

'Definitely. My life was very bad when I first arrived here four years ago. Ed had to persuade me to come. I was a mess. I didn't want to go anywhere. Not even to the corner shop, never mind getting on a plane to Venice.'

'Why were you so low, if you don't mind me asking?'

'Divorce. Disappointment. Depression.'

'And when you got here?'

'It was quite extraordinary. As if from the first moment I was on a journey of transformation.'

'Go on . . .'

'Well, I distinctly recall feeling as if everything I was worried about before didn't matter now. As if my mind was opened up to a different way of living, to a new way of being happy. The tiniest things took on more significance and I cared about everything: the people, the trees, the food, the flowers, the stars in the sky . . . I'm sounding like a proper earth mother now.'

'No. You're not.'

'I had never been so happy. And for a while, I didn't even recognise that feeling. I thought I was mad, or being slipped drugs, happy pills, or something. I couldn't quite believe it was being generated inside me.'

'I get it,' I reassured her. 'Can I ask you, what was your husband like?'

She thought about this for a while. 'He wasn't a bad person, not at all. I think the whole notion of living with a person forever is so bizarre. It has to be exactly the right person, and you have to be exactly sure.'

'Yes. I've certainly never felt that way about anyone.'

Diana gazed wistfully into the middle distance.

'Are you okay?' I asked.

'Yes, I was just thinking how pleased Umberto will be that you're coming to the festival. He really misses – there is this one sadness . . .'

But she trailed off.

'Did he have a daughter?' I asked. 'I saw a photograph. Perhaps of his wife and –'

'Sorry, Charlotte.' She became quite flustered. 'I can't . . .'

'I'm sorry.' I touched her arm, gently, embarrassed to have distressed her. 'I didn't mean to pry.'

'You're not prying. I know I can tell you anything and trust you, but I mustn't. It's not my story to tell.'

At which point, Rosa approached and poured us both some more coffee.

'So, Venice for you today?' Diana said, breezily, glad to move onto safer ground.

'Yes. I must get ready,' I said, seeing that it was nearly nine o'clock. 'I need to get into town around eleven o'clock.'

'Have a great day, my dear,' she said.

'You too. Pilates.' I grinned. 'No wonder you look so amazing!'

I went up to my room, wondering what the big deal about the festival might be. And what had happened to Umberto's wife and daughter? Judging by Diana's reaction, and the snatches I'd overheard Michael telling Marthe on my first day at the Rossini, it was hard not to conclude that they had somehow died tragically.

18

Marcella's

Umberto dropped me at the station in Montecastello at ten o'clock.

'I'll collect you later,' he said.

'Really? You don't mind?'

'For sure, it's my pleasure.'

'Thank you. I'll be back about four o'clock,' I said.

'Send a text,' he said, handing me a card with his details. 'I'll be here. Or one of the guys will come.'

It was ages since I'd been this well looked after. Not since my family life ended. And I loved the feeling of being cared for.

He took my hand, warmly. 'We're so fond of you, Charlotte. We don't want you to go home,' he said.

I squeezed his lovely, weathered hand in my own. 'That's a very sweet thing to say.'

*

I arrived in Venice about eleven. I had more time to consider the beauty of this unique city. It seemed unchanged through the centuries, the charm of it being that all its history was in its Byzantine bones. I used my phone to find Casa Doges and after navigating shady alleys, canals and quaint bridges, located the Villa Veneto, which I soon found was a grand little palace of sorts, part Gothic, part Moorish in architectural style, set back behind a pair of extravagant gates. I decided I wouldn't worry about those, as I was due to meet the lawyer outside. I had an hour for preparation, so found a nearby café, Marcella's. Very traditional, bustling with locals. I ordered coffee plus iced water and, taking a pavement table, began to make some notes for the meeting. Then, distracted by the sight of cakes on other tables, I popped back inside to see what snacks they had. The sweet smell of pastries seduced me; the *cannoli* looked divine. While the sight of a cabinet of filled Italian rolls, baked to golden perfection and groaning with cheeses and salads, made my mouth water, even though breakfast had not been that long ago, I gave in to a local temptation, ordering a sweet *bussolai* cookie. I knew my sharp, bony angles were turning to curves. But there would be plenty of time to get back to the gym routine once I was in New York. And even though I could feel extra flesh on my bones, I didn't dislike it. I went back to my table where a waitress served the cookie. It tasted divine, every buttery mouthful of it. Even more heavenly, I could observe the people of Venice as I ate it.

Every few minutes, I found myself dreamily people-watching as stylish Venetians walked by – Nice shoes! That bag! Less Botox than London. Father/daughter, surely? I loved the way Venetians greeted each other with feeling, and laughed heartily, disagreed passionately but without malice, and kissed each other goodbye like they would miss each other forever. I liked how all the emotions were on the outside, not buttoned up. I found myself dreaming strange thoughts about living in Venice, or even Montecastello, and coming to the city once or twice a week. The fact that riding Calandra, the elegant black mare, each morning and evening was part of my daydream made it a little too detailed, too believable, for my liking.

I drew myself up short. This was disgraceful behaviour on my part. I had hardly prepared for this meeting at all, and I *never* went into meetings unprepared. Bryony thought that she'd recognised a fellow Trojan that April day in New York, but here in Venice, I wasn't in that mode at all.

It was while I was sitting out there, on that hectic pavement, that I first noticed a beautiful pair of sandals at the next table. Simple, flat, but elegant, with an ankle strap and cute buckle. Italians can do footwear like no one else, I thought. I didn't even look up, and went back to my notes for a few minutes. The sandal-wearer was on the phone now, apparently talking to a friend called Lucia, who was late, which was a source of concern. Still I didn't look at the sandal-wearer's face.

It was a few minutes later that I looked up, and recognised her immediately. I'm not sure how I hadn't realised sooner. Her cloud of fabulous dark hair, stylishly un-styled, topped an outfit of white linen trousers with a denim corset top and Armani sunshades. I supposed it wasn't so very odd to see her here, because her mother lived virtually next door in Villa Veneto. But recognising someone in Venice really played into my fantasy of becoming a local. Someone I knew on my first trip into the city!

She was texting, so didn't see me at first. I carried on with my vacuous notes.

Within minutes, another girl, quite young, arrived. She was also incredibly pretty, with lustrous long hair cascading down her back, and endless tanned and slender limbs. I wondered if I'd seen her before, but where? She was more fragile than Lily, looking a little anxious, her complexion almost luminous.

'Ciao, Lucia,' said Lily, embracing her friend.

'Ciao, Lily,' said Lucia. 'Nice eyebrows.'

Lily pointed to some sandwiches on the table. 'Eat!' she said.

Lily and Lucia. What a spectacular pair. Lily and Lucia. Yes. Stylish. Contemporary. Complex. Friends. Co-warriors. City girls.

That's when it came to me. My next fragrance. *Lily & Lucia*. Younger, fresher, wilder. For young women who led these intriguing lives. I ran a fantasy marketing campaign in my head. We would shoot the ad right here on Casa Doges, with Lucia arriving at the café, all hair and limbs and angst. The narrative wouldn't be about the fragrance ensnaring your man. No, it would be a scent for young women, with a storyline about other young women; driven by a passion, a drama and a gaze that were exclusively female.

When Lucia settled down and started to nibble on a sandwich, Lily spotted me and broke into a wide smile.

'Hey, Charlotte,' she said. 'Good to see you.'

I got up to say hello properly. 'Hi, Lily! Great to see you again.'

'What a coincidence.' Her smile was a million dollars. 'I was just about to tell my friend, Lucia, about you, actually.'

And that's how I met Lucia.

19

Lucia

'Hi, Lucia,' I said, shaking hands with her. Fragile, bony fingers, painted nails with cracked polish.

'Hi,' she said, shyly. I noticed that she was almost trembling.

'Why not sit with us? Do you have time?' said Lily.

I glanced at my notes, and thought, What the hell? I pulled up a chair and moved my stuff over to their table.

Lily ordered some cakes to follow on from the sandwiches. How these girls stayed so slim was a mystery to me.

'This really is a cool place?' I said. 'I came upon it by accident.'

'Most places in Venice are quite cool,' said Lucia. 'But I hate them all.'

'Really? I seem to be falling in love with it! I'm so bored with London –'

'And we love London!'

'Familiarity really does lead to contempt, I guess,' I said.

'Lucia is a model,' said Lily. 'But she's tired with the life it brings. So dark. Manipulative. She wants to try a new career.'

'Right, I get it. In London, obviously.'

'Yes. Exactly.'

'You certainly look as if you'd be in demand for modelling, for all big design houses,' I said. 'But if you're not happy –'

'I don't want to do more modelling. I'm over it,' said Lucia, bluntly. 'The shoots, the bookings, the fashion weeks, the abuse. It pays well. But, yeah, I hate it. It isn't a proper job; I mean, I do nothing with my brain or my creativity.'

'I've heard a few models say the same thing,' I said. 'It's something you desperately want to do, then you grow tired of it, of the way you are treated.'

'Exactly,' agreed Lucia, smiling for the first time. 'I want to be known for my creativity. Like Lily. She's so smart. She's interesting.'

'But I'm sure you're interesting too,' I said. 'Don't be hard on yourself.'

'She's very hard on herself,' said Lily. 'It's crazy that she got like this. She used to be so confident.'

'Lots of models find they can use their career as a force for good,' I said. 'But, forgive me, Lucia, you don't know me at all – I spoke with Lily the other evening when we met at the Rossini party.'

'Right,' said Lucia, turning to her friend. 'The birthday thing you mentioned?'

'Yup,' said Lily. 'Charlotte might be able to give us some help with moving to London.'

'Really, wow, that would be incredible,' said Lucia. 'I don't know the good areas in London. I've always been in hotels for Fashion Week. I have an aunt in Knightsbridge. But I don't think I could afford anything there.'

Before I could respond, she turned to her phone, her expression anxious. She looked to Lily for help.

'Is he coming here?' said Lily, in a low voice.

'Yes,' Lucia breathed.

'Say you will meet him across the road. We don't want him in here, okay?'

'Okay, okay,' said Lucia, almost frantic.

Lily turned to me. 'Lucia is expecting one of her contacts to drop by,' she said. 'He books her modelling jobs.'

I wanted to move us away from Lucia's seeming distress and so we chattered on about London, the best bars, the cool places, how much for a nice apartment.

'Do you have an idea of the sort of job you'd like?' I asked.

'Hm, I was thinking of training as a florist,' said Lucia, barely above a whisper. 'I'd love to design wedding flowers for those country churches, the medieval ones in little villages, like Chipping this or that.'

'Yes, lovely,' I said, wondering at her innocence and optimism. 'I've met some impressive florists through my business. If I can help, I will.'

We were talking about shopping opportunities on the King's Road when Lucia got a text. Next thing, with no warning, she was flying across the street at top speed, taking her bag with her.

'Come right back,' called Lily, as she shook her head in sisterly despair.

I looked across the street a few moments later, and saw two men talking to Lucia. One, a large man with a Frankenstein head, blocked my view of the other.

Lily watched anxiously, although she tried to smile and

make chit-chat all the while. The big guy was doing all the talking. To my mind, he didn't look like he worked in fashion, booking modelling jobs for a gorgeous girl like Lucia.

After a few minutes, Lily got up from her seat, and walked to the edge of the pavement. 'Lucia!' she called. 'We need you here. We've had a call for you.'

It was an excuse, but it worked, and Lucia came back to join us a few minutes later.

'Everything okay?' said Lily.

'More or less,' Lucia replied, flustered, pulling a face. 'Same.'

I was beginning to see why it might be a good thing for these girls to change city for a while.

'Well, I must get on with some work,' I said, careful not to mention the meeting with Lily's mother in case it made the girls nervous of trusting me. Just from the glimpse I'd had, I thought it was important that they got away from those guys. Permanently.

'Sure, it was great to see you,' said Lily. 'I've got your card, so we can get in touch soon.'

'Perfect,' I said. 'Just so you know, I'm moving to New York at the end of September.'

'Wow. New York is awesome.'

And I suddenly had a thought. 'You could perhaps rent my flat?' I suggested. 'While I'm away –'

'Could we really?' said Lucia, her eyes eager. 'That would be perfect. When can we go?'

'Well, I'd have to pack it up and everything...'

She looked disappointed, almost crushed, as if she was set to get the first flight out of Venice, ready to start this new life.

As I was getting up from the table, Lily leaned in. 'Charlotte?' she said. 'Please don't mention this at the Rossini. That you've met Lucia. The family don't want me to go to London and –'

'Ah, don't worry,' I said. 'I won't mention this to anyone. I promise.'

Lily sighed with relief. 'Thank you.'

My God, Lucia really is in need of urgent help, I thought as we said our goodbyes. But I hardly knew them, nor did I know what those men wanted. And I certainly didn't know at that point that I'd come across one of those men before.

20

Ariana Pisani – the lawyer

I went back to my notes. I felt hopelessly chaotic and unfocused. What should I be asking the Countess? What should I tell her about Damselle, and Florinda? How could I swing things to conclude the deal? I took a breath.

Focus, focus, focus.

For half an hour, I wrote nonstop in my notebook. I had to get this deal through. It was going to change my life, my finances, my future. My sore ankle and being seduced by this beautiful part of Italy had briefly snuffed out my ambition, but I could surely summon it back. 'Come on, Charlotte, do this for Mum and Dad,' I urged myself.

By the time I left the cafe, Lily and Lucia had gone. Their table was empty and cleared as if they'd never been there. I still couldn't make sense of how Lucia had got caught up with those guys and why Lily was the only person helping her.

I met Ariana Pisani at ten minutes to noon outside Villa Veneto. I loved her on sight! Small, plump, matronly. Coils of glossy hair supposedly caught in a ponytail but bouncing in all directions, she wore a purple dress with big gold jewellery. She carried a wodge of notes, slightly dog-eared, and she seemed to have bags of food shopping with her. And, incredibly, a mop. A new one, with the tag on. She saw me and laid down her bags and mop, charging towards me.

'Charlotte Alexander?' she said, holding out her hand.

'Yes, Ariana! Good to meet you.'

'How nice to meet you,' she said. 'Excuse all this shopping, I had a spare few minutes and I have to go to another meeting before I go home. My mop was a disgrace.'

'Good use of your time. Anything I should know before we go in?'

She looked at her watch. 'Just a couple of things.'

'Yes?'

'She has a reputation, the Countess. I mean, some people say she's a kind person with a big heart. But when she gets in these vendetta things. She's notorious. Don't align yourself with the Rossinis.' She looked me in the eye. 'I don't know how to put this ...'

'Don't hold back, please. I want to know everything.'

'I heard she's a bit annoyed you're staying at the Rossini. That's how trivial she is. My source said she cancelled our meeting and a party at the hotel because she thought you were in the Rossinis' pocket.'

'My God. I had no idea of the feud before I arrived.'

'Exactly, and she must know that too. But she can be irrational.'

'I see. So, what approach do you advise?'

'That's a very good question. I've been taking advice on this. My understanding is that she's not driven by money but simply by power over the Rossinis, especially Alessio Rossini. He's quite a difficult guy.'

'So I've gathered. I've, well, I've encountered him.'

'So, you know his ways?'

'To an extent, yes.'

'She hates him with a passion!' said Ariana with a flourish of her plump, bejewelled hands. 'But, there's something odd about this, I must admit,' she added. 'Still, let's hope for the best. We've got this!'

*

I was nervous as we went towards the gates. I hadn't really considered what would happen if I didn't settle a deal on Lavandula. What would Bryony and the team at Florinda say? Would they give me more time to find another place? Would they insist on the fake lavender oil option?

'Don't look so worried,' said Ariana. 'You might be just what she's looking for.'

'Hope so,' I said.

She looked at her watch again. 'We can go in now. I've never been here, but my colleague says it is splendid. Trust me to make an entrance with a mop!'

'If it goes badly, we can offer to do the floors,' I said.

'I'm not too proud,' said Ariana with a chuckle.

I took a deep breath. I hadn't got to this point in my business without knowing that progress pivots on meetings like this, moments in time, a throwaway word, a friend in common, a book you both love. Perhaps even a lawyer with a new mop.

I was curious to see if she would trash Alessio, and how that would make me feel. Whatever the case, I thought, I have to ensure I walk out of here as the new owner of Lavandula.

21

The Countess

Ariana pressed the buzzer at the gates and, without a word or sound through the intercom, they started to open. Inside the grounds, the villa looked even more impressive. With a palatial façade, but relatively small gardens, we were up close to its ornate beauty; the stone carvings and pillars gave it an imposing grandeur.

'What is the Count like?' I whispered, as we went to the front entrance.

'Dreadful. A playboy,' she replied, in low voice. 'He won't be here. He prefers Rome.'

'I see. And does her daughter, Lily, live here?'

'The writer? Yes, I think she does. Even though she famously fell out with her mother for writing her first book about the Rossinis and not the Morettis!'

'So even though the Countess remarried, she now thinks of herself as a Moretti again?'

'Well, more so than as a Rossini, for sure.'

The heavy wooden door opened and an informally dressed housekeeper greeted us.

'Hello,' said the lawyer. 'I'm Ariana Pisani, and this is my client, Charlotte Alexander. We're here to see the Countess.'

'Hi, come in,' said the housekeeper, casually. 'Gabriella is expecting you.'

The reception hall was circular, crammed with dramatic paintings – I looked for the famous Titian but couldn't see it – and antiques. The floor was chequered with black and white squares, but the overall impression was a little gloomy, perhaps museum-like, and I felt tense with the heavy atmosphere.

Ariana left her shopping with the housekeeper, then we were taken through to a drawing room which looked onto a leafy side garden. We could have been anywhere; there was no sense of being in central Venice. Apart, that is, from the Canalettos on every wall! Within a few seconds, the Countess came into the room, dressed in gym gear, showing off a fabulous lithe figure, with a pack of small dogs following.

There was definitely a steely look in her eye, and my hopes were not high as we shook hands, before sitting on cobalt-blue brocade sofas. The Countess's gym clothes were incongruous against the opulent interior, yet, very, very cool. She smiled as she fussed over her dogs and I saw how much like her daughter she was.

Come on, Charlotte, I thought, you can do business with this person. You must get to New York. You must get to the next stage of your life. She wants to sell a farm – you want to buy it. It's not as if we're squabbling over a Titian. We both want the same outcome.

The conversation began in English, for which I was grateful, my Italian not stretching to high-level negotiations and legal terminology.

'My client would like to settle the sale as soon as possible, if everything in our offer is to your liking,' said the lawyer.

'I'm in a hurry as well,' said Gabriella. 'But, tell me, is there a connection with the Rossinis?'

She looked at me directly.

'No, not at all,' I said. 'I am simply a guest at the hotel.'

She narrowed her eyes. 'Were you not at the birthday party on Sunday?'

I gulped. 'Yes. As Diana's guest.'

'I see. I heard you were quite in the heart of it.'

'I enjoyed it, yes,' I said. 'It was the first time I'd met the family.'

I wondered if Lily had spoken to her mother about meeting me. But Lily was so secretive, I doubted it.

'Is the money safe?' Gabriella continued. 'It's not dependent on this and that and the other? I hate that.'

'The money is coming from Miss Alexander's bank, via a US company, Florinda. There is no problem with payment.'

'That's good. What else do we need to do?' asked Gabriella.

'Everything seems in order from our point of view,' said Ariana. 'I have ordered the deeds and expect them any day.'

'This is a relief,' said Gabriella. 'It's been dragging on.'

'Why is that?' asked Ariana.

'I've only had one other proposal and I didn't want to accept it,' she said. 'For personal reasons. That's why I was thrilled to get your offer.'

'So, there is no reason we cannot proceed swiftly?' said the lawyer.

'None at all,' said Gabriella. 'I'm not playing games with you. I need this sale.'

'I see,' said Ariana, looking around the room. 'Do you and your husband jointly own Lavandula?'

'No, thank God; look, I'm fifty now,' said Gabriella. 'I want to simplify my assets. I don't need a lavender farm, pretty though it is.' She leaned in towards us, putting her forefinger to her lips. 'Sshhh,' she whispered. 'Walls have ears. Come closer.'

We moved our chairs towards her.

'I'm going to divorce that evil son of a bitch,' she said, pointing to a portrait of the Count, who looked like an unfortunate cross between Prince Charles and Tarzan. 'And I want all my assets in cash. Except my Titian. I will never sell the Titian. That was from Dante. The most sweet-natured, good-hearted man I've ever known. How different things would have been had he lived.'

The famous Titian. It obviously meant a lot to her. As did Dante Rossini; perhaps she really had loved him. She continued:

'I'm going to buy a place for Lily and me, a modern apartment, get out of this mausoleum. Enjoy my life.'

Suddenly everything clicked into place. She wanted the cash, she didn't want her enemy Alessio to have Lavandula, but she did want me – an uncomplicated outsider – to get it. It wasn't difficult. Thank God.

'I understand,' said Ariana. 'It sounds like both sides will benefit from this deal.'

'Yes,' said Gabriella. 'I know it sounds spiteful of me, not selling it to Alessio. But I have my reasons. I am not normally a vengeful person. The Rossinis treated me so badly when my first husband died.'

'That's a pity,' said Ariana, soothingly.

'It's no secret,' said Gabriella with a dramatic gasp. 'You probably read about it. They tried to keep my Titian.'

'I did read that in the press, yes,' said Ariana.

'Yes. But Umberto, dear Umberto, he did the right thing.'

'And Lavandula,' Ariana asked, 'did you inherit the farm from your first husband?'

'He wanted me to have it,' said Gabriella. 'And now Alessio thinks he can take it from me. He's not civil to me, or to anybody. But he can't always get his own way. There are so few people who deny him what he wants. But I am one of them.'

I said nothing while nodding inwardly, full of optimism that we were so nearly there.

'Well, it looks like we are free to proceed,' said Ariana.

'The sooner, the better,' said Gabriella.

I cleared my throat. 'I'm delighted,' I said. 'Thank you.'

'My pleasure,' said Gabriella. 'Will you have some coffee?'

As we chatted over exquisite cups of espresso, I saw how easy Gabriella was to talk to, speaking lovingly of her daughter and her first husband, Dante Rossini. Why was Alessio so mean to her? Surely it was his own fault that she wouldn't sell Lavandula to him. I knew he'd be raging when he discovered I was definitely buying it. But that was too bad. I had a deal. New York awaited. Gabriella was right; it was good that someone stood up to him, because those he employed were always going to be his Yes People.

I couldn't stop smiling as we chatted in that palatial sitting room in central Venice. We were like a scene from an intriguing painting of our own.

The Countess, the lawyer and the perfume-maker.

22

Penelope's Story

Ariana and I went to a café near her office following the meeting. There wasn't much to discuss, but we were excited by how smoothly things had progressed.

'What do you think?' I asked.

'It went fabulously well. I will draw up the paperwork this week, as soon as the deeds arrive. When do you fly back to London?'

'I was thinking of Friday?'

'Could you drop by before you leave, to sign some papers?' she asked.

'Yes, of course. I'd be delighted to. That means I don't have to come back a second time.'

'Exactly. What a great meeting. She's not as bad as I've heard.'

'I agree. I liked her.'

'Unless she is a superb actress, of course,' said Ariana, gathering up her mop and shopping bags.

We said goodbye about quarter past one. I walked along Casa Filippo with mixed feelings. I was relieved. Bryony and her team would be happy. Lara would be proud. My time here was coming to an end, which could only be a good thing, as I'd been so distracted from day one. My personal fortune would be secure the moment I signed the papers – and the next phase of my life would begin.

However, there was another feeling in the mix. I could hardly identify it at first, it was an anxious feeling. I unravelled it back to source and realised that I was actually nervous of Alessio's reaction to the news that I'd done a deal with Gabriella. Although I had every right to buy Lavandula, as far as I knew, I worried about it. You are being pathetic, Charlotte, I told myself. He's irrelevant.

Just at that moment, I caught sight of myself in a shop window. God, I looked rough, a proper country bumpkin, compared to Lily and Lucia. It was time to sort out my appearance. I needed to find a beauty salon. After googling places in the area, I decided on Salon Aphrodite just a couple of blocks away, and conveniently near the train station.

Minutes later, I opened the vast glass front door of the spectacular Salon Aphrodite. I was greeted by a curving steel and glass desk, supporting two huge steel vases of white lilies. Apart from one white leather sofa, there was nothing else.

Behind the desk was Claudia, according to her badge.

'Hello, can I help you?' she asked.

'Hello,' I said. 'I would like to have several treatments, straight away if possible?'

She glanced at the screen in front of her. 'That should be okay. Which treatments?'

I explained. 'Haircut and highlights. Nails. Facial. Eyebrows.'

'I will ask the stylists if they can. You will be here until five o'clock. Is that okay?' said Claudia.

I would let Umberto know that I'd make my own way back to the hotel, or maybe he'd fetch me from the six thirty or seven o'clock train. I knew I was treating him as if he was my father or Grandpa Alexander, but he was such a sweetheart I couldn't help it.

I spent a lovely afternoon in Aphrodite, in the care of the gorgeous Penelope. She was a real extrovert: bouncy, hilarious. Blonde, huge dark eyes with endless lashes. She told stories about local people, mimicking their expressions and voices, rolling her eyes at their antics.

'I hope you won't tell your other clients all about me,' I said.

'No offence,' she said. 'But there's nothing interesting to say about you.'

I laughed. 'How true.'

While I was having my freshly highlighted hair bouncily blow-dried, a young woman sashayed through the salon on her way out; so graceful, tall and elegant; the closest thing to a goddess I've ever seen. Such poise, and although she looked a bit aloof and mysterious, she smiled sweetly and chatted amiably to her stylist. They disappeared into the Reception area and that was the last I saw of her.

'Wow, she's a beauty,' I said.

Penelope leaned forward so she could be heard over the hairdryer, telling me, with raised eyebrows: 'That's Bianca Borlotti. Beautiful, yes. And it's all natural. But. Problems? Yes! Many problems go with that beauty.'

I knew the name Bianca Borlotti. I should have realised.

'Wow. The supermodel? Does she live in Venice?'

'Now she does, yes.' More eyebrow raising, more pursing of lips. A story, I felt, was imminent.

'*Now* she does?'

'Yes, she used to live out of town.'

'Did she?'

'Yes, somewhere near Toretto – no, Montecastello, I think . . .'

'Ah, quite far out.' I tried to stop my eyes popping at this revelation.

'Yes. I have never been. But she lived there – until her love life went wrong. Spectacularly wrong.'

'Oh, poor soul, we've all been through that.'

'It was a terrible mess,' said Penelope. 'It was in the newspapers every day. We felt so sorry for her. Sometimes we had the paparazzi outside here. Her life was hell. We let her use the back door for a while. When it was really bad, we went to her apartment to do treatments. Some days she was trapped indoors, sobbing, with all the photographers in a pack on the street.'

'That's awful. It must be terrible to be hounded like that.'

'Yes, but the story was selling, you know. People loved to read about it. They were such a stylish couple. In fact, it was more of a love triangle. Those are always . . . juicy, you know? People think, if the rich and famous can't get it right, then I'm doing okay.'

'True. Gossip always appeals.' I was living proof of that, as I sat on the edge of my seat waiting eagerly, nosily, impatiently, for more details of Penelope's salacious story.

'It all started,' she said, 'when she met an artist, and they fell in love.'

'Oh. A well-known artist?'

'Yes, quite well known here. But you probably won't have heard of him.'

'Try me.'

'Cosimo Moretti. He's quite classical. Part of the new Renaissance here in Italy. He's very good.'

'Ah. I'll look out for him.' I gulped. 'So, they were dating?'

Poor Penelope thought she was on safe ground, telling secrets to a boring Londoner with no connection to these people. I felt a little guilty, but much nosier than I was guilty, I urged her to continue.

'Yes, that's right,' she went on. 'And he lives on a pretty lavender farm, as I said, near Montecastello. He likes to paint in the tranquillity. So romantic. But when Bianca was visiting him there one time, she had her head turned!'

'Hence the triangle?'

'Yes. By one Alessio Rossini. He's quite famous here.'

'Is he? For what?'

'Making frizzante. Making love . . .' She laughed throatily.

'A playboy type then?'

'Alessio Rossini? A playboy? Not quite. He's not had many girlfriends, but it always hits the gossip columns when he does. Every woman in Italy wants to marry him. But he's picky. And difficult.'

'God. He sounds awful.'

'Yes. Awful man. But. Wow, he is so SEXY. He's so bad tempered, I will admit. But he's very handsome. And RICH. He's crazy-rich. He used to come in here occasionally to wait for Bianca, and we would just stare. Bianca said he was very kind. She adored him.'

I swallowed hard. This gave him more context. To think all the girls in Italy fancied the man who'd thrown me effortlessly over his shoulder. This was getting properly bizarre.

'And then? She ended up with this Alessio, from what you say?'

'Apparently, Alessio seduced her away from Cosimo, then he got bored of her and threw her out! Just like that!' She snapped her immaculate fingers above her head.

'Threw her out?' I gasped. 'That divine goddess! No way!'

'He grew tired of her, they say, then he packed up her stuff saying he was too busy with work for a relationship. She came back to the city. Very fragile for a few months. Of course, Cosimo now hated her too. Things were bad. I mean, everyone knows the Rossinis and the Morettis hate each other. The last big problem was years ago, when Dante Rossini married Gabriella Moretti. My mother told me it was a big story.'

'Insane – there's nothing like this in London!'

'I know, but we love these stories here in Venice. So, Bianca was all washed up. She still came in for her treatments, but she was low. Until she met Salvo one night in a club, just over the road from here!'

'Salvo?'

'Salvo Gallo! The hottest footballer in Italy! He's off-the-scale HOT.'

'Ah, right. I must look him up.' I guessed Lara would know him already.

'But they say she's just trying to make Alessio jealous. That she still wants him. That's what her stylist thinks.'

'And what do you think?'

'I don't know. I wouldn't kick Salvo out of bed.' She winked and I nearly blushed. 'But he's more of a boy. Alessio is a man. You could imagine he'd be *deeply* heroic you know?'

I googled Salvo on my phone. Yes, he was cute and boyish. 'Not bad. I see what you mean.'

But Penelope wasn't finished. 'Apparently, Cosimo Moretti would do anything to payback Alessio Rossini. Steals his girl, then rejects her. Harsh.'

'Awkward, for sure.'

'Definitely. Because they're still more or less neighbours, you know?'

'Yes. This Alessio guy should have thought it through . . .'

'Yeah. I don't know what went wrong. He was serious about Bianca. I mean, they were engaged.'

'Engaged!' I spluttered.

'Yes. She had this stunning antique ring. They say it belonged to a French queen originally. Which, personally, I could totally believe. I remember the day she walked in here, wearing it. We were all green with envy. A big diamond rock, literally weighing her hand down.'

I felt a stab of irritation at this news. But it was probably just because I love antique rings.

'And do you think they *will* get back together?' I asked.

'No. Never.'

'Why are you so sure?'

'Because Alessio Rossini's going to marry me,' said Penelope, throwing her head back wildly as she laughed.

I laughed along with her.

'Seriously,' she gasped. 'I don't think they can go back now. It never works, does it?'

'Not usually. That's true.'

I felt a rush of sympathy for Cosimo. Imagine losing your girlfriend to a neighbour. And then that neighbour got fed up with her? No wonder Cosimo hated him. What was *wrong* with Alessio Rossini?

While I was on the train back to Montecastello, feeling a bit fabulous after Penelope had worked her magic, I received a text. From Allegra, the journalist I'd bumped into the day before.

'Are you free to meet for coffee tomorrow?' she asked.

I thought about it. The fight I'd witnessed between Alessio and that man back at the hotel. Penelope's compelling story – what a way to treat Bianca and Cosimo! His enraging manners. But there was a little voice in my head saying: What harm has he done to you? Didn't he turn back for you when your ankle was hurt and lift you into his trailer and then drop you at the hotel? Didn't he accept you as a guest at his private birthday party, then bring a camera as a gift for you?

These were all gestures of kindness and decency, true. But what if he had ulterior motives? What if this was all about Lavandula? It was obvious my arrival had been anticipated. And what if he really *was* a bully, harassing those who crossed him. As the Countess said, he was, at the very least, someone who no one dared say no to. What harm could a coffee do? And it sounded like my deal on Lavandula was going to glide through, so I didn't have an awful lot to do before my flight on Friday in any case.

I agreed to meet Allegra the next afternoon in a café called Titian's Elbow in a quiet district of downtown Venice.

23

Calandra

Umberto and Diana met me at the station at a quarter past six, and Diana exclaimed over my hair, nails and eyebrows.

'Thank you,' I said. 'I suppose it was to celebrate a good day.'

Diana looked over her shoulder from the front seat. 'Mission accomplished?' she said.

'It would seem so, yes.'

'Well, I'm very glad for you,' she said, sincerely.

Umberto smiled. 'I'm pleased your trip has been successful. We would like to see more of you at the Rossini. As I told you, you have cheered us up.'

'You have cheered me up! I love it here. But, yes, I would love to visit again. I think this place has got under my skin. I've got the lavender festival in my diary for the end of August!'

'Diana told me,' said Umberto. 'I am delighted. We've got something special planned.'

'So I hear.' We played these games. As if we didn't know what the other meant. I think I always knew, deep down, that they planned to marry that day. And I wanted to be there. They'd been so kind to me during my stay.

'Any plans for the evening?' Diana asked.

'I thought I might go out for a ride on Calandra when we get back,' I said.

'Calandra?'

'Yes, she's the mare at Lavandula. She's lonely, I think.'

'Ah, the black mare,' said Umberto. 'She's been there for many years.'

'Has she?' I said. 'I think she needs some love.'

'It's very sad that we don't go near Lavandula, apart from festival day – when Cosimo is out of town,' said Umberto. 'He doesn't much like us.' He hesitated. 'Or any of the Rossinis.'

I didn't want to be drawn. 'Calandra is a beauty. And there's tack and riding kit in the stable block. I can't resist.'

'Sounds like fun,' said Diana. 'As long as you get back before dark.'

'Yes, I was thinking that I should get moving.'

'So, a later dinner?'

'Yes. But please don't wait for me. I can always have something in my room.' Then, as we pulled up in front of Umberto's garage: 'Thank you so much for the lift.'

Umberto looked at the sky. 'Don't stay out too long,' he said.

*

I dumped my bag in my room and went out to the balcony to bring in some swim stuff. I could hear Diana and Umberto chatting below on the terrace.

133

'Cosimo Moretti certainly has a way with him,' said Diana.

'Yes. Poor Alessio,' said Umberto. 'Another disappointment for him.'

What was the disappointment, exactly? And didn't they know how Alessio treated Cosimo and Bianca? It was frustrating that no one acknowledged how brutish he was. Poor Cosimo, more like.

I quickly changed and practically ran along the paths to the stables, guessing I had only an hour or two of full light left. I really should have called Bryony to tell her how well the meeting had gone, but I didn't. I felt as if Calandra was calling me, cooped up in her stable, while I'd been gadding around the city.

I thought it was time for a catch up with Lara, however, and I rang her as I approached Lavandula.

'Good news,' I said, a little breathlessly.

'Yeah?'

'The deal is on.'

'Yes! Well done! Nothing can go wrong? We now own it?' she said.

'Not yet, but there's nothing stopping us from owning it by the end of the week. I am going to sign some papers before I leave on Friday.'

'Charlotte, this is WONDERFUL news,' she said. 'But where on earth are you, I can hardly hear you?'

'I'm nearly at the stables. I have to take Calandra out before nightfall,' I explained.

'What? Who's Calandra? What are you talking about?'

'Can we talk more in the morning?' I said, the stable block now in sight.

'Charlotte, you know something?' said Lara. 'You sound really unlike yourself.'

'Do I? In what way?'

'Like you're not very present.'

I laughed it off.

'Seriously. You've just had great news, but you're so relaxed. So . . . unagitated.'

'Unagitated?' I pondered her words. 'Am I *usually* agitated?'

'*Always* agitated. I've heard you tired before. But I've never heard you like this. I'm worried.'

'I'm almost at the stables. Sorry I'll have to go. Catch you later.'

'Yes, bye for now. Let me know how you get on with Bryony. She'll be delighted.'

'Oh God, yes, Bryony. Will do. Bye, Lara.'

I was so excited about riding out on Calandra and, even though the sky was heavy, I brushed it aside, supposing it was dusky rather than menacing. I approached the stables quietly. The Alfa Romeo wasn't in the courtyard, so I assumed Cosimo was out. I wasn't disappointed by that. I wanted some time with Calandra, that was all. But I did feel more warmly towards Cosimo after learning all that he'd been through.

Calandra was delighted to see me, dancing on the spot, neighing with pleasure. I kissed her nose.

'We're going out!' I told her, and I'm sure she knew what I meant as she began to charge around her loose box, with a 'let me out of here' expression. She then reared on her hind legs and looked like she might just barge her way out.

'Wait there a moment,' I said. 'I won't be long. Promise.'

I went to the tack room, searching impatiently through

all the bits and pieces and found some jodhpurs and boots that roughly fitted. I took some brushes and the tack along to Calandra's stall. After a quick brush down, I put the numnah, saddle and bridle on her, checking she was comfortable.

'Come on, girl,' I said. 'Let's have some fun.'

I led her out to the courtyard – she danced all the way – and mounted her using a box there for that purpose; she was taller than I realised, at almost seventeen hands. It felt lovely to be back in the saddle, and she was a sweet and responsive horse. I had no other thoughts in my mind as we set off, besides enjoying the scented air, the warm breeze, the feeling of freedom. I think Calandra felt the same.

I glanced at the heavy sky, but it didn't look too bad, I decided. At first, we walked sedately along the pathways edging the amethyst fields, strolling past peach trees, olive trees and wildflowers. We then broke into a trot. Trotting through a gap in a wall, we went out onto the hills beyond Lavandula; the hills I could see from my balcony, and then gathered pace to a canter, building to a flat gallop. The heat dropped and a fresh wind blew in my face. I felt energised, exhilarated, excited. I realised we weren't far from the remains of the Rossini castle at the top of the hill. I thought about turning back and returning another day. It was near to nightfall. But I didn't want the evening's adventure to finish just yet.

24

The Drama

We pressed on to the castle and, as we got close, I saw the magnificent turreted building dead ahead. Admittedly, it lacked its former glory, but it was still impressive. I imagined it had been a look-out fortress to protect the region, once upon a time, with a moat and drawbridge. I dismounted and tethered Calandra on a long rein allowing her to graze and take a drink from a pond, as I went to explore further.

There was a sign explaining the history of the castle. The English version read:

This castle was built by Roberto Rossini, local lord, in 1187. The Rossini family lived here until they built the Rossini Villa, now the Rossini Hotel, in 1769. The wealth of the family came from lavender medicine sold across Europe, and later wine-making as well as production of honey. Historian Matteo Marconi describes Roberto Rossini as: A noble and brave knight, loved for his benevolence and compassion.

I climbed some steps, going into the building through a huge entrance hall. The roof was partially missing, but it was still possible to see the layout of each room and imagine how it had been in medieval times. It was vast, a sign that even back then, the Rossinis had been a family of considerable wealth and power. There was a chapel to the north of the castle, almost perfectly intact. I went inside. The atmosphere felt intense; I could smell incense and the recent burning of candles. Statues at the altar were of marble and gold. There was even a vase of fresh flowers at the font and confetti by the door. I was surprised by this; I hadn't realised it was in use for weddings.

Back outside, Calandra waited contentedly by a tree. The sky was black, so I jumped back in the saddle and we cantered, carefree and happy, back towards the purple fields. About halfway down the hill, I felt a spot of rain on my arm. I ignored it. A few minutes later, another drop, more definite this time. By the time the rain was coming down quite steadily, I heard a clap of thunder, which made Calandra rear with fright.

I held on tight and managed to stay in the saddle, but I was on high alert; I'd almost fallen from her.

How am I going to get back in this, I thought, as darkness fell and rain cascaded down. We were still on the hill, but I couldn't see where we should join the pathways to Lavandula. I didn't know the area well enough, and I couldn't see more than a few feet in front of us. We rode through a thicket of bracken. I stopped, unsure if my face was soaked with rain or tears or a mix of the two. I knew I'd been very foolish bringing Calandra out like this in the evening. She wasn't even my horse. I shone my phone torch, and gradually we got back on smooth ground.

At least I had my phone, I told myself, if I start to feel really desperate. But I was determined to solve this problem on my own. As I neared the estate, I considered stopping to shelter, but decided against it.

I was drenched through, but not cold. I reassured Calandra, speaking softly to her, as we cantered on steadily. Surely we couldn't be far from safety now? But she began to slow, and her smooth stride started to falter. I pulled on the reins so she knew she didn't have to soldier on.

'What's wrong, sweetheart?' I said.

I suspected that something was hurting, maybe her leg. Or foot. She slowed to a walk, then stopped. Rain still pelting me, I jumped down, and using the torch again, I examined her legs. The back legs looked fine but as soon as I saw the front right leg, I saw a cut on the shin.

'Poor girl,' I said, kissing her nose. 'I'm sorry.'

I decided the best thing to do was to lead her back to Lavandula, which was bound to take a while. I didn't want to put my weight on her back and cause any more strain. Using the torch to see ahead, we trudged along on the footpaths. I was shivering and we were both bedraggled and feeling a bit sorry for ourselves, when I heard the beat of hoofs approaching. Who else was unlucky enough – or silly enough – to be out in this dreadful weather?

I could tell the horse was getting closer, so I pulled over to the side of the path to let it pass. I threw my arms around Calandra's neck, murmuring to her not to worry, I'd put a bandage on her leg as soon as we were back.

The rain was easing off a bit as a familiar chestnut horse came into sight. I recognised Alessio's horse, Bruno, at once.

The rider shone a light our way and I snuggled into Calandra, both of us drenched and exhausted.

'Is that you, Charlotte?' The confident voice of Alessio Rossini.

I groaned inwardly. Of course, it had to be him of all people that I bumped into at a time like this.

'Yes, it's me.' Despite myself, my voice cracked.

'What's happened?'

'Calandra has an injury on her leg. I'm leading her back to the stables at Lavandula. We're fine. We'll manage.' I hated seeming so helpless.

'Why did you go out in a storm?' he demanded.

'It wasn't like this when we left,' I said, crossly. 'I could ask you the same thing!'

'I have known this area all my life,' he said. 'And I'm not the one in trouble.'

Typical! There was no arguing with that. I looked away in frustration.

'Am I not allowed to explore the area –?'

'But the forecast . . . it was already getting stormy when you walked by.'

He'd seen me heading over. Did he come to check on me, to see if I was with Cosimo? Or, did he see Umberto who'd mentioned my plans to ride out on Calandra?

'Never mind all that,' he said. 'We have to get you two back to safety.' He thought for a moment. 'We'll have to bandage her up at the stables.'

'Yes . . . I hope she can make it.' It wasn't going to be fun to be with Alessio at Cosimo's stables, but all that mattered was the horse. I couldn't allow her to suffer through my own idiocy.

He jumped down and looked at her injury. 'It's not too deep. But it's sore. Poor girl.' He patted her neck.

'I shouldn't have let her get hurt like that,' I said. 'It's my fault.'

'No. It isn't,' he said. Then he went on: 'You look tired. Why don't you ride on Bruno, and I'll lead Calandra?'

I sighed inwardly. Pathetic me, again.

'I'm sure I can lead her,' I said, unwilling to allow him to be the shining knight once more.

'It's about two kilometres. You should ride, rest your legs.'

He was right. I was shaking and shivering.

I swung around towards Bruno, and realised my head only went up to his shoulder. 'How am I going to get up there?' I said.

'I'll help you,' said Alessio, taking off his waterproof jacket and handing it to me. He then lifted me by the waist while I grabbed the saddle and pulled myself into it. I don't think it was my most dignified moment, equine or otherwise.

Even so, I couldn't help thinking, was it on a night such as this that he won over Bianca Borlotti? Maybe this was his style.

There was no conversation as we went slowly along the pathways; Bruno waiting patiently at times for Calandra, Alessio refusing to rush her.

I was pleased to see the stables ahead. I wanted to comfort Calandra, and to get rid of Alessio before Cosimo saw him acting all heroic. I could imagine how upsetting – and inflammatory – that might be.

'Let's dress her leg,' said Alessio, entirely unfussed. 'I can send for my vet if she needs stitching.'

'I hope it's not that bad,' I said.

We got her inside and, in the light, we saw that the cut on her leg was definitely quite superficial.

'Are there any bandages?' said Alessio.

'Yes, I think I saw some in the tack room.'

I came back a few minutes later with everything. I handed the bandages to Alessio.

'Let's clean this first,' he said, plunging a spare bandage into cold water and tenderly cleaning around the wound, while I held Calandra steady and, pointless as it was, whispered in her ear about all the adventures we would have in future, when we would take picnics of apples and carrots, and canter across the hills for miles.

'There. She'll be fine,' said Alessio, stroking her neck.

'What a relief. Not a great start. Our first ride out together.'

'I have a horse you could ride,' said Alessio. 'But I can see you are very taken with Calandra. And I don't blame you.'

'It's because she seems so lonely here,' I said.

'I've offered to stable her,' he said.

Ignoring his comment, I put down some fresh bedding and filled her water bucket, as well as giving her some oats.

'Thank you for your help,' I said. 'She seems very happy now. I think she enjoyed the outing, despite the drama.'

I was relieved that things seemed calmer. But as I was shutting up the stables, Cosimo zoomed into the courtyard. He jumped out the car to find out what was going on.

'Charlotte! Look at you! Did you get caught in the storm?' he asked.

'Yes, stupid of me, I took Calandra out for a ride and went too far. She's fine, she got a little injury.'

But Cosimo wasn't listening; he was too busy glowering at Alessio. I felt I should explain.

'Alessio was out on Bruno. He saw us in trouble and brought us back. She's comfortable now.'

'Come into the house to get warm,' Cosimo instructed, taking charge. 'Then I will drive you back to the hotel.'

'Yes, sure. That would be nice.'

I turned to Alessio, who was back on Bruno already. 'Thank you for your help,' I said. 'I'll go into the farmhouse and get warmed up.'

It wasn't the best turn of phrase. He gathered up the reins and bolted off into the night without another word. Even the sound of Bruno's hooves had a fury to it.

'That man turns up fucking everywhere,' Cosimo griped. 'Come inside and let me make you some supper.'

I followed him in with a little trepidation.

'My other clothes,' I said, looking at the soaking jodhpurs and boots. 'They're back in the tack room.'

'Not to worry,' he said. 'I have a kimono you might like.'

25

The Silk Kimono

Cosimo was a perfect host. He gave me a silk kimono to wear and he ran a scented bath for me. While that was filling, he began to cook pasta and reduce a tomato sauce with garlic, olives and anchovies, in the messy but welcoming kitchen, where almost-wilting lilies in a vase filled the air with a heady scent. He poured chilled Chianti into glasses, and sang along to Leonard Cohen's 'Suzanne' as he worked. Sometimes he shouted noisily, though affectionately, at his saucepans, calling them cretins when they spilled over or their lids popped with boiling point pressure.

After the bath, I asked if he would check on Calandra. I looked out from the door, my feet bare, as he went across the courtyard. I peered anxiously until he came back into sight.

'Okay?' I called.

'Fast asleep,' he declared.

By the time he lit candles and served dinner, it was ten o'clock.

It was so cosy, and I was famished. What a night!

The kitchen table looked lovely, with rustic napkins and mis-matched plates and flickering candles. I was ravenous after my eventful day. The pasta sauce was delicious, the Chianti perfect.

As I devoured the food, I felt that Cosimo was watching me. I blushed as I looked up.

'Is anything wrong?' I asked.

'You have sauce around your lips,' he said.

'Oh.' I took my napkin and wiped my mouth, and still he watched me with a piercing gaze. I blushed again.

'Don't be self-conscious,' he said.

I took a sip of wine.

'You may as well stay here,' Cosimo said. 'And I will take you back in the morning.'

'But they might be worried about me,' I said.

He interrupted: 'Are you not a grown-up?'

'Umberto and Diana are . . . they have taken great care of me.'

'Well, call them or text?' he suggested. 'Say you got very chilled in the storm and you are going to stay at Lavandula until morning.'

I wasn't sure.

Cosimo cleared the plates, filled up the wine glasses, insisted I didn't move, then worked away in the kitchen with black cherries, mascarpone and limoncello, which he served in antique china sugar bowls, the luscious cream swirled with scrolls of dark cherry juice.

'This looks wonderful,' I said.

'You need to eat,' he said. 'For the portrait. Goddess of Abundance. Remember?'

I laughed. 'You're still on about that?'

'I am deadly serious. You are perfect for her. I've been looking for someone for years.'

'I'm flattered, but it's not the sort of thing I'd normally do.'

'Would you normally take a beautiful black horse out in a storm, and stay the night with a stranger on a nearby farm?'

'No.' I hadn't said I'd stay.

'You see – nothing is normal.' He raised his glass to his lips, the crystal catching the candlelight. 'No one will know you posed for Ceres. I will not depict you exactly. Will you consider it?'

'I'll think about it,' I said.

'Good. Now let's eat this dessert and then go through to the sitting room?'

'Sounds perfect.'

Every spoonful of that pudding lingered on my tongue. The heavy mascarpone cream, the sweet, distinctive cherry, the sharp lemon. I felt as if I was tasting food for the first time in ages, as if it was nourishing parts of my body that needed this rich goodness. I'd always associated the pleasure of food with my mother. My mother's food tasted this way, shot through with layers of flavour. I had loved her cottage pies and fruit crumbles, the spiced lentil soups and frosted carrot cakes, and I was reminded there in that kitchen at Lavandula, of the way that I relished every spoonful of my childhood dinners and lingered over them. But, for the last few years, I'd been eating avocados and peanut butter, tomatoes and green soup, crackers and mushroom pâté. When my mother died, I believed that I would never enjoy food again. But something was happening to me. My inhibitions were breaking down, my senses reawakened. I was re-connecting with my pleasure zone. God, I realised, this could be damned dangerous.

We went into the front sitting room, which I hadn't seen before. The walls were painted cerise, hung with Cosimo's work, most of the paintings presented in ornate gold frames. There were some older portraits – of Moretti forefathers and mothers, I decided. The floor was covered with Persian rugs, mostly threadbare, but gorgeous. There were two purple velvet sofas, piled with cushions. A vase of wildflowers sat on a low chest between the sofas. The chest was piled high with fine art books and magazines. In the corner, by the window, was an easel with a palette and paints to one side of it. Next to that, a record player.

'Sit where you like,' said Cosimo. 'I will play some music.'

26

Ceres, Goddess of Abundance

'This house is utterly wonderful,' I said, captivated.

'I know. That's why I have stayed so long.'

We sipped wine as we listened to his vinyl, mostly romantic ballads.

'I would like to paint you,' he said. 'Really.'

'So you said.'

'It's not a throwaway line. I think you would be perfect for me.'

'Where would you paint me?'

'Right here, in this room. Right now.'

'Now? And can I decide if the painting is ever seen outside of here?'

'No. That is my choice.' He smiled. 'Of course, I will hope you will love it. I will paint your beauty, your curves. You will look magnificent.'

I was tired, tipsy, so easily persuaded. Surely it wasn't that big a deal. 'Why not?' I said.

His face lit up. 'Let me get organised,' he said, going over to his easel.

'Where will I sit?'

'I'd like you to stand. I will show you holding wheat in one hand, and fruits in another ... let's approximate that for now.'

He went off in search of props, returning with long stalks of lavender and a bowl of peaches.

The Cohen song, 'Suzanne', was playing soothingly again in the background.

*

'Take the kimono off,' he said softly.

I did so.

'Perfect,' he said, looking at my body. 'Perfect for Ceres.'

He placed the lavender and peaches in my hands, then ran his hands through my hair.

'Stand like this,' he said, demonstrating the pose of offering. 'Wonderful. Soulful. You are spiritual, generous. It's your spirit that's perfect for this. You are abundant with love and kindness.'

I almost giggled, but I realised he was serious, intensely serious. So I stood like a statue as he took photos of me on his phone. Naked photos, with tousled hair, and ripe, fleshy peaches.

Then he sketched for ages, using a small pad with charcoal. And I was tired of standing, but I didn't move, or complain. Finally, he laid down his charcoal.

'Time for sleep,' he said.

And to my relief, we went to sleep soon after that. Me, in a spare room, which seemed to be unchanged since 1955, and him in his own room, which I didn't see. My double wooden bed was clothed with an old-fashioned eiderdown and plump feather pillows. There was a bible on the bedside table, and an old-fashioned lamp. I climbed into the bed and stared at a black and white photo of a couple, gazing into each other's eyes. Maybe Cosimo's parents. I had such vivid dreams that night. I was a giant goddess of a woman, walking the hills around Montecastello, distributing fruits and wheat. Then I rode on Calandra and she took off, winged, across the skies, to a place I didn't know, and my mother and father were waiting for me there.

27

Truths

Wednesday morning began with the sun leaking in like golden honey through a chink in the chintzy curtains. I heard birdsong through an open window and smelled the scent of lavender in the wind.

Cosimo was still fast asleep, it seemed. His door was closed, but I could hear his steady breathing. The storm, the drama with Calandra, then posing as Ceres seemed to belong to a dream. I brimmed with energy and was dying to get up and say hello to Calandra, to check on her leg. I piled my hair up on my head and fastened the kimono round my waist. There was a china sink in the corner of the spare room, and I ran the tap. Only cold water, but I splashed my face with it.

I resolved to make pancakes for breakfast, as Cosimo had been so kind to me. I went downstairs, astonished to find it was already eleven o'clock. Before I went out to the stables, I decided to make coffee, and see if there was flour and eggs. While I waited for the coffee, I looked out to the secluded back garden, thinking how pretty the combination of flowers looked, and how they would all work together in a fragrance; the jasmine, the wild rose and the lavender. I felt a flutter of excitement as I considered my ideas for the Lily & Lucia fragrance. It was as I swung round to check on the coffee, that I saw the studio door was open. The house slept on; the only sound was the coffee dripping through the machine. Cosimo was still sleeping, I guessed. I was curious. He would have locked the room if it had been private, I reasoned.

I found myself in there, looking at scores of his impressive paintings. There was a still life I loved; a striking picture of a single peach. Many life drawings. Figure drawings, portraits, classical statues. Some paintings were packaged up for galleries in Rome, Paris, Milan and Florence, according to the labels. I looked at his paints, his easel, his brushes and cloths. I was fascinated by his process. As I examined a range of brushes, I could smell the coffee brewing to perfection.

Just as I was leaving the room I saw some canvasses leaning face to the wall. I thought I shouldn't look, but that made me want to all the more. It felt odd that they were the only pictures not on show.

Tentatively, my heart fluttering in my chest, I turned them over one by one.

I wasn't surprised or even hurt at the images I found.

They were all of different women as Ceres, Goddess of Abundance.

In fact, I was glad. Relieved. Because it broke the spell. Reality flooded the dream. I was glad I'd slept alone. I'd had a lucky escape.

I had to see Calandra. She was injured. I'd been busy posing naked with stalks of lavender, while her poor leg was most likely pulsing with pain! It was unforgivable! I ran through the hallway, threw open the front door and crossed the courtyard to the stables.

'Good morning, Beautiful!' I called as I approached the loose boxes.

I expected to hear her feet dancing in the stall.

No dancing.

'Calandra! Hi!'

Still nothing. She must be sleepy, I thought.

'Hey! Calandra.'

No response. My heart boomed. Where was she? What had happened to her?

I heard no sound as I approached the loose box. No! Please no!

I was almost afraid to look over the door into the stall. I closed my eyes for a second, swallowed, then looked in.

She was lying down, motionless.

'Oh no!' I gasped, fearing the worst.

I opened the latch to the door and walked towards her.

'Calandra,' I breathed, as I crouched by her side.

She made no response.

I said her name again, stroking her softly.

I listened carefully. I could hear her gentle breath.

She raised her head slightly, with difficulty.

'Oh, thank goodness,' I said, kissing her forehead. 'You're alive.'

After nuzzling into each other for a few moments, I went to check her leg. I undid the bandage. Blood-soaked! The wound on her leg looked much worse. Alessio had mentioned his vet last night ... but could I ask him to help? I felt deeply awkward about staying at Lavandula.

I dipped my fingers in her water bowl and transferred some of it to her mouth. I then washed around the wound and covered it over again with a fresh bandage. I was in a panic when I ran back to the house, calling on Cosimo.

'Cosimo! Where are you?'

'I'm here.' Still upstairs.

'Calandra isn't well.'

He came down from upstairs, hair standing on end, wearing shorts with a vest.

'What's the matter with her?' he said, sleepily.

'She's lying down, listless. And her leg looks infected.'

'Poor girl,' he said.

'I think she'll need to see a vet. Can you organise that?'

'I have a number somewhere ...' He went to look.

I tried the number he came back with. No reply. A message which was a bit garbled. In short, the vet was on holiday.

Cosimo went to get showered, leaving me to think through our options.

I got my phone. Thank goodness Alessio had saved his number to it. He picked up immediately.

'Hello,' I said. 'Alessio?'

'Yes. Who is this?'

'Charlotte.' I gasped. 'Please, Alessio, it's Calandra!' I said, gulping down a sob.

'Oh God. Is she okay?'

'No. Please can you get your vet to come? Please. I would be so grateful.'

'Of course, Charlotte. Wait with her. I'll call Isabella and I'll be over soon.'

*

I went back to join Calandra, who seemed pleased to see me, her ears twitching. But she was clearly struggling.

'We'll get you some medicine soon,' I told her, as I lay down next to her.

I forgot that I was in a kimono with a messy web of hair and no make-up. All that mattered was getting this horse well again. I felt so responsible for her. It was so selfish to have taken her out at night when I knew so little about the area.

She was a horse not a baby, but still I started to sing lullabies and nursery rhymes to her, which I recalled my mother singing to me when we were waiting for an ambulance once, when I cut my foot badly on the beach. Foolishly, I found myself apologising to Calandra that the songs were all in English, but the tunes seemed to soothe her.

I was singing 'Rockabye Baby' when Alessio let himself into the stable block, as stealthily as a spy. It was a second or two before I realised he was watching us, as we lay in the straw.

I jumped when I saw him.

'Did I give you a fright?' he said.

'Yes. No. Sorry. I was away in another world,' I said, leaping up.

I realised the kimono was not fastened well, so I adjusted the belt and tried, in vain, to smooth my hair a bit.

'Thank you for coming,' I said.

'Isabella should be here any minute,' he said. 'She lives nearby.'

'That's great, thank you,' I said.

'Has she drunk anything?'

'A little,' I said.

He sat down at the other side of Calandra. 'Don't let me stop you singing to her,' he said.

I blushed.

'I don't mean to embarrass you,' he said.

There was an awkward silence.

'I stayed over at Lavandula to be near her,' I said.

He looked at my attire and said nothing. I imagined Cosimo would be furious when he came across to the stables to find Alessio Rossini was here. And let's not even think about the naked photos of me on Cosimo's phone.

Luckily, we heard tyres out in the courtyard within minutes.

'That should be Isabella,' said Alessio.

The vet greeted Alessio warmly and got on with examining Calandra. She looked at the leg for ages, then did some standard tests, temperature readings and blood pressure.

'She's struggling,' said Isabella. 'She's in a lot of distress. Part of me thinks we should put her out of pain.'

I yelped, distraught. This was all my fault.

Alessio looked at me. He almost came towards me but he checked himself.

'And what does the other part of you think?' he asked.

'We could admit her to the equine hospital and try to stabilise her,' said Isabella. 'But it would cost a lot and the outcome might still be a negative one.'

Alessio did not miss a beat. 'We'll do that,' he said. 'We'll try the equine hospital. Put it on my account.'

'Thank you,' I said, softly. 'Thank you so much.'

'I'll wait here while you get dressed,' said Alessio. It was an order, but this time I didn't mind. He turned to talk plans with Isabella as I left them to get organised at the house.

I explained to Cosimo that Alessio had turned up and that Calandra was going to hospital.

'Bloody typical heroics,' he complained. 'Is he dispatching an equine helicopter?'

I ignored his sark. 'Heroics or not, we must do whatever is best for Calandra.'

I went to wash and dress. When I got back to the yard, Alessio had gone and Isabella was on her phone, guiding in the equine ambulance.

I looked at my phone. A text from Alessio:

'Charlotte, I have returned to work. Calandra is in safe hands. Please let the experts do what they can, and call the hospital about five o'clock.'

I said goodbye to Cosimo, who didn't even try to hide the fact that he was in a totally foul mood, and then I walked back to the Rossini.

It was on the walk that I decided I really didn't want to sleep over at Lavandula again.

28

The Call

I was anxious to see Diana and Umberto. I wanted to tell them all my news and hear their thoughts.

I looked everywhere for them, but only found Michael and Marthe, sunbathing, and they told me they hadn't seen them. I soon discovered from Rosa they'd set off for the airport in Venice.

'Oh. The airport? Do you mind me asking why?'

'Diana is going to London. To check on her elderly mother who had a fall,' said Rosa. 'It was all very sudden. She will get back tomorrow night, all being well. She does these little trips from time to time. Umberto said he'd be back here by three o'clock.'

'I see.' I couldn't help but feel disappointed.

'Never mind,' said Rosa, very sweetly. 'Would you like something to eat?'

I remembered I hadn't made the breakfast pancakes after all. 'Maybe some bread and cheese, thank you, if it's no trouble.'

'Of course, take a table,' she said. 'I won't be long.'

'Did you have a nice evening away?' she asked a few moments later, as she set down a platter of bread and hard cheese, along with figs.

'No, to be perfectly honest, it's been terrible!' I said.

'Forgive me, Charlotte, but I could have guessed,' she said. 'I don't trust the Morettis.'

It was clear that although Rosa wasn't an actual Rossini, her loyalty was pinned to them. I realised her views on Cosimo might be skewed, but because I was so keen to distract my mind from thoughts of poor Calandra, I encouraged her to chat.

'Just because he's a Moretti or because of something he did?' I asked.

Rosa didn't hesitate. 'I'll never forgive his aunt, the Countess, for what she did to the Rossinis,' she said. 'And then she put him in that farmhouse out of spite for Alessio.'

'It does seem a little strange to have a Moretti living on the Rossini estate,' I said.

'Exactly. But there is, how should we say it? Method in her madness.'

'The Countess you mean?'

'Yes, exactly. He lives there to guard Lavandula,' she said.

Not for the first time, I wondered what on earth I had walked into. How would the Rossinis feel when the sale went through? I would be out of town by the time they realised, so I tried not to worry too much about their reactions.

'She inherited Lavandula from her first husband. I believe?'

'I shouldn't say any more,' said Rosa. 'I've said too much already.'

I kept quiet and, naturally, she carried on.

'Everybody knows she forged a document so she could claim

a Titian, worth millions. It wasn't left to her in the will,' said Rosa. 'And she established ownership of Lavandula by forging her husband's signature on a letter willing it to her.'

I wasn't sure how Rosa could possibly be so sure about this.

As if reading my mind, Rosa leaned in and said, 'Mr Alessio dropped the court case to save young Lily's blushes. It was all there, in black and white. The Countess should have gone to prison. She changed her husband's will after his death on two counts. *Quello che una cagna.*'

'Gosh. Well, Lily seems such a sweet girl . . . I'm glad Alessio did that.'

'She is very sweet. But she also has a very kind cousin.' Rosa checked her watch. 'I must get on with my work!' she exclaimed, as if I'd forced her to stand around gossiping.

If I thought through the consequences of that conversation, I'd be completely overwhelmed. I decided instead to dismiss it as idle gossip. Surely no one would dare alter a will with such brazen impunity?

The day was becoming rather intense and I felt quite lost without Diana to chat with, so I called Lara from my seat on the terrace.

'Ah, you're still alive!' she said. 'Have you been busy?'

'You might say that.' I took a deep breath before telling Lara everything that had happened in the last twenty-four hours, starting with Calandra.

'Sounds like there isn't much you can do until five o'clock,' she said. 'But it was pretty nice of this Alessio guy to help out.'

'Yeah. It was, I guess,' I said.

'Why do you say it like that?' she asked. 'You don't like him?'

'No, to be honest, I don't.'

'Why?' she pressed. 'Whatever has he done to upset you?'

I capitulated and told her about the ankle, my undignified rescue by the 'tractor driver', the fight in the grounds, the birthday party, Cosimo Moretti and Ceres, Goddess of Abundance, Diana and Umberto, Lily & Lucia, the Aphrodite beauty salon, Penelope's tale about Bianca Borlotti. And then I finished off with more about Calandra and her injury.

'Whoa. Slow down,' said Lara. 'Sounds like a movie.'

'So much has happened in such a short space of time,' I said. 'Maybe the countryside is richer in action than cities?'

'Profound.'

'But on a more mundane note, I swim twice a day and eat olives and peaches and drink frizzante whenever I like.'

'Can I come over to join you? Sounds idyllic.'

'I'd love you to come. But who will run the office?'

'I know when I'm not welcome. You want both those Italian hunks for yourself.'

'I don't want either man for myself. They are both equally annoying.'

'You'll be home soon anyway. We'll see you on Monday morning then, back in the office?'

I felt flat at this thought. 'Yes. I guess so.'

'Charlotte?' said Lara. 'What do you think that fight was about, when you first arrived?'

'I don't know. Maybe a business dispute. Or something about a woman?'

'Perhaps, yes. Either of those things.'

'There's something Alessio keeps from the rest of his family, I'm convinced of it. I met a journalist who's trying to work out what he's hiding – it was a fascinating discussion.'

'And you'd trust a journalist?' said Lara. 'You know better than that, Charlotte.'

'True,' I conceded. 'But he's so annoying. You have to meet him.'

'But so far he's rescued you *and* a horse you nearly killed. I'm not seeing the annoying,' she said. 'Sorry.'

'It's impossible to explain,' I admitted, realising my assessment of his character did, for sure, sound a bit unfounded.

'I'm going to google this Alessio Rossini,' said Lara.

She was silent. Then: 'Wow! Smoking!'

'No, not smoking, he's awful.'

'He's on actual fire,' Lara insisted. 'Are you sure you don't secretly fancy him?'

'No! He treats people very badly.'

'This is based on Penelope's story? A girl in a beauty parlour who loves to gossip. Who gathers her info from tabloid stories most likely? Written by people like the journalist you met snooping round his estate?' said Lara.

'What about the fight?' I said. 'Explain that in a good light.'

'That's hard to explain, I will grant you that.'

'There's no chance of me ever being interested in Alessio Rossini, so let's be totally clear on that score.'

'Whatever you say, boss.'

Maybe I did protest too much. I laughed and we chattered on about Salvo Gallo, the football star Bianca Borlotti was now dating.

'He's a clear ten. Keep me posted,' said Lara. 'I'm loving this Italian news.'

We said our goodbyes. I thought about getting my book from my room, but I was so worried about Calandra that I knew I wouldn't focus. I found myself thinking, too, about what Lara said about Alessio. Was he really as annoying as he seemed? It's true he'd been helpful. But he was so arrogant in person.

I decided to do a bit of internet research, and found some of the newspaper articles Penelope had referred to. I became engrossed in the romance between Alessio and Bianca. They looked incredible, like a classically sculpted god and goddess. I found myself thinking it was inevitable they'd get back together – surely they were destined for each other. I also tried to research Umberto, but while I found sad news of his wife dying in childbirth with a second child who also died, I could see nothing about a surviving daughter.

My reading was interrupted by a call on my mobile.

'Hi,' I said, picking up at once.

'Hello, Charlotte? It's Lily. Lily Rossini.'

'Hello, Lily,' I said, taken aback. 'How are you?'

'Not good,' she said, sounding troubled. 'I'm really worried.'

'Oh no. How can I help?'

'Can you talk?' she said. 'Privately?'

'I'm at the hotel. Can you wait until I get into my room, please? I don't have much privacy just now.'

I bolted up to my room, while she stayed on the line.

'Are you okay?' I asked once I got there.

'Not really,' she said. 'We're at the airport, about to board a flight to London.'

'Oh. Already?' I felt really alarmed. 'Right. Is Lucia okay?'

'No. She's in so much trouble. We have no choice but to get out of town. That's how bad things are.'

'Oh no, Lily. I'm so sorry to hear that.'

Silence. I cleared my throat. 'Do you mind telling me what kind of trouble? Maybe I can help.'

She hesitated, and mumbled that she couldn't.

'I understand. But I want to help, if I can.'

'I really need help.'

'I can tell you are feeling desperate . . .'

'I am.'

'It's your choice. I don't want to pry.'

'You promise you won't mention this? To anyone?'

'I swear.'

'The guys you saw? They started out supplying her. Now they're trying to blackmail her. It's beyond awful. The worst. I fear for her life. For her sanity.'

'How terrible. What are they trying to blackmail her with?' I asked.

'They're going to tell her father she's a drug addict and a prostitute. She doesn't want to hurt her family. They are already worried out of their minds about her.'

'And are those things about her true?'

'Drugs, yes. I'm trying to help her get off. That's at the bottom of all this. It started with the modelling, trying not to eat, taking coke. And her habit got so bad that she fell into debt with them.'

'And they want her to pay back the debt by . . .'

'Yes, exactly. Hateful. But she's not like that. Yet. She's running out of options. She was supposed to meet a top client tonight, they insisted, and she can't face it.'

'And don't you think they might just continue their threats even when she's in London?' I asked.

'If Lucia disappears off the radar for a while, they can't really do much. It will be like she's gone missing. That's what we're hoping. However much they bully and threaten, they're just cowards, really.'

'I understand you're in a panic but, Lily, I don't think running away from the problem is going to help. It needs to be confronted.'

'I know, but right now, we just want to get away from this client. A flabby old corrupt politician. Lucia can't bear the thought. She's so tortured.'

'Poor girl. But what if she just has a big talk with her family? Comes clean, admits everything, then the blackmail threat will hold no power?'

'I suggested that, but she doesn't want to break her father's heart. I told her she already has – and she just sobbed so hard that I didn't press the idea.'

'Okay, let me think,' I said. Then, getting practical: 'Do you have a safe place to stay in London?'

'We're going to a hotel in Bloomsbury at first, but nothing permanent.'

'Right. Stay safe. I will be back soon and I promise to help you then.'

'Thank you. Lucia will be so relieved.'

'But you must be careful. Do you think there's any chance they will follow her to London, these guys?' I said.

'I don't think so, if we leave no trail. You're the only person who knows of our plans. We're going to disappear.'

'Okay.' Their plan seemed a bit sketchy to me, but they were resilient kids. 'Look after each other and I'll see you in London.'

29

A Legal Point

Despite my reassurances, I was desperately worried about Lily and Lucia. At that moment, they didn't seem like the sort of glamorous duo to inspire a perfume, yet the complexity added to my interest in the two girls. Wealth and family status had not handed them an easy life it seemed. And I couldn't help but reflect on whether or not money would bring me joy. Still, I needed to get myself organised. I called Allegra to ask if she could meet nearer Montecastello as my plans had gone awry since Calandra was injured.

'Sure, there's a café in town, the Vineyard. Near the market square. See you there at two o'clock?'

'Yes, perfect, thank you.'

I figured the meeting would keep my mind off Calandra.

*

Allegra was waiting for me when I arrived.

'Thanks for coming, Charlotte,' she said, as we ordered coffee. 'I really appreciate it.'

'I'm not sure I can be of any use, really.'

'I think you can. Everything you hear about that man is of interest to me.'

I hesitated. Now that I was in front of her, I was having some doubts. I couldn't decide what was dishonourable about him, versus what was just plain annoying. Once gossip was in print, it was read as truth – and I didn't want to be part of that.

'I realise you're an incomer,' she said, 'but people here know Alessio Rossini is an entitled bully. I'm determined to prove it.'

What if he was genuinely a bad person? I didn't really share her point of view but I was still in two minds about him. Maybe I should say what I saw . . .

'I mean, there was something I witnessed . . . but I don't know what it was all about.'

Her eyes lit up. 'Yes. What?' She checked that her phone was recording.

'It was the first day I arrived, actually, in the gardens at the Rossini.'

'What did he do?' she asked, leaning in closer.

'I was inside, halfway up the stairs, looking out –'

'And what did you see? You have to tell me, Charlotte. We need to put a stop to his bullying ways. What did you see?'

Her tone was turning quite aggressive now. I couldn't explain the fight, and that troubled me. After all, Alessio had been punched by the other guy. And I hadn't really seen him act in an aggressive way at any other time. I was confused. What did I *really* know about Alessio Rossini? Did I dislike Alessio, or did I simply like him too much?

Suddenly, I felt quite sick.

'I'm not sure that I should have come here,' I said. 'I'm very preoccupied about the horse I mentioned earlier. Really, I should go, but if I do think of anything relevant, I will call you.'

She almost glared at me, intensely annoyed that I was backtracking.

'But you said you wanted to help.' Her face was turning livid. 'I've come up here specially.'

'I'm sorry,' I said, but that anger so plain to see helped me stick to my decision. It hadn't taken long for her to lose patience.

'I know it's hard,' she said, trying another approach, 'but you have to think of other people you'll be helping by sharing your story. It's very brave of you, Charlotte. You must speak up. You'll be back in the UK by the time the article is printed.'

As if that would make it okay.

I couldn't stop thinking about Calandra and how gentle and thoughtful Alessio had been with her. And how he hadn't tried to blame me for my foolishness.

'Charlotte.' Her voice was forceful again. 'What did you see in the garden?'

'I didn't see much in the garden, when I think of it,' I said.

She looked furious. It was my mistake; I should never have met her. I could see why she was riled, but . . .

'So, you've wasted my time, and you're okay with that?' she said, fuming. 'Invited me here for a laugh, did you? I've come up here from Venice, remember.'

'No. I'm sorry. It's Calandra. She's taking up my whole mind. I was riding her last night, and we got caught in that storm –'

She sneered at me with disdain, unable even to fake interest in my horse story.

I looked away. It was hopeless. I just couldn't speak badly of someone I didn't know. Alessio was a mystery, true, but he'd given me no reason to be sure he was anything resembling a bad person. I had to get away. I sipped the coffee and tried to change the subject.

'Do you come this way much? It's curious that we met on the train the first day I arrived.'

Allegra ignored me, flicking through images on her phone with irritation.

I couldn't work out what she was up to. 'Are you looking for something?' I said.

She continued flicking.

'Perhaps I can encourage you to talk?' she said, finally.

I was nonplussed. 'What do you mean? There's nothing I can tell you. I'm sorry. Please, let's not fall out about it.'

She turned her phone to me, shielding the screen from others in the café with one hand.

I looked. I looked away. I choked. I struggled to process what I was seeing.

'Why? How? What? Did he?' Words came out in a jumble.

'You're very easily confused,' she said nastily.

'How did you get these?' I asked. They were the photos Cosimo had taken of me, naked, posing as Ceres!

'I'm building a loyal network of people who want to reveal Alessio for the bully he is,' she said. 'I'm not working alone.'

I choked. 'So, you're blackmailing me? With Cosimo Moretti's assistance?'

'I just want to tell the story. I have an editor breathing down my neck and I need you as my perfect, reliable witness. It's a simple enough scenario.'

'What's the plan? You're going to release the photos if I don't dish some dirt on Alessio?'

She lifted her shoulders in a nonchalant shrug. 'Maybe. Oh, come on, Charlotte. For the sisterhood. We need something, one last thing, to get this story to stick. Charlotte, you know he's a terrible man, don't you?'

I took a deep breath. 'Not as terrible as you are,' I said, standing to leave. 'And nowhere near as terrible as Cosimo Moretti.'

'So, you won't object when these *intimate* photos go viral?'

'Not really, no. It's just me and my body in an *artistic* pose, that's all. Let's face it, Cosimo's the one who'll look like the lowdown he is when I say he released them without my permission. So, yeah, on you go. I can't wait.'

As I turned to leave, she jumped up, distressed all of a sudden.

'Charlotte, I am sorry,' she said, changing tone. 'That was heavy-handed of me. Come on, let's talk. I need more evidence. I'm ashamed of that trick I pulled, really I am. Please forgive me. I don't want you to hate me.'

'Allegra, I don't hate you, but I won't be talking to you again. I'm sorry I came.'

As I left the café, she came after me, desperate for one last piece of the drama. 'I bet you don't know about the drugs scandal,' she hissed. 'They play that close to their chest.'

I ignored her, feeling a sense of sheer relief that I hadn't got in any deeper with her. And as for Cosimo, teaming up with dodgy journalists! Unless Allegra had something on him and was controlling him too? Maybe he was more stupid than wicked. Most likely he had walked into her trap as I so nearly had.

I strode back to the Rossini, my nerves jangled. I found myself thinking about that first train ride into Montecastello. Was it possible that Allegra knew even then who I was, why I was coming to town? Possibly Cosimo had been briefed by his aunt? She knew when I was arriving and where I was staying, as Lara had sent all the details to her lawyer before I left. I shuddered to think that my arrival had been so anticipated.

My thoughts moved on to Allegra's final comment about a drugs scandal. Was it possible that, as Marthe had implied on market day, there was some drug connection to the fight in the garden? It was feasible, but I just couldn't see how Alessio would need to get involved with drugs when he was running what seemed to be a hugely successful wine business.

It was all so baffling and I couldn't make head or tail of it. I was just glad I'd kept my head steady around Allegra. In my heart, I knew I would be letting Umberto and Diana down if I spoke badly of Alessio.

And then my mind turned back to Calandra. She was much more important than this petty subterfuge. I called Isabella on the way back, and the vet told me that the mare was fragile still, but stable. She was hopeful she'd be back in her stall about six o'clock. That put a spring in my step.

I walked into the Rossini, feeling such a sense of comfort. It was as if I was home.

I was reading in the hotel lobby when Umberto finally got back from the airport, at about five o'clock. I expected him to chat. But he was different, not himself. He waved, almost like a salute, but went straight to his office and closed the door. Had he been crying? It looked like it. I assumed he felt lost without Diana, or that he had a lot of work stuff getting him down, but Rosa came by and confirmed that something had shaken him. Badly.

'What sort of thing?' I said.

'I can only guess,' she said. 'I checked the newspapers but there was nothing as far as I could see. Thank goodness. Press would finish him off. One day that story will break. Mark my words.'

Newspapers? 'What story might break?' I asked.

'Forget I said anything,' she told me sternly, as she scooted off with a tray of glasses.

Was this linked to Allegra? It was a puzzle: one in which there was much I didn't understand.

*

I went to check on Calandra before dinner. Cosimo's car was there, but there was no sign of him in the courtyard. I tiptoed into the stables.

'Hello, Calandra,' I called. 'It's me!'

She neighed from her stall and I was so happy to see her looking so well, head over her stable door, as if to say, *hi, what's happening?* Flicking her hair like a minx. I was thrilled that she was so much better. Alessio's vet had done a great job and I would be eternally grateful for that.

I went inside her stall, hugging her and brushing her down gently.

I spent about an hour there, quietly telling her the whole saga about Allegra. I was fully aware that this was a very one-sided conversation, but she did seem to disapprove of the journalist, snorting haughtily just at the right part of the story. I was reluctant to leave her, but I had to go.

'Bye bye, baby,' I said, kissing her nose as I left. 'I'll see you before I go home, I promise.'

Even when I was halfway back to the Rossini, I felt I could hear her still neighing, calling for me. I had to steel myself not to go back to her. I really didn't know if I could leave her there.

But what choice did I have? She wasn't my horse and how could I arrange for her to be moved without offending Cosimo? Although I didn't care about him after what he'd done with my photos, Calandra was in his charge and, though I wished it was otherwise, technically not my responsibility.

Back at the hotel, I missed Diana, and Umberto was still out of sight. I chatted to Michael and Marthe for ten minutes after dinner, which was more than enough, but they did give me one interesting piece of information.

The conversation started when they asked about my horse-riding escapade in the storm. I don't know who told them, but news had clearly galloped fast.

'Of course, that mare belonged originally to one of Cosimo Moretti's girlfriends,' said Michael.

'Really?' I asked. 'So why did the girl leave Calandra behind?'

He simply rolled his eyes.

'You don't like to say?' I said.

'That's right. But I will. The thing is,' he said, leaning in, 'they had a terrible falling out, Cosimo and the girl.'

'Did they?' More gossip; I couldn't help but be intrigued. 'Can you elaborate?'

'It was all about his aunt. The Countess. From what I heard.'

'Ah.' Why was I not surprised?

'From what my source said, and I really shouldn't repeat this, the girlfriend fell out with the aunt, over money. And that's why the aunt insisted on keeping the horse. And now Cosimo has to take care of the horse. And he's not an animal lover, as you might have gathered.'

'That sounds so petty and spiteful.' I couldn't help but be shocked. 'To keep a horse away from its owner?'

'That's nothing. She's like that,' Michael said, hitting his stride. 'She was unspeakable over the Titian. There were no legal grounds at all for her getting that painting. None at all.'

'Yet she owns it now?'

'Well, yes, but that's because her daughter Lily plays such a big part in the Rossini thinking.'

'Ah. They adore Lily.'

'Yes, she's family. But she's also so kind. So helpful to them. Lily is a great girl; no one would want to see her hurt.'

Michael chattered on, but I was preoccupied now and excused myself. It was remarkable how the Titian always cropped up. If it was true that Gabriella had lied about that painting, then she was capable of being deceitful about other things surely. I was even more worried about Calandra now. If Cosimo wasn't attached to her, perhaps someone else should look after her?

I went up to my room. This place was a hotbed of intrigue. But I was here on business. I pushed away the idea that Gabriella was malicious and unreliable. I had done a commercially significant deal with her and that was all that mattered.

*

I slept badly that night, convinced something was going to go terribly wrong with the purchase of Lavandula. I tried to make myself see reason. The meeting with Gabriella had gone so well. I understood her motivation to sell. She had to divorce that horrible, cheating man. There was nothing to worry about. My mother would have said I had an overactive imagination and embellished facts with fancy. It was the dark hour before dawn and I was dramatising, that was all.

The next morning, around nine, as I ate breakfast alone, missing Diana's bright company, a call came through.

'Hello, Charlotte? It's Ariana Pisani.'

'Ariana! I was hoping to hear from you,' I said. 'Still on for signing tomorrow before my flight?'

There was a pause. She cleared her throat.

'I'm sorry to say I have some very bad news.'

My heart sank. What sort of bad news?

Surely the Countess could not have changed her mind so quickly. This could not be happening. No!

'What's wrong?' I managed to croak.

'I called the land registry to chase the deeds.'

'And?' Surely if there's an issue we could order duplicates, I told myself.

'Well, the land registry have the deeds. But, I'm afraid that the fact is that the deeds are filed with the lawyers of Alessio Rossini, and they won't release them.'

Alessio Rossini? How did he come into it? I should have known he would ruin it all.

'Does this mean ... he owns Lavandula?' I said, my voice shaking as the penny dropped.

'It turns out that, technically, factually, he does, I'm afraid. His lawyer said they had seen no need to be heavy-handed with Alessio's aunt before now, as she likes to pretend it's her farm, and they allowed that conceit, out of respect for family members, but they can't sit back any longer, not now that we've asked for the title deeds. She cannot legally sell it, as it's not legally hers to sell.'

I felt myself turn cold with fury, disappointment, disbelief.

'Basically, now that I've gone to all the bother of coming here, agreeing a deal and spending a pile of money, Alessio decides to reveal that he had the deeds all along?'

'Yes, you can read it like that. Or –'

'Or what?' I almost snapped.

'You could say that Alessio hoped the deal might falter some other way, and he could avoid embarrassing his aunt, and most importantly, his beloved cousin.' Ariana's voice was thoughtful, soothing. 'Maybe the Countess genuinely thought the deeds were with her lawyer, or that they were missing, but maybe, and more realistically, she knew Alessio had them and was hoping he would release them to her when it came to the crunch, to protect Lily. Much in the same way that Umberto capitulated over the Titian painting.'

'But surely she knew Alessio wouldn't go that far, to quietly sign the deeds over to her so she can sell?'

'No, they are clear that they can't allow her to gain family wealth and property by the back door again.'

'This should have been aired the minute she put Lavandula up for sale,' I said.

'Yes, I have to agree. But do remember that Mr Rossini had a truly terrible time with court cases over the Titian. Maybe Alessio thought the Lavandula problem was best left to lie dormant. I suppose he couldn't believe she would try to sell it. Then he might simply have hoped the whole thing would conveniently go away. It's not one of his most pressing concerns, I'm sure. But then you came along, with the cash and in a rush ...'

I could see the sense in Ariana's rational words, but I was deeply upset. If Alessio had made it known he had the deeds, I reasoned, then his aunt would surely never have felt bold enough to put Lavandula up for sale. It seemed to me, at that moment, like a plan to teach her a lesson, to humiliate her and anyone who stepped up to buy the farm. Such as one Charlotte Alexander.

If he wanted to cut deep, he had succeeded.

'Are you there?' came Ariana's calm voice.

'Yes, sorry, I'm just knocked sideways by this.'

'I can imagine. The farm was never the legal property of the Countess. It's really shocking, even for me. There is nothing we can do. I've never been in this situation before.' She paused. 'I am appalled that her lawyer didn't check this out before allowing the farm to be marketed. Excuse me, but he's a pathetic puppet to her wishes.'

'Unbelievable,' I said. 'So, there is no recourse?'

'No. Unless . . .' She hesitated and I knew I needed to wait for her to speak. 'Unless Alessio Rossini would sell Lavandula to you? I got the impression he might.'

I almost choked. 'I very much doubt that. We don't exactly see eye to eye. And it's quite clear he wants to hold onto it. Plus, he doesn't need the cash.'

'Ah. Perhaps you're right. But he might approve of what you want the land for. He may like the idea of a perfume business, and the lavender continuing for his honey. I would ask him just in case. After all, there's nothing to lose.'

'I'll consider it.'

'The process could take a bit of time though, if we were to start again from scratch. As I recall, you are against the clock?'

'Yes. I certainly am.'

Her voice became brisk and business-like again. 'Well, good luck, Charlotte. I'm sorry there's nothing else we can do at this stage, but I'm always here if you need me. I must go into a meeting now.'

30

Reality

Waves of choking frustration engulfed me. Alessio Rossini owned Lavandula? Why, oh why, had the Countess advertised it for sale? Why invite someone over from London to discuss terms! For the love of God, I had a whole team of American corporates waiting on this transaction going through. Bryony was going to be LIVID.

I could imagine how smug Alessio would be, basking in his glory. I had known from minute one that he was going to spoil this deal, from the moment he splashed me and humiliated me by transporting me in a trailer. He saw me arrive in town, he knew who I was and what I wanted. And now, it seemed he knew all along I couldn't buy Lavandula. My brain was generating conspiracy on top of conspiracy, but I could find no sense in any of it.

I couldn't think straight. This was a disaster. A catastrophe. My house in New York, my life-changing lump sum. Everything had turned to dust.

I flopped on my bed. I didn't sob. I was too angry for that.

Angry with Alessio Rossini, for always holding the winning card. Angry with Gabriella, for closing her eyes and hoping she could wing a complex legal sale by improper means. I was angry with her errant lawyer. And with my parents for not being here to help. And with Diana for being away when I needed her steadying perspective.

But, most of all, I was incredibly angry with myself. I'd been so irresponsible since I arrived in Italy. I'd ignored signs that Lavandula was a pawn locked into the Rossini and Moretti vendetta. I'd been in holiday mode, sunning myself by the pool, reading trashy novels, and riding Calandra into the stormy sunset. I'd allowed Cosimo to chat me up, I'd fallen into Allegra's trap. It was time to fly back to London and get my wise business head back on. But first, I'd have to call Bryony. I'd been very remiss about staying in touch with her. This level of let-down deserved a phone call. I looked at my watch. I thought she'd still be in the office. It had to be done.

I was trembling as I called.

Her assistant picked up. 'Amy Corniche speaking,' she said.

'Hi, Amy. This is Charlotte Alexander. Is Bryony there, by any chance?' I asked.

'Yes, Charlotte, she is. Please hold the line a moment.'

Every second ticked like a time bomb that was about to explode.

After what seemed like an age, Bryony finally came on the line, all chirpy and tickety-boo.

'Hey. Charlotte. I've been expecting to hear from you. Good news from Italy, I hope?'

I hesitated. Best to blurt it right out, I decided. 'No, I'm afraid it's bad news, Bryony. The worst. I'm so sorry. Looks like the deal on Lavandula is off. It's gone completely belly-up on a technical issue over title deeds.'

A brief silence and then I explained the story.

She was quiet for a while. 'There is only one possible course of action now,' she said, her voice cold as ice.

'Which is?'

'We use synthetic lavender oil. We've worked with you on this, Charlotte, more than we normally would. But this is a grade one disaster. We need to maintain our momentum. I'm sure you will understand. We have to protect our investment.'

'I understand.'

'We have deadlines to meet.' She adopted a fiercely bullish tone. 'We're talking about a huge investment here, Charlotte. This is not artisan anymore, you know? We're against the clock.'

'I do understand.' I took a breath to stop myself stammering. 'But can we discuss –?'

'Not now, I have to dash, Charlotte. I'll email the contract for signing. This means we can get the deal through within a week or so now. You did your best, but we have reached the end of the line with this. Speak soon.'

The phone clicked off.

I struggled for breath. The room was spinning. No, no, no. This could not be happening. I didn't want to use fake oil in my beautiful, delicate, natural, wild fragrance. It wasn't just a matter of principle; synthetic oil would unbalance the perfume's harmonious composition entirely.

This was fast developing into the most distressing work-related event that had ever happened to me. I felt as if I couldn't process it away from my office, away from Lara and my trusted team. I called Lara and told her the news, my voice shaky and unclear, my storytelling lunging wildly from fact, to conjecture, to conflating, to catastrophising.

'Oh Charlotte,' she said, as kind and grounded as ever. 'We'll fix this. We always do. Are you going to fly back today?'

'I should. I need your help. But I have to say goodbye to Calandra. And Diana and Umberto ...'

'So. Why not come back tomorrow?'

'Yes. I'll do that.'

'Breathe. Relax. It'll be okay.'

'Will it? Oh, I suppose I'll come round to the idea of the synthetic oil. It does have its green virtues, after all. And I have a house waiting for me in New York.'

'Focus on New York. It's what you've always wanted.'

Thank God for Lara.

31

Suspicion

I spent the rest of Thursday in a trance, packing up my room, not telling anyone what was happening. Diana returned from London and although it was lovely to see her and we had tea on the terrace together, she commented that I was very quiet.

'I'm thinking,' I explained.

'That's what I feared,' she replied.

She knew that I was leaving but, somehow, we didn't discuss it. I'd chatted through my departure with Umberto who looked so sad I thought my heart would break. Diana and I couldn't bear that discussion. We'd only been together for a short time but we'd forged an intense friendship.

To make matters worse, Umberto was still very low, following whatever had shaken him on the day he took Diana to the airport. He was as courteous and helpful as ever, but he'd lost his sunny smile.

'Is Umberto okay?' I asked Diana.

'No. But I can't say much about it. I'm sorry.'

'I wish I could help.'

'We're all down at the moment,' said Diana, smiling warmly. 'I live in hope of a solution for him.'

If the people at the Rossini *had* known all along that I wouldn't be able to buy Lavandula, they showed no pleasure in my disappointment. But it was possible they didn't know the details. Had Umberto and Diana known that Alessio had the title deeds securely stored? Probably not, but even if they had, there was nothing they could have done to help. I knew in my heart that if they'd tried to warn me off Lavandula, I wouldn't have listened.

My flight was at noon on the Friday, so I arranged for a cab to collect me from the Rossini at nine o'clock sharp. At breakfast, I found Diana on the terrace, reading. She looked up, very much like she'd done on the day I arrived, when she took such good care of me: 'the girl with the injury'. My heart hurt at the thought of saying goodbye.

'Charlotte, lovely to see you, sweetheart,' she said. 'Come and join me. I have a pot of coffee here. Bread and peaches coming!'

And two cups. She'd been expecting me.

'We will miss you,' she said. 'Very much.'

'And I will miss you.' I paused. 'Can I ask you something? A favour.'

'Yes, of course.'

'Can you find someone to look after Calandra, if it's okay to remove her from Lavandula? I don't think Cosimo wants her over there. She's a lot of work. He's not a horse lover and he's very busy with his painting . . .'

'Sure. Maybe we could bring her over to the stables here.'

She had a quick think. 'Oh. Fear not! I've a girl in mind. She lives on the estate. Jasmine Pirelli. Her mother is one of the accountants in the Rossini office. Jasmine is horse-mad, but her mother can't afford a horse – she's on her own with three children.'

'Sounds perfect. What age is she?' I asked, as I poured the now familiar-smelling coffee into a large cup.

'About seventeen. She's very sweet.'

What a relief. 'Wonderful! I'm so grateful.'

'I don't want to pry,' said Diana.

'But you're wondering what happened while you were away?'

'I just want to know if you'll be back? Will you come for the Lavender Festival?'

I wanted to be honest with her. 'I'm not sure,' I said. I didn't want to say to her that I was so angry with Alessio that I wanted to leave this town for good.

'You've had a big disappointment here?'

I nodded. 'Yes. I have to go back to London without Lavandula. Turns out that Gabriella doesn't own it.'

'I'm sorry, sweetheart. I'm so sorry.' And she really was sorry. 'It's a mess, that side of things. Gabriella makes things messy. She's a victim of sorts, but also a culprit.'

'I liked her. But she's really let me down. It's changed things. I'll still go to New York, though. I have to go ahead with my deal with Florinda. That's why I can't be sure about coming back here later in the summer.'

'So, Damselle will no longer be independent?'

I hesitated. 'That's right.' I pushed away thoughts about the synthetic oil and new branding, trying to focus on the business side; the money and the opportunity. And, I reminded myself, Cooper Dean. Delicious Cooper Dean.

'Do you have another source of lavender? Your original source?'

'No, that's too expensive for them.'

'What then? Surely not artificial oil? You said your brand excelled because it was natural.'

'I know.' My words were a barely audible whisper. 'I have no choice. I've been badly let down over Lavandula.' I flinched, ashamed of that spiteful comment as soon as I said it.

She paused. 'I'm sure it will work out for the best,' she said. 'Business is all about compromise. The scent will still be wonderful.'

'But will it, Diana?' I could feel myself becoming petulant, needy. 'What if it changes it? What if it smells different?'

'It means so much to you as you've developed it from scratch. To them, it's just a –'

She stopped there. I knew she was right. I was overly attached to Damselle. Bryony and her associates felt differently; they were simply working to maximise a business opportunity.

'You know,' I said, 'if Alessio had shown his hand earlier, I could have avoided wasting a whole week –'

'Is that how you see your time here?' She sounded hurt. 'As a waste?'

I rushed to reassure her. 'No. Actually, I've really enjoyed it.'

'So maybe there was some other, larger purpose to you coming here.'

We both looked out to the pool, smiling as we saw Marthe sitting on Michael's knee.

'Quite the centre of romance, this place,' said Diana.

'Seems that way.'

'Alessio's going to miss you.'

'What? Are you kidding? We've never got on.'

'He likes you,' said Diana. 'It's obvious.'

'No. He doesn't.' I laughed. 'Quite the opposite.'

'Trust me.'

'Even so,' I said. 'He has a young girlfriend, doesn't he?'

'No. He's single,' said Diana emphatically. 'He got into such a mess with Bianca. And the stuff with Cosimo. He takes relationships very seriously. When Cosimo took Bianca away from him –'

'Cosimo? Took her away from Alessio?'

'Yes. It was awful.'

'I didn't know that. But I've definitely seen Alessio with a pretty young girl?'

Diana's face went through an animated sequence of expressions. Surprise. Alarm. Confusion.

'I know who that is,' she said. 'She's not his girlfriend.'

Surely the mysterious, pretty girl couldn't be Alessio's daughter? I hadn't seen her face on market day.

'Is she his child?' I asked.

'No,' said Diana. 'But it feels that way.' She didn't continue.

'Diana, do you mind if I ask something else?'

'Sure. I don't know if I can answer though.'

'There was a fight. The day I arrived. I saw Alessio being punched by a guy near the lake.'

Again, she looked pained. 'That's connected to the young girl. I'm sorry to be so vague.'

'Is that girl connected to whatever upset Umberto the

other day? He's been so morose since he got back from the airport.'

'Yes.'

I was beginning to piece things together. So, the girl wasn't Alessio's girlfriend, and she wasn't his daughter either . . .

32

Umberto

I thought about Alessio as I went out to my balcony one last time. I looked at the orderly vineyards stretching out as far as the eye could see. The Castello, the towers of the Rossini headquarters. All owned by that scruffy farmer who rescued me in his tractor! It was, I supposed, quite commendable that he pottered around town in a tractor, looking like he'd been working in the fields. Maybe it showed a lack of conceit. Or, maybe it showed enormous conceit. There was a lot I couldn't be sure about with Alessio Rossini.

And then there was my failed bid for Lavandula. Maybe he didn't mean to ruin my deal. It wasn't his fault that Gabriella didn't have the right to sell Lavandula. But I blamed him for his secrecy, which seemed so unnecessary and had really wasted my time. And yet, his love for Lily might be behind that.

However, none of it mattered now. I would never see him again. I was quite sure that Diana was mistaken when she said he had feelings for me. She and Umberto were probably keen for him to settle down, that was all. I wouldn't be back for the festivities, but I would always think fondly of Diana and Umberto.

The last minutes before the cab arrived seemed never-ending. I had said a sad goodbye to Diana and Umberto. And, having given my last goodbye kiss to Calandra, I couldn't bear to see her again. She reminded me so much of my childhood, and all the happy memories of my parents taking me to horse riding lessons. Diana had negotiated with Cosimo to bring her over to the Rossini stables at the weekend. I don't know how she'd managed to persuade him, but I was glad she had.

I tried to read one of the romantic novels. But I'd only enjoyed them while I believed in Lavandula. I gazed out to the grounds and thought more about my parents. About our last family holiday. I was reminded of that feeling of waiting around in the holiday location while the holiday is over, and that sense of dislocation. We'd had half a day to kill in Madrid one time, and we'd played Scrabble in our apartment, watching the city go by, strangers in it once more. I felt like that at the Rossini that morning. My sense of belonging there had vanished and I could feel myself choking up.

*

I sat in Reception, taking in all the little details so I could think back on this place. The paintings, the rugs and antiques. I noticed some Rossini family photographs I hadn't spotted before. A father and son on horseback. Alessio and his father, I presumed. A beautiful little girl, so like a younger version of Lucia . . .

189

Oh my God. It *was* Lucia. I thought back to all that Lily had told me, about Lucia being afraid to let her father down. I'd vaguely suspected from what Diana said that Lucia was Umberto's daughter, but now I was sure. I felt absolutely terrible that I had encouraged the girls to flee to London. Their departure must have been what had upset Umberto so much. But, I told myself, I hadn't suggested the idea and at least I had proposed confessing all to Lucia's family first.

It was clear to me now. Lucia was Umberto's beloved daughter, caught up in modelling, drugs and exploitative sex. And I supposed that seeing her leaving for London broke his heart all over again. Lucia was such a lovely girl, really, and Umberto such a wonderful person, surely there had to be a way of reuniting them? But it wasn't my job to do that. And if Diana had failed to bring them together, then what chance did I have?

I was staring out of the window, expecting to see the cab arrive, asking myself if I really wanted to leave at all, when a terrible piercing shriek came from the back of the hotel, maybe from the pool area. It wasn't the sound of people having fun. It was a shriek of anguish, pain or fright. I couldn't be sure, but I thought it may have come from Diana. What on earth had happened out there? It sounded like a murder had been committed!

I got up to investigate, torn between running to and from the scream. At that very moment, Rosa came flying through the doors from the terrace, waving her arms in the air.

'Charlotte! Charlotte!' she cried. 'Can you come quickly?'

I jumped up and sprinted out with her to the pool area, my heart pounding. I was terrified. For some reason, I started to imagine Umberto hanging from a tree still strung with bunting. No, please, no. Don't let him be dead.

*

At first, I couldn't see anyone. I lowered my gaze and saw Diana, kneeling by the box hedge, stricken. I ran towards her. Umberto lay on the grass, motionless. She clutched his hand to her heart. Oh no! Umberto! God, no!

I raced over to them.

'I'm here. What can I do?' I said. 'What's happening?'

Diana was in shock. 'Rosa is calling an ambulance,' she said, her face smirched by falling tears, words juddering out one by one.

'What happened?' I asked, gently. 'Do you know?'

She trembled and I placed an arm around her shoulders. 'He was weeding. I was watching him from the side of the pool. He just collapsed in front of my eyes. Sort of slithered to the ground. Quite elegantly.' She gasped for breath.

My heart raced. *Not Umberto, please God.* 'Is he conscious?'

'I . . . I don't think so,' said Diana, sobbing.

Rosa ran back. 'The ambulance is coming.'

Meanwhile, Silvana brought pillows and blankets from inside the hotel.

'Rosa, can you call Ed and Alessio?' said Diana, taking a deep breath. 'I'm sure there's more first aid we should be trying. Do you know what we should do, Charlotte?'

Me? I was hopeless. But I found strength from somewhere. We *had* to save Umberto.

'Can you feel a pulse?' I asked, trying to remember the basic first aid training I'd done years ago.

'I'm not sure. It's so faint.'

I kneeled next to Diana, feeling for a pulse in his neck. Thank God, there was a slow, faint throb.

'I'm not sure that he's breathing,' I said. I closed my eyes as I tried to focus on what to do next. It was like a horrible dream from which there was no waking up.

'I'm going to try CPR,' I said, sounding braver than I felt. I trembled as I turned to Diana. 'I'm going to take off his glasses and check his airway; is that okay?'

'Of course! Anything. I'm so glad you're here.' Poor Diana was in a terrible state.

I'd never done CPR before, except in my training classes. I was quivering with nerves, but I placed the heel of my hand in the centre of Umberto's chest, then placed my other hand over it, interlacing the fingers. With arms straightened, I pushed down with my upper body weight. I did it again. And again.

Diana couldn't watch.

'I'm sorry, Diana. This looks rough but I have to make lots of these compressions.'

'Please, carry on, Charlotte,' said Diana. 'Thank you.'

I was becoming exhausted, but I kept going, praying that the professionals would soon arrive – and that I was doing the right thing. What if I was making things worse? But it was all I could do. I wasn't confident enough to try rescue breathing.

I was still trying my best with CPR when Ed and Alessio arrived, firing out of the hotel onto the terrace like rockets.

'Oh my God! What's happening?' said Alessio, distraught, but taking immediate charge.

I was relieved to see him, I had to admit.

Ed comforted his mother as she spoke. 'We can't be sure, but seems like a heart attack. Charlotte has been amazing, she's been performing CPR for a few minutes. The ambulance should be here soon.'

'Good God!' said Alessio, his voice breaking.

'I'm not sure that I can go on,' I murmured, breathless.

'You've done well, Charlotte,' said Alessio, tenderly. 'Let me take over.'

'Please.' I moved aside. 'I think I can hear him breathing.'

'Charlotte, your cab is waiting at the front of the hotel,' said Ed.

'Oh, I completely forgot about that,' I said. 'I'm not going for the flight while Umberto is like this. I'll go and tell the driver to leave.'

I ran to the front of the hotel, paid the driver for his trouble, and by the time the cab was driving away, the ambulance had arrived.

I explained to the medics, in a garbled fashion, what we knew so far. They brought the stretcher with them. Alessio was in full command of the situation when we got to the poolside, shirt sleeves rolled up, directing operations.

'Suspected heart attack,' he said. 'Airway is clear, no history of blood pressure or diabetes . . .'

So, he's a fully trained doctor as well. Amazing.

We all cleared the area and we heard Umberto splutter, which raised a cheer from us all. The medics gently manoeuvred him onto the stretcher.

'We will take him to Emergency at Mestre,' said one of the medics. 'Who will travel with him?'

'I will,' said Diana. 'I'll just fetch my bag.'

'I'll get it, Mum,' said Ed. 'Is it in your room?'

'The rest of you can follow us,' said the medic, as Diana and Ed sorted out their arrangements.

'I'll follow in my car,' said Alessio. He turned to me: 'Do you want to come too?'

'Yes,' I said. 'I do.'

33

Suspending Enmity

'At least he's alive,' said Alessio, visibly shaken. 'Thank God. The Rossini brothers have a bad history of fatal heart attacks without warning. My father. Uncle Filippo.'

'Poor Umberto,' I said, tearfully. 'He's been so stressed.'

'Very true.' Alessio let out a heavy sigh. 'And that's been going on for a while. I should have helped more.' His face looked drawn with guilt.

Umberto was stretchered through the hotel, which was thankfully quiet as most of the guests were away at the market.

We watched them leave; Diana in the ambulance with Umberto, whose eyes had flickered open a few times on the way through the hotel. Ed went back to work as he had left clients unattended when the call about Umberto came through.

'Do you need to do anything before we leave?' said Alessio.

'I'll bring my case,' I said. 'I can get a later flight, perhaps.'

I'd seen that he was driving a convertible Ferrari, so I

picked up a scarf and sun cream from my bag while I was inside. As I came out, a text pinged on my phone – from Diana. My heart thundered in my chest. I could hardly bring myself to read it.

When I did, my heart skipped a beat.

'He's talking to us!' she wrote.

I relayed this to Alessio immediately. He stepped forward and I thought he was going to hug me, but he stopped short, leaving us suspended in an awkward moment.

Instead, he looked at my feet. 'Sensible shoes, I see,' he said. 'Makes a change.'

I ignored him and we both got in.

'Can you put the hospital postcode into my satnav please?' he asked, handing me his phone.

'Yes, sir.'

'You think I'm bossy?'

'Yes.'

'But I have to be. I am a boss. The clue is in the word.'

'But I am not one of your employees.'

'That's a valid point.'

I put on my shades, applied sun cream and wrapped the scarf round my head. We set off silently, and now that the shock of the situation was wearing off a little, I found myself wondering how on earth I'd ended up on a road trip with him. It seemed as if fate kept pushing us together, disastrously so. I turned away from him until my neck cricked so much, I had to revert to sitting normally.

'Poor Umberto,' said Alessio eventually. 'He's a saint of a man. He doesn't deserve what life has thrown at him.'

'He's always so professional. I hope he will take a rest now.'

'Yes, if God spares him. I hope so.'

'Don't say that. He will be fine,' I said with determination. 'He's talking! That's wonderful news.'

I had to be upbeat, however forced I sounded. My mind was churning with so many thoughts of my own father and grandfather, it was almost unbearable.

'I hope so, Charlotte. I can't imagine my life without him.' Alessio looked completely anguished at the thought. I felt an overwhelming urge to comfort him, but told myself that it wasn't my place.

We sat in silence as he drove swiftly, expertly, through the country roads towards the outskirts of Venice.

'Would you like to listen to music?' he asked. 'I have a playlist.'

'The Macarena?' I couldn't help asking.

'Yeah, that's on there. My party piece.'

It was all quite retro: Dusty Springfield, Bob Dylan, Bryan Ferry, Velvet Underground. Even so, it was good not to have to talk.

After a while, he turned the music down just as Lou Reed was singing about his perfect day.

'Have you had a nice time in Montecastello, Charlotte?' he asked.

'If you call gaining three kilos in weight and making a fool of yourself in business and at play having a nice time ..'

'Even so,' he said, 'you've made a big impression on my uncle.'

'I like him very much. Hence making this journey with you.'

He looked like he was going to explain something but then

decided against it and turned the music up again. We spent a while not speaking.

Then, at one point, we thought we were lost, as we circled one characterless roundabout after another. We were both feeling tense and, as we approached Mestre, getting closer to the hospital, we began to get seriously anxious.

'Do you think I've taken the wrong turning?' he asked, checking the satnav.

'It's adjusting,' I said. 'I think we're still okay.'

'I just so much hope Umberto is on the road to recovery.'

I nodded. I felt as if I wanted to pray, but I really didn't know how to.

How ill would we find him? Would he have rallied? We had no idea. I felt an urge to reassure Alessio, but I pulled back from that. I hardly knew him, or his uncle for that matter. I didn't want to be crazily over-connected; it wouldn't help anyone. Even though I felt so worried for Umberto that my heart ached.

In the end, we navigated the last few kilometres to the hospital quite easily.

'Ready?' said Alessio as we parked up.

I nodded, feeling so choked up again that I couldn't quite trust myself to speak.

34

The Patient

We walked so fast we were almost running, arriving in Reception in a big fluster. The hospital was modern, very new-looking, and somehow all the more reassuring for it, with its expanses of white pristine marble, vast windows and array of equipment.

'We're here to see Umberto Rossini,' Alessio told a nurse on the ward desk.

'Come this way,' she said. 'He's expecting you.'

'He must be conscious in that case,' said Alessio.

I nodded, allowing myself to smile.

Umberto was in a private room, with dropped blinds and a fan turning in one corner. His eyes were closed when we went in, and he lay motionless.

Diana was at his side, looking worn out. I thought he'd got worse and gasped and reached out for Alessio, shocked by the sight of him. The scene was unbearable. Alessio caught me as my legs wobbled.

'It's okay, Charlotte,' said Diana. 'He's pulled through.'

I steadied myself.

'Umberto,' said Alessio, as we approached the bed together. 'It's me, Alessio. Charlotte is here too.'

There was no response, but I could see now that he was breathing, although he was wired to so many machines, we couldn't be sure he was breathing for himself.

Alessio took his hand and, slowly, Umberto opened his eyes.

'My boy,' he murmured.

'What a shock you gave us,' said Alessio, still holding his uncle's hand tenderly.

'I gave myself a fright,' he said, becoming more awake, and catching sight of me. 'Ah! Charlotte.'

'We were so worried,' I said.

'I'm fine,' he said, trying to sit up. 'I'll be better when I get out of here.'

'Shh now. Stay where you are,' said Alessio. He turned to me: 'Too bossy?'

'No, just right,' I assured him.

'This is all about Lucia,' Umberto said, his face distorted with pain.

Alessio glanced at me in a way that suggested I should leave.

'I must get some water,' I said. 'I'll be back in a few minutes.'

'I'd like some too,' said Alessio. 'Please.'

*

When I got back, a nurse was there and informed us that Umberto would have to stay in overnight, maybe for two nights, for observations. With a bit of luck, he might be allowed out on Sunday.

When we left the ward, Alessio went to talk to a senior member of the medical team.

As we headed to the car, he seemed much more relaxed. 'You look happier,' I said, not wishing to pry about what the medics had said.

'I am. I think he's going to be okay. In some ways this was inevitable with the stress he's been under.'

'Thank goodness it wasn't worse.'

'I know. He was so stressed about his daughter. We just need to make sure he doesn't get so worked up again.'

I recalled the day I'd heard him weeping in his office, but thought it better not to mention it. It wasn't really my place to know all their business.

We arrived silently back at the car. Another hour with him. I'd obviously missed my flight and I wasn't in the mood to rush to the airport, so we'd have to head back to Montecastello together.

'I'm starving,' said Alessio, as we buckled up. 'Do you fancy a bite to eat before we drive back?'

'Why not?' I said.

'We could park at the Tronchetto and catch a boat into Venice? Go somewhere nice?'

'Sure. But please choose a place that's not too... supermodel-ish.'

'I don't like supermodel places,' he said. 'The portions are too small.'

'Exactly.'

'It's nice to enjoy food, is it not?' he said. 'It's one of life's joys.'

'Yes. That's true. Here, I feel like I'm tasting flavours for the first time in ages.'

'Why have you not enjoyed food at home?' he asked as we drove towards the parking zone.

'Good question. Business pressures, I guess. Wanting to be thin. Feeling in control of food makes me feel in control of everything else.' I paused, deciding to trust him. 'But, if I'm honest about this not eating thing, it started when, you know, when my parents died.'

'I didn't know – both your parents?'

'Yes.'

'Sorry. It's rough. I can talk about that with authority.'

'You talk about everything with authority.'

'I know. It's something I should work on, I guess. A bit of humility.'

'Perhaps.'

He looked at me kindly then. 'Do you mind if I ask how your parents died? What happened?'

I told him the whole story on the way to the Tronchetto and he listened carefully. He didn't say a word, but I could sense his support.

35

Marco's

After we left the hulk of the parking terminal behind, the boat ride into the city was magical.

The wide lagoon began to narrow and the mysterious, exotic buildings, influenced by thirteenth-century Byzantine Constantinople and Islamic Cairo, emerged before us in a dancing gossamer heat haze. It felt as if we were in a painting and I couldn't imagine how anyone could resist a city with such otherworldly charms.

I looked over at Alessio, who was watching me. Smiling, evidently enjoying my wonderment. 'I'll take you to Marco's,' he said. 'He's a friend of mine.'

When we got off the boat, he gently guided me through side streets and alleys, pointing out a sumptuous array of bridges, galleries, churches and statues.

Finally, we arrived at Marco's, where delicious smells of garlic and rich pesto-parmesan sauces were wafting through the warm air.

'It *is* pretty fancy,' I said, peering into the restaurant from the street, then taking out my compact mirror and applying some lipstick.

'Let's go,' said Alessio. 'Stop fussing. You look nice without lipstick. Let me introduce you to Marco. He means a lot to me.'

I really would have to talk to him about that ordering-around thing he did. But it wasn't the right moment. I took my time with my lipstick, then pouted his way.

'I get it,' he said. 'You'll wear lipstick if you want to. And take as long as you like.'

'Exactly.'

The owner, Marco, approached us as soon as we entered, wreathed in smiles for Alessio, welcoming us as if we were family.

'Alessio!' he said. 'Wonderful to see you again, my friend.'

'And you!' said Alessio, embracing the restaurateur, slapping his back, seeming more animated than I'd ever seen him before, with the exception of when he was playing Dinosaurs with his nieces and nephews at his birthday party.

'This is Charlotte,' said Alessio. 'She's a friend of the family, here from London.'

'Ah, welcome to Venice!' Marco said. 'Do you like it?'

'Thank you. Yes, I love it.'

We were shown to a discreet booth table and, as we browsed the menu, some delicious nibbles of warm crusty bread, cheese and olives arrived.

'I usually have the pappardelle,' Alessio told me.

'I'll try that then,' I said.

'Are you sure? I mean, the fish is also great ... whatever you prefer. Listen to me! I'm sorry.'

It was the first time he'd been intent on not seeming overly bossy or authoritative. Noted.

I relaxed a little, deciding to celebrate that Umberto was going to be all right after the awful scare this morning, and put all thoughts of the strange subterfuge around Lavandula behind me.

Alessio and I made some small talk about the history of the restaurant, how hard it had been for Marco, when his father died young, to take over the place and modernise it.

'So, you both had to learn fast?' I said.

'We did. So true.'

He smiled at me. It was so unexpected and disarming that I could do nothing but stare. I then remembered my manners and smiled back at him.

No one could have missed the awkwardness or, for that matter, the charge between us. This man was almost too handsome to look at.

It was while I was ordering, the fish as it happened, that I noticed a commotion at the entrance. It was impossible to ignore. Two guys had arrived and it didn't seem as if they were welcome. Marco and one of the waiters were literally showing them the door.

Alessio glanced over as well and his face turned such a strange colour that I looked again at the kerfuffle.

Two tough characters were standing stubbornly at the desk, glaring our way. I recognised one of them as the Frankenstein man who was on the street outside Marcella's, when Lucia had to discuss something horrid the previous Tuesday. And the other was the man involved in the fight with Alessio at the Rossini. Definitely; the sleeve tattoo on his arm confirmed it.

Alessio's face clouded with concern.

'Go to the washroom and don't come out until I text you,' he commanded, shaken.

I was frozen to the spot, not able to process what he said.

'Now!' he said, urgently. 'Please. Go!'

I grabbed my bag and did as he said.

I looked over my shoulder before I went down some steps, following a sign to the washroom. Alessio was leading the two men out into the street, away from the restaurant. I carried on towards the washroom. But I was terrified they were going to harm him. Why now, just when he was starting to behave like a decent human being? I couldn't run away like this. I had to protect him. Guilt brimmed over inside me, for ever believing he was to blame for the fight in the gardens, and my guilt made me feel even more protective towards him. When I thought of my conversation with Allegra, I shuddered. Imagine if I'd contributed to an article blaming him for that fight.

I noticed a door opening onto the narrow alley behind the restaurant and, without a second thought, snuck out through it.

Out on the street, I heard raised voices. They'd obviously come around to the alley to discuss whatever business they had with each other. Thank goodness Alessio hadn't been bundled down a dark alley with a hood over his head. The Frankenstein guy was seriously HUGE. I crouched down behind some bins, sharing a corner with a sleeping tabby cat, who checked me out through one eye. From where I hid, I could see the three men. Alessio, Frankenstein, and the smaller one, with the tattoo.

'Lucia has disappeared,' snarled Frankenstein.

'Has she?' said Alessio. 'I know nothing about that.'

'Yes, you do. Where is she? You *will* tell us.'

'I honestly don't know. She doesn't tell me much.'

'She owes us money,' said Tattoo. 'Fifty thousand euros, to be precise.'

'No way,' said Alessio. 'I don't believe you.'

I heard a violent smash as a punch was thrown. Alessio fell against a wall, making me flinch.

'That's for lying. And for attacking my friend here,' said Frankenstein. 'Bastard.'

'I've told you before, don't go near my uncle, he can't bear it. In fact, he's in hospital right now.' At least Alessio was able to speak.

'Oh, my heart bleeds,' snarled Tattoo.

This enraged Alessio, who swung a punch at him. But Frankenstein waded in and I thought they were going to beat Alessio to death as they both started to smack him around. He was slumped like a dummy against the wall. I felt help-less. What could I do to save him? I couldn't watch him being beaten to a pulp, right there behind his friend's restaurant in Venice. No. I looked round for inspiration. There were bins everywhere. Cardboard lay against the wall, tied in a bundle. Hopeless. What good was that? I needed a weapon.

Then I spotted a huge broken aluminium saucepan lying near the bins, within reach. It was worth a try. I reached out for the pan, which still had some tomato sauce in the bottom, causing a bit of a clatter which made everyone realise they were not alone, although they still couldn't see me.

I didn't have time to hesitate. Without really thinking, I

charged towards the brawling trio, the pan lifted high above my head. Using all my strength, I hit Frankenstein square in the face with the pan. He was more startled than anything, but looked dazed, almost comedic, before collapsing to the ground. Tattoo approached me and I knew he was going for my wrist, to wrestle the pan off me. But I was quicker than him – and switched it to my other hand, then brought it down on his head before he could act. Stunned, he fell to the ground next to his friend. They lay side by side like a malignant Laurel and Hardy act. They didn't move for a few seconds and I was terrified I'd somehow killed them. But after a few moments, they began to moan and groan and splutter.

'Where did you come from?' said Alessio. 'I thought I told you to hide in the WC.'

The gratitude!

'*Thanks for saving my life, Charlotte*, would have been nice,' I said.

We stared down at the gruesome pair who were now trying, and failing, to get back up.

'We need to get out of town,' he said.

'Yes, let's get a move on!' I said.

I could see that the guys were determined to get on their feet, although they were still dazed, and maybe even concussed. I really had smacked the pan over their heads with some force.

'Come on,' Alessio urged.

He grabbed my hand and we started to run down the narrow street, bordering a canal. 'Are you okay?' he gasped, still running.

'I'm fine. But you're injured.' I went to examine the wound on his left cheekbone, but he shook his head.

'No time for that. There's no way I'm letting you get hurt.'

Laurel and Hardy were now staggering around behind us, hurling abuse, while bumping into each other, smacking each other like toddlers. We lost sight of them, but we both sensed there was every chance they'd soon appear ahead of us, as they surely knew more short cuts around this maze of a city than Alessio did.

'Alessio, over there.' I nudged him and we both turned towards a young man with luxuriant dark curls who was starting up an exquisitely varnished Riva speedboat on a small jetty.

'Can you take us to the Tronchetto?' Alessio said. 'Please? We're in a hurry!'

'Sure thing,' said the guy, amiably. 'The fare's a hundred euros,' he added, clearly recognising an opportunity when he saw one.

Alessio was already counting notes out from a money clip when, sure enough, the clowns appeared from a different direction.

'It's time to jump,' said Alessio, grabbing my hand.

And together we leaped – gracefully, I like to think – onto the Riva, just as our enemies bundled towards us horribly fast.

'Go!' Alessio instructed the driver, who deftly adjusted the collar of his shirt as the boat picked up speed.

I took in the Riva's sleek lines and cream leather trim, finding it hard not to imagine we were actually in a James Bond film.

Then, as we pulled further away from the jetty, we dared to glance back.

In fury and frustration, we saw Tattoo shove Frankenstein into the canal, where he splashed about, gulping and shouting obscenities – at us, at his partner, at the world in general.

Alessio and I laughed till tears ran down our faces. I couldn't help but notice the young Venetian man's elegant shoulders shaking too.

I felt such relief that Alessio was okay, but I also felt a sense of equality. He'd rescued me a couple of times, but now I'd saved him.

'Nice work, Charlotte,' he said. 'I like your style.'

'Not bad going, I agree.'

'But seriously, that was so brave of you. A woman with a saucepan – every gangster's worse nightmare.' He laughed again, but we both knew the situation had been deadly serious.

He then called Marco and asked him to alert the police so they could lift the guys.

'They've a thousand charges against them,' Alessio told me. 'They'll be kissing their freedom goodbye for a while...'

Back at the Tronchetto, we thanked our dashing saviour. I felt nothing but relief at how lovely it was to get back into the car together.

'Phew,' Alessio said. 'We're safe.'

As we left the city behind, we finally began to relax.

'That was quite the afternoon,' I said. 'Do you often get into scrapes like that?'

'Only since my cousin got involved with those nutters,' said Alessio, shaking his head. 'I don't know what I'm going to do with her. I mean, she and Lily have gone to London now, and Lily's mother is going crazy with worry, blaming Lucia. Just another thing Gabriella has against the Rossinis.'

'It's pretty alarming, though, that those two young women are tangled up with creeps like that.'

'More than alarming. We've been devastated. Desperately worried since Lucia –'

Now was my chance. I had to speak up. 'I should tell you,' I began, 'that Lily asked my advice about going to London ... about the two of them moving there.'

'Did she really?'

'Yes. She was being very responsible. Trying to find out the best way to go about it. Where to live. How to get a job for Lucia.'

'She's amazing, young Lily. Kind and sensitive. She takes such good care of our cousin. That's why ...' His voice trailed away. I knew what he was thinking of saying. That's why he tried not to embarrass Gabriella, over Lavandula. It would upset Lily. But he didn't say it. I guessed he realised that bringing it up would lead to talk of my failed Lavandula deal, and we couldn't risk that topic. Not yet.

'I told them they could rent my flat when I go to New York. That's if I do go,' I said. 'I don't really know what's happening.'

There was a little silence after that.

'You still want to come back to Montecastello?' he asked.

I'd checked flight times to London. There was one boarding, but that was the last of the day.

'Yeah. I think I'll need to stay at the Rossini for the night,' I said.

'Okay, I'll take you back. It's the least I can do. After all, you saved my life.' He grinned. ' With a saucepan.'

As we drove out of the suburbs, we got back onto the subject of New York.

'Sounds like it could be fun,' he said. 'Living in New York.'

'It's something I've always wanted to do.'

'I've been there a few times. But have never had the desire to live somewhere else. I love it here.'

'That's no surprise. Your family goes back a long way.'

'True. But sometimes I think we just keep repeating the same old patterns.'

'In what way?'

'Looking after the land. Looking after our family.'

'Hating the Morettis.'

'I try not to.'

'I can't imagine being in your situation. With real-life enemies. But I've had to stand up to a few business adversaries before. I've found that usually bullies hate being met with strength and integrity.'

He nodded. 'You've done well in business. I admire that.'

'Thank you. I sometimes think it was more by hard work than genius or courage, but I know I've achieved a lot.'

'You have. And I feel terrible to have stood in your way.'

I actually flinched. He was going to bring it up. I *so* wasn't ready to discuss business with him.

But he obviously wanted to clear it up and pressed on. 'I should have warned you as soon as you arrived that Gabriella was playing games.'

'That would have been helpful.' My tone was matter-of-fact, not a hint of our earlier laughter. 'Why didn't you?'

'Because I thought you'd assume I was trying to put you off for selfish reasons.'

'I suppose that's exactly what I would have thought.'

'I behaved stupidly. I hoped the whole problem would go away. That you'd decide the farm wasn't big enough, or that the locals were too miserable, and you'd never need to know that it didn't belong to Gabriella at all. That would have been simple.' He sighed. 'But life is never simple. It's all been so unfortunate. I'm truly sorry.'

I thought for a moment before speaking. 'In some ways, your actions were quite noble. I understand why you wanted to spare Lily's feelings,' I said. 'But my time has been wasted.'

'I know. That was the outcome that I desperately didn't want,' he said. 'But of course I could sell you –'

'Please, Alessio,' I interrupted. I believed him. But still, it was too late now to create a new deal – Bryony had moved on to synthetic oil. The lavender farm plan was over. I said firmly, 'I don't want to talk about it.'

'Okay. But, please, it was not my intention to harm your plans. I hardly know you. I only wish you well.'

He glanced at me as he drove. It seemed for a second or two that we would reach out and take each other's hands, but we didn't, and the moment passed.

36

Lovebirds

'Shall we take the country route back?' Alessio said. 'It's slower, but more scenic.' He'd just got off the phone with Diana, who had reassured him Umberto really was okay, no longer in danger. We were safe to head back to Montecastello.

'If you think there's time, then, yes.'

'We're not in a rush, are we? If you're flying tomorrow now?'

'True. I'm all packed up and have nothing more to do. Yes, let's take the slow route!'

'Great. Now you can relax for a few hours in my spectacular company.'

'I am honoured to be in this beautiful car with you, instead of a tractor and trailer.'

He laughed. 'It was pretty funny, wasn't it?'

'Hilarious.'

'I felt bad that your dress got splashed.'

'Did you? You didn't show it.'

'I don't give anything away to people I don't know.'

'That's for absolute sure.'

We went through a few small villages, admiring the scenery, now listening to Alessio's favourite opera, *Rigoletto* by Verdi. Occasionally, he would pull over to point out places of interest, historical sites, interesting features, beehives, wildflowers, a certain type of goat. He had a story about most of the restaurants we passed. I guessed he'd been on plenty of journeys between Venice and Montecastello.

He also had a great knowledge of churches in the area.

'Do you like churches?' I asked.

'Yes. More than I like religion,' he said.

'Same. I like the peacefulness but not the doctrine.'

'Precisely.'

The sun shone down on us, and it was remarkable how quickly we forgot about the drama at Marco's. We had entered our own world. The only reminder was the injury to Alessio's handsome face.

I caught myself looking at his hands as he drove, registering how much I liked them. How much I liked him.

Then, as we drove through a tiny picture-perfect place called Spello, there was a great commotion in the centre of the village.

'Oh, look!' I said, spying a beautiful church. 'It's a wedding!'

There was an assortment of fabulous cars, glamorous couples in sophisticated clothes, and an abundance of flowers and ribbons. It was quite a spectacle.

'Do you want to stop and watch?' he said.

'I would love to. If you don't mind?'

'No, I don't mind. I'd like to see the cars. Let me find a place to park.'

'Let me look at your cheek,' I said, as he parked on a little side street.

He turned to face me.

'Not too bad,' I said.

'And the cheek?'

'You've got plenty of that,' I said, flirtatiously enough for him to have kissed me if he'd chosen to, but he didn't.

The sun was shining high in the sky as we walked across to the church. As we got closer, Alessio exclaimed, 'I don't believe it!'

'What is it?'

'I went to school with the groom!'

'Really! Do you want to say hello? Did you get on with him?'

'Yes, sure. We were good friends. I'd heard he'd moved out here but we lost touch. Amazing.'

'This might be a chance to catch up with some people?'

'Yes. This is incredible. Paulo's a football agent, a bit of a lad. He's been dating Leonora for years but I didn't think he'd settle down. Imagine that. Married. Wow! I can't believe it. I always thought they'd go their own ways.' He shook his head. 'Shows what I know about relationships.'

'Sometimes the teen sweethearts do the best,' I said, thinking of my own parents, and a couple of friends from Ambler who were blissfully happy in young married life. According to their social media feeds, at least.

'True.' He looked wistful, vulnerable somehow. I wondered if he was hurt that he hadn't been invited, or maybe it was a shock to him that even the more laddish of his school friends were getting married? A reminder of his own loneliness perhaps.

But it wasn't long before another school friend spotted Alessio and came bounding over, beaming. Quite unexpectedly, Alessio draped an arm around my shoulder as the friend approached. It would have been churlish of me to object. The whole atmosphere was so friendly and love-filled, and I was quite carried away by everyone's energy.

'Alessio! Great to see you!'

'David!' said Alessio. 'It's been too long.'

'It has! You never came to any of our reunions? We thought you'd had enough of us.'

'No, not at all. Sorry. I was too busy with the grapes. Boring of me, I know.'

'Never known as boring, my friend,' said David, slapping Alessio on the shoulder – which looked painful considering his recent back-alley fighting – and glancing my way.

'Oh, how rude of me,' said Alessio. 'This is Charlotte Alexander, visiting from London.' His arm went from being draped to drawing me firmly closer towards him. I got the message. I was going to be his girlfriend for the next half-hour. I didn't mind. I knew how it felt to be unexpectedly shaken by witnessing the personal happiness of others, especially your peers. No amount of business success could match that.

'Hi, Charlotte,' said David. 'Well done to you for taming this one!'

'I don't think he'll ever be tamed,' I said, playing along. 'We've already been fighting in the street today.' I pointed to Alessio's bruised cheek.

David laughed. 'She's got a great sense of humour as well,' he said.

'Oh, she really has,' said Alessio, looking at me with a glint in his eye.

David turned to me: 'He was always a wildcard. But, believe me, he's the guy you'd want by your side in a crisis.'

'I think he's referring to a specific incident at the leavers' ball. I'll tell you later, *cara*,' said Alessio, looking into my eyes as if to say: 'Thanks for this.'

'I know Paulo will want to see you,' said David. 'Why not join us in the garden for a few drinks? You'll know everyone.'

'I'd love to, but I won't stay for long,' said Alessio. 'I'm driving.'

'Damn. Stay the night in the little hotel?' said David, as he pointed across the street. 'We're all in there. They're bound to have an attic room or a shed or something?' he said. 'What's stopping you?'

Alessio shrugged. 'Nothing, I suppose. What do you think, Charlotte?'

'Sounds great – I do have a flight home tomorrow,' I said. 'But a party sounds like much more fun!'

'It's going to be awesome,' said David.

I looked at Alessio. 'I'm in if you are,' I said.

'Okay. Let's see what they say at the hotel.'

We congratulated the bride and groom, who were genuinely delighted to see Alessio, and then went over to the hotel to ask about accommodation. It was a small place, very traditional, tiled floors and not much furniture, but spotlessly clean.

At first, they said they had nothing, which was hardly surprising, but what was surprising was how crestfallen Alessio seemed at this news. As we turned to leave the hotel, the owner called us back.

'Actually,' he said, 'we do have a little room. Number sixteen. But it's very small?'

'We'll take it,' said Alessio and we were handed a huge old key.

'Shall we take a look?' he said.

'Yeah. Let's see what "very small" means.'

We went up a winding staircase, the ceiling getting lower on each level, so eventually Alessio was practically bent double. The key looked as if it was going to prove as big as the door itself.

'Here's room sixteen,' he said. The door was indeed tiny.

'You'll have to crawl in,' I said, laughing.

He tried the key. The door opened to reveal a room which, although small, had a reasonably high ceiling, and it was furnished nicely, but with a tiny double bed.

'What do you say?' he said.

'Snug.'

'Yes, I like that word. I've never had the opportunity to use it. *Snug*.'

We both looked out of the window, from which we could see the wedding party laughing and clinking glasses.

'Are you happy to share this?' he asked. 'Truly?'

'Yes. I'll sleep on the floor.'

'No. I will.'

I didn't think we needed a stand-off on the subject of sleeping arrangements. 'Do you mind if I get changed?' I asked. 'My case is in the car. Didn't quite know I'd be attending an Italian wedding when I set off for hospital. Well, strictly speaking for my flight home.'

'It's been a mad sort of day, hasn't it?'

I nodded. 'The highlight of which was surely the fight in a Venetian alley.'

'I really am sorry about that drama. But you were very heroic,' he added with a wink.

'I suppose I was.' I paused. 'It isn't the first time I've seen you in a fight, of course.'

'What? What do you mean?'

'At the Rossini. I saw everything – the day I arrived.'

37

To Know All

'Oh God.' Alessio looked more worried than I'd seen him all day. 'What did you think?'

I sat on the end of the bed, and he joined me, then took a bottle of water from his bag, offering me a sip.

'Thank you,' I said, grateful for the cooling effect on my parched throat.

'So?' he said. 'The fight at the hotel?'

'I thought you were a brute,' I said.

'No wonder.' He looked at me. 'But do you get it now?'

I nodded and he went on.

'He'd come for money. He knew I'd been giving Lucia money. She can't bear to ask her father, you see. But I didn't like that guy coming to the hotel. I can't have that. It was getting out of hand and I wanted to scare him off.'

'I understand. You don't have to justify . . .'

'No, but I want to explain. I felt bad about it all. I was protecting my family. I even told Lucia not to come too close to home while she was involved with them. She liked to meet me in a church in town. We'd remember her mother there. She's buried in the grounds at the back of the church, along with the child.'

That explained market day. There was so much I hadn't understood.

'I shouldn't have judged a situation I knew nothing about.'

'It's natural. You walked into a complex family.'

'But an amazing family,' I smiled.

He looked thrilled. 'Thank you. I think so. This is the worst thing that's happened to us in recent times. Even all the dramas with Gabriella aren't so bad compared with this. Lucia is just a child. We miss her. And Lily has been dragged along by her big heart.'

'You are a loving family –'

'Believe me, we've tried everything to help her. But the more we tried, the more we pushed her away.'

'Lucia's very fragile, I can see that. When did she and Umberto stop getting along?'

'It was gradual. Started when she got the modelling work in Venice and Milan. She was only sixteen and so excited.'

'Of course, she's very beautiful.'

'I know, but so tiny! She was known for being so skinny, childlike, and she had to keep that going. That was unfair, cruel really. She needs to be allowed to become a woman.'

'So, did she starve herself?'

'Yes, but she also told me that she started using, to kill her appetite.'

'That's awful. I saw her with Lily in Marcella's on Tuesday. She was terrified. And those two brutes I just knocked out – single-handedly with my saucepan – were intimidating her.'

'Bastards! They never leave her alone. They sniff out opportunity, vulnerability. The family wealth, her looks, her fragility . . . But also, I think the monster one tells himself he's in love with her. Makes it even worse.'

I shuddered. 'I'm glad she's safe from him in London. I'll see them when I get back there.'

'Thank you. It just broke Umberto's heart when he approached her in the airport and she wouldn't even look at him.'

'Poor man. I'm guessing he raised Lucia alone?'

'Yes. He took her to nursery every day after Marianna died. Then school. Holidays. Ponies. Funfairs and beaches. They used to be inseparable.'

'I hope they can resolve things,' I said. 'She's probably too ashamed of herself to face him just now.'

'I agree. She turns shame to anger.'

I nodded.

'Anyway,' he said with a deep sigh, 'back to this wedding. Shall I get your case from the car?'

'That would be kind, thank you.'

I headed to the bathroom, washing my hands then taking my make-up bag from my handbag and touching up my eyes and lips, while I waited for him to come back.

When he returned, he was very helpful, running to fetch an iron when I decided to wear my Bluebell maxi dress, which was all crushed. Then he held one section of my hair patiently while I attempted a chignon in the cramped little bathroom, with attic eves proving a challenge. Finally, he fastened my mother's locket round my neck, his fingers brushing against the nape of my neck. As he came closer to fasten the catch, I shuddered at the sense that he was going to kiss my neck.

'You can leave now, while I get dressed,' I said, somewhat breathlessly.

'Okay,' he murmured. 'I'll be out in the street, waiting for you.'

'Won't be long.'

'Thanks for this, Charlotte. I feel like the odd one out. Unmarried, love life in the tabloids. You're providing me with my dignity here.'

'I get it.'

As he went out of the door, he turned to smile. 'Nice ankles, by the way!'

Yes! At last my ankles were back.

Once dressed, I couldn't quite see how I looked as there wasn't a full-length mirror, but I thought I should get on with it, so with one last tweak of the chignon, I made my way downstairs.

*

I emerged on to the sunny street where he was waiting, talking on his mobile to Diana.

He clicked off his phone, turned to look right at me and said: 'Wow. Beautiful.'

'Thank you. Shall I keep the room key in my bag?'

'If you wouldn't mind. Please.'

As we went over the road to join the wedding party, he reached out with his hand, which I took in mine. Silly play acting, but in some ways, it was quite good fun. What am I saying? In every way, it was good fun. I felt very happy in that moment. Buoyant and grounded all at the same time. Either way, much happier than I had felt in years.

When we joined the wedding crowd, the party had just started.

We walked through the entrance to the garden, decorated with an arch of flowers; jasmine, lilies, pink roses and wild blue geranium. The place was vibrant with laughter and love. Endless trays of drinks were spirited around by waiters and waitresses in black and white outfits. There were platters of lobsters, oysters and langoustine, garnished with lemons and parsley, protected from the sun under gazebos. Music played in the background. People laughed joyfully. I was sure I glimpsed the handsome footballer, Salvo, who Penelope had gossiped about as Bianca's beau, but thought nothing of it – everything was such a thrill, so intoxicating and novel.

As I hadn't eaten a thing at Marco's, my head was turned by the food. The dishes looked divine. Mushroom and asparagus risotto, prawns in sharp tomato sauce, pesto chicken pieces, pan-fried gnocchi with duck sauce and parmesan. Venison stew in red wine, braised pork with apple and Grappa sauce, as well as baked bass with herbs. But we weren't even proper guests so I felt we'd have to wait until invited to eat.

The bride and groom, Paulo and Leonora, zoomed right over when they spotted Alessio again.

'Alessio! It's so great you could stay,' said Paulo.

'Alessio, when are *you* getting married?' Leonora exclaimed as she wrapped him in a hug.

'I can highly recommend it,' said Paulo. 'It's the best thing ever!'

'Err. You've only been married for ten minutes,' said Alessio.

We all laughed, that crazy way when everyone is jolly, and everything seems hilarious. Alessio and I started to mingle, enjoying the champagne, chatting to the groom's parents and various old friends from Alessio's school days. Even a few of his teachers, one of whom was determined to tell me that he was 'always strong-willed'.

As we fled the teacher in a fit of giggles, Leonora insisted that we help ourselves to food.

'We should send them a lovely present,' I said, feeling a bit of a gate-crasher, but tucking in, nonetheless.

'Sure. They'd like a crate of fizz, I'd guess,' said Alessio, before quickly adding, 'I'm not hugely imaginative about presents.'

I laughed. Clearly.

Lemon cake with figs and fresh cream, then coffee and raw chocolate truffles followed the superb main dishes. After that, some serious dancing kicked off.

'Want to dance?' said Alessio.

'Sure. Why not?'

At first, they played Italian rock and pop and I could see that Alessio loved to dance. After a brief break for the band, they struck up again, and this time, everyone rounded on Alessio.

It was his favourite: The Macarena! This turned out to be a request from the groom; evidently it was an old joke from their school days where Alessio was famed for this dance. Some of the women – who were once schoolgirls with him – made a beeline for Alessio, and he got immersed in his routine as he'd done at his own birthday. I started to dance with one of his school friends, Filippo. Alessio very sweetly came to ask if I was okay.

'Of course, carry on. This is your moment.'

'It's a pain. Follows me everywhere I go. I'll be back. Promise.'

'I'm fine,' I said, sorely tempted to kiss him, but managing to resist. Just.

I was totally relaxed, chatting to Filippo as we danced, when I glanced over to see that Alessio was now dancing with a girl. Just one girl. Very tall. Very elegant. Goddess-like.

She was as graceful as a gazelle.

Bianca Borlotti.

I gulped, privately distressed, but unwilling to show it.

38

Dirty Dancing

And, anyway, what was it to me? We were only pretending to be a couple, but they looked so perfect together, I almost choked. They really were made for each other. It was clear to anyone who saw them that she was the love of his life, and they'd just been waiting to be reunited. I looked around and noticed that Salvo seemed uninterested; he was chatting up another stunning girl at the bar.

'Are you okay?' said Filippo.

'Yes, sorry, I just need some water.'

I took a seat while he kindly went to get some. I saw that Bianca was dancing very close to Alessio now. He seemed entirely relaxed, moving in perfect time with her. I couldn't stand it. There was a burning, agonised feeling in my heart. The truth was, I was consumed with jealousy.

Filippo returned with the water. I thanked him and excused myself. How stupid I was. Had I started to imagine there might really be something between Alessio and me? We were just on a high about Umberto being okay. And about playing at being vigilantes. Yes, we had bonded in the car, but who wouldn't under those circumstances? We were still strangers. I'd only known him for a week and we'd been enemies for most of it.

I went for a stroll in the gardens, recalling our first meeting with the tractor, then the market day subterfuge. The red bikini on the Sunday and the shock of my life later that day, when I discovered he was the boss of the whole Rossini empire. I blushed as I recalled him catching me under the peach tree with Cosimo. I melted when I recalled the way he helped me with Calandra during the storm, and the next day when she needed care. I marvelled at how supportive he was of his uncle, how mindful for his cousin's feelings about the Countess's behaviour. The way he had overlooked his rights to Lavandula. His school friend had said Alessio was someone to have on your side in a crisis, and that was so true.

I reflected more on the reasons why he'd kept quiet about the deeds for Lavandula. They did seem honourable, as he'd explained them. I sat down by a pretty river running along the bottom of the garden and I realised with a crashing, terrifying bolt to my conscious mind that I might be falling in love with Alessio Rossini. I was shocked at myself. Clearly all my loathing of him had been to mask my attraction, to push away the chance that he could upset my plans. I had to stay on course, get to New York, live my dream life. Alessio Rossini was no part of that.

I tried to find my rational self, not easy after wine and dancing and laughter in a picturesque Italian village. I asked myself what I was doing at a rural wedding with a man I hardly knew, imagining that I had feelings for him. It was all part of the summer madness that I'd experienced since I arrived in

Montecastello. It was fate that he'd come here and been reunited with Bianca. Penelope, the beautician in Aphrodite, had told me Bianca wanted him back. And Diana had implied he'd been heartbroken. I was nothing to him. The sooner I realised that and got away, the sooner I'd stop feeling this terrible burn of jealousy. I gathered up my dress and started to run to the little hotel. Maybe if I got my case and asked them to call for a cab, I could get an airport hotel for the night. Yes. That was my plan.

After all, it was New York I wanted. It was time to get over this silly crush on Alessio Rossini.

My mind was made up. I needed to follow my destiny, not be side-tracked, derailed by the warmth and beauty of this seductive place.

I took a long route round to the hotel, avoiding the wedding party. I knew I was doing the right thing. And I told myself now that he'd been reunited with irresistible Bianca, Alessio would only be relieved that I'd left.

Stealthily, I crossed the road to the hotel. I asked at Reception if they could call a cab.

'Can you ask them to wait by the town hall?' I said.

She nodded, pressing the number. I heard her make the arrangement.

'It will arrive in fifteen minutes,' said the girl. 'Meet by the town hall. A white SUV.'

'Thank you.'

I went quietly up the steep staircase, letting myself into the room. I half wished he was in there, waiting for me, like in a film. But the room was empty. I changed into a simple dress and mules, repacked, fastened up my suitcase and went downstairs and out onto the street.

Darkness was falling as I skulked along the main street, pulling my case behind me. I told myself I didn't want him to see me. And yet I hoped, childishly, that he would be searching for me.

I thought about my arrival in Montecastello. Pulling the case, hearing the tractor, meeting Alessio for the first time. He was right, it was hilarious.

The cab was waiting. I jumped in and leaned back into the seat.

I decided to see if I could book a room in an airport hotel. I reached into my bag. But where was my phone? Damn! I realised I'd left it in the hotel room. Idiot! What should I do? I knew there'd be a real chance of seeing Alessio if I went back. But I'd decided on this course. The car was turning around, away from the village. Should I ask the driver to stop and turn back? I decided to leave it. I'd email hotels from my tablet or wing it. My time was up in Italy. I'd soon forget this place and these people.

I looked out of the back window and I thought I saw Alessio outside the hotel, running his fingers through his hair distractedly. Or maybe I imagined it. Who knew? It was hardly important anymore.

I leaned forward to the driver. 'Can you go via the hospital in Mestre, please?' I said.

'Sure. But weren't you going to the airport?'

'Yes, but only after I've been to the hospital,' I said.

'Okay. I will wait for you outside.'

39

London

On the flight back to London the next morning, I was glad that I'd seen Umberto and that he looked so well. He'd asked where Alessio was. I'd blushed and told him I'd left him with Bianca at a wedding we gate-crashed.

'Bianca?' he said.

'Yes. They seemed so perfect for each other.'

'No,' said Umberto, giving me a direct look. 'They're not.'

I wavered slightly and changed the subject. 'I need to get back to London,' I said.

'Will you check on the girls?' He reached out and took my hand. 'Lily and Lucia have gone to London.'

'I will. They'll be fine. But of course I'll look out for them.'

'Thank you. And, Charlotte? Will you promise me something?'

'Yes. What is it?'

'Don't tell Lucia that I've been ill. Please.'

'Okay, I won't mention it. But she might hear some other way, through Lily?'

'Maybe. But I don't want her to worry about me. She's got enough of her own problems.'

It was typical of Umberto to be so selfless and thoughtful. But still, I did wonder if it might be good for Lucia to know, that it might bring them together. But, considering the situation with the brutes, I reflected the girls might be best to lie low in London for a long while.

During that flight back to London, I began to worry about Lily and Lucia. I hoped that they'd feel free and alive and inspired in a new city. I wanted to help them as much as possible. But I'd be going to New York soon. Wouldn't I?

Thank goodness I'd put them in touch with Lara. She had already met them for coffee and given them top tips on where to go, and not to go. 'They said Alessio likes you,' Lara messaged me.

I sighed. Diana had said the same. But everybody had got that wrong.

Lara. A godsend. I was really looking forward to seeing her again. She had organised a phone for me which she said would arrive at the office on Monday. I'd decided to get a new number. I wanted to tell myself that maybe Alessio had tried to contact me, but that I'd never know. It was stupid of me, but I felt as if he was going to be hard to forget, so I would do everything possible to erase him from my mind and from my life.

*

Lara came to my little Chelsea flat, overlooking the park, on the Sunday, to discuss what to do about the New York deal, and bring me up to date on things in the office.

She used her key and found me buried under my duvet.

I was having serious withdrawal symptoms from my heated Italian adventure. London felt cold, the light was so empty and grey. My heart was so full. It was going to take me a while to get back to normal.

'Welcome home. I brought breakfast!' she said, standing at my bedroom door, proffering a bag of buttery croissants.

'Great, thanks,' I mumbled. 'I'll come through to the kitchen in a minute. Can you put the kettle on, please?'

My lovely breakfasts on the sunny terrace with Diana were no more!

'Hurry up, boss,' said Lara. 'There's a lot to discuss!'

'Okay. Okay. Give me ten minutes. I'll shower.'

When I finally got through to the kitchen, about half an hour later, she'd made coffee, heated the pastries, and chopped a pile of fresh fruit.

'Thank you!' I said. 'I don't deserve you.'

'Yes, you do. You've had one crazy week in the sun. You're allowed.'

'And it really was crazy.'

'I'm starting to think so,' she said, a cheeky grin on her face.

'What do you mean?'

'Oh, nothing . . .'

'Tell me!'

She laughed, relishing her secret.

'What is it?' I asked. 'What's funny?'

'Just something that might be of interest to you,' she said.

'Oh, stop it. Tell me. Please.'

'I spoke to someone you know this morning.'

'And?'

'Someone you know in Italy.'

'Lily?'

'No, not Lily.'

'Who?'

'Alessio Rossini.'

'No!' My throat seemed to close over.

'Yes! *The* Alessio Rossini.'

'Oh my God. What did he say? How did he get your number?'

'He has your phone. I rang it and he picked up.'

My breathing got faster. 'Oh no. What did he say? I left so abruptly.'

'Calm down. Have a coffee and I'll tell you.'

'This is like a nightmare.'

'No, it's not. No drama required. He's very concerned about you. Apparently there was a misunderstanding.'

'There was.'

'He said he'd like to speak to you.'

'I don't want to keep in touch with him,' I said, with complete finality.

'Oh, really? Are you quite sure about that?'

'Yes,' I said. 'But I'll keep his number just in case,'

'Yes. Do that,' she said. 'Good idea.'

I looked hard at her. 'Shut up.'

'Oh come on, tell me what happened. He sounded worried, honestly. Wanted to know that you'd got home safely.'

I sat down at the breakfast bar. 'Okay,' I said, 'here's what happened.'

Lara listened carefully, like she always does. Not interrupting or giving opinions. Just tilting her head this way and that, nodding, raising an eyebrow.

'So that's it,' I concluded. 'I left the wedding without telling him.'

'You shouldn't have done that,' she said. 'That was childish.'

'I know. But it was easier. To get away, put all that behind me. The trip was a disaster from start to finish.'

'Or, to look at it another way, it was a triumph.'

I looked at her quizzically. 'What do you mean?'

'You enjoyed yourself. Let go. Got involved. For the first time in ages. Your heart has fired itself up again.'

I considered this. Maybe she was right. 'Yeah. But for now, I need to get back to how I was before Montecastello. What are we going to do about the Florinda deal? Are we going to go with the synthetic lavender oil?'

'What choice do we have? We've run out of time.' She held my gaze. 'Plus, I think they will give you very little say.'

'You're right. But maybe when I get to New York and I'm in the office every day, I will have more control.'

'You need to establish that,' said Lara. 'You've fought really hard to protect that brand. Remember what we went through when Gorgeous Girl copied our bottles? Remember that court case and the horror story we had when they threatened us?'

'I know. I know. But there's so much money on the table, Lara. We could start over again with a new fragrance and a new design approach with that kind of capital. Any financial worries would be over.'

'It's so tempting. But only if you're sure you can live with the changes they're going to make.'

I took a sip of coffee. 'I have to try. The sooner I get out there, the better.'

'Okay. Let's get the flights sorted.'

'Plus, Cooper Dean is waiting for me,' I said, desperately looking to change the subject away from Alessio.

'Cooper Dean?'

'Yes. He asked me to dinner.'

'Did he really?' said Lara.

'Well, he said when I arrived in New York, we should go to dinner.'

'And you're going to bet your life on him?'

'Yes. No. We'll see.'

'Meanwhile, what are we going to do in the London office?'

'Work on the new brand.'

'What new brand?'

'It's called Lily & Lucia. It's innocent but a bit wild. White peach, cotton candy, ginger ...'

'I love it. And the packaging?'

'Ink and pen, sketchy. Very Italian.'

'Gorgeous. Your trip definitely wasn't a waste of time. Lily and Lucia are going to be thrilled. An iconic fragrance named for them.'

'I like that you already think of it as iconic.'

'Anything you make will be iconic. You have a real flair for this business.'

'Thank you, Lara, that means a lot.'

After breakfast, Lara left and I googled Alessio. I just had to see him again.

A news story popped up.

'Tear-stained and emotional, Bianca Borlotti flees Paulo Marconi society wedding ...'

40

Back to Business

Back in the office, my new phone arrived on the Monday. Firstly, I called the Rossini and Rosa gave me Diana's number. I hadn't thought it through well. Leaving my phone behind in that little hotel room proved to be a very annoying thing. I messaged Diana to check on how Umberto was doing. She replied immediately.

'He's fine! We miss you! Are you coming back for the festival? It's on the twenty-eighth of August.'

Over a month away. There was so much that could happen before that. But I did want to go. I just wasn't sure I could stand the tension with Alessio.

'I won't promise, but I will try my best,' I said. 'I could be in New York by then.'

'Okay. Alessio is in a foul mood these days. What happened after you two left the hospital? He said some guys who've been harassing Lucia upset you?'

'Yes, there was a scene. And the time had come for me to get back to my desk. But I want to stay in touch with everyone.'

'You MUST. Let me know how everything goes with your perfume deal. Lots of love, D.'

Lara had Lily's number, so I called her to check that she and Lucia were okay, and they seemed to be loving London. We planned to meet up the following week. I also had an awkward call with Bryony, when I told her I'd be in New York within three weeks.

'Good,' she said. 'We need to press on with things. The manufactured oil will be great. You know this is the best way to proceed, don't you?'

I said a swift, 'Must dash', as a response to that.

Lara and I invited our designer, Nathan, into the office to talk about the new fragrance and we made some progress. I felt as if Italy had touched me and ignited my creativity. Lara was right about that. I didn't admit it to anyone, not even Lara, but I missed Montecastello. The weather, the views, the people and, not least, Calandra.

And, well, for sure, Alessio was on my mind. I didn't text him from my new number. I wanted to see if I could stop thinking about him. I was sure that when normal life resumed, and I was entertaining in my Upper West Side house, I'd think of my Italian feelings as nothing more than a silly holiday crush.

*

Despite my efforts to write off my Montecastello experience, as I made plans to leave the London office, it was never very far from my mind. It started to seem as if that intense, eventful week had been an illusion, one long daydream, but with very real consequences. None of it seemed quite of this world, but I knew it had changed me, healed me, in some significant way. When I wasn't busy, an image of Alessio Rossini would float into my mind, and I could now laugh at the ludicrous scenario of this successful Italian businessman carting me onto a trailer and pulling me through town in a tractor. I couldn't decide if his humility was greater than his arrogance, or if my attraction to him was based on the mixture of the two.

With each passing day, I thought more positively about him, recalling little events, looks and incidents between us with the advantage of hindsight and a type of close-at-hand nostalgia. In my most truthful moments of night-time candour, I admitted I'd been hasty to leave the wedding like that. I knew the truth was that I couldn't bear to see Alessio with Bianca. I was jealous and I asked myself what this meant. Was it more than a crush? Had I been starting to fall in love with him?

I tried to work out what he thought of me.

An image which I replayed was the look in his eyes when he saw me with Cosimo that day at the peach tree. Had he felt a surge of jealousy too? How could it be so? We hardly knew each other. Unless I went back to Montecastello for the lavender festival, there would be no need to see him again. I supposed I'd hear a bit about him from Diana, and from his cousins. Lily and Lucia were very much on my mind back in London. It was best to leave any feelings in the past. I had a new life to get on with after all. No for time distractions.

Early in my second week, Lara and I organised lunch with the Rossini cousins. We wanted to see what they thought about the name of our new fragrance. And I wanted to sound them out about a black and white photo shoot for promoting the range.

41

Countryside

Lara had booked a table at our favourite place, Sophie's, on Brougham Place, for an early lunch.

Lily and Lucia were already in the restaurant when we got there. It was lovely to see them. Lucia looked better already. From the friendliness of their chat and laughter at one another's jokes, it was clear that Lara had already bonded with them. I should tell Diana how well they are, I thought, so she could report back to Umberto. It was clear that Lucia had no idea about her father's illness, just as he wished.

The girls literally jumped for joy when I told them the name of the new fragrance we were planning.

'That's so cool. Can we be the face of it?' said Lily.

'I was going to ask that. Would you be up for that? Some photographs?'

They giggled, delighted. As they sat side by side on Sophie's pink velvet banquettes, wearing denims and white frilled shirts, their hair loose, a smudge of rosy lipstick, I thought how perfect they looked right there – and for the brand.

'I was only joking, actually,' said Lily. 'But I would love to get involved. How about you, Lucia?'

'Yes! I can't think of anything more fun.'

'It will be ages before we get to the promotion stage. Developing a perfume takes forever. But, great to know you're in. Thank you. Let's order lunch, my treat.'

We didn't talk about family things back in Italy. But gradually the conversation got around to the reasons they'd left Venice in such a hurry. Lara was curious.

'We were in big trouble back home,' said Lucia. 'Poor Alessio tried everything possible to get those guys to stay away. But it was getting more and more dangerous.'

'They looked pretty mean when I saw them opposite Marcella's that day,' I said.

And that was when Lucia suddenly became animated.

'Alessio says he's sorted out those guys for good. Though he didn't make much sense. He was so weird. Said they'd been silenced by a minx of a girl hitting them with a saucepan! I think he was just trying to shield us from the details. He says the funniest things.'

'He really does,' I smirked.

Lara looked at me askance.

'They've been arrested on drugs charges, apparently,' said Lily. 'They're going down.'

'And you're going up,' I said, delighted to hear that justice had been dealt to the creeps.

'We sure are.'

'Which means you must try not to think of the past now,' I said.

'We won't,' said Lily. 'We love London and really want to stay here!'

'We can definitely help you with all the logistics,' I said. 'Lara is a whizz at that.'

'That's so kind of you,' said Lily. 'But, actually, Alessio is coming over later this week to help!'

'Right.' I gulped, but regained my composure quickly. 'Well, that's very good of him.'

'Yes. He asked if we could all meet up. If you have the time?'

I paused. This was totally unexpected. I couldn't picture Alessio anywhere other than Italy. I was torn between excitement and panic, and automatically searched my brain for a plausible excuse. 'I'm actually going to the countryside later this week. For a break. What a shame.'

Lara looked at me as if to say, what are you talking about? She knew I absolutely never went to the countryside. I'd always assured her that I hated the countryside.

'Wow,' said Lara. 'The countryside?'

'Yes. I'm going horse riding back in Ambler, where I grew up,' I said. Get me, what a cracking excuse. I'd only thought of it in that moment.

'Ambler!' said Lara. 'It's so beautiful there.'

'Lucia loves horse riding,' said Lily. 'She really misses her horses.'

There was a little silence.

'Maybe we can all come to Ambler?' said Lara with a grin. 'I'm sure I've got an old pair of jodhpurs somewhere ...'

*

The weekend in Ambler took on epic proportions. Before I could say giddy-up, I was looking for accommodation for six people for a weekend in my childhood village. Me, Lucia, Lily, Alessio, plus Lara and her boyfriend, Jack.

'It's completely your own fault,' said Lara, gleefully.

'Why did you have to go and invite everyone?' I said.

'Because, you want to see Alessio again but you won't admit it. Also, it will be nice to get out of London. Maybe if you enjoyed the Italian countryside, you will enjoy the English countryside, too.'

'I haven't been there for ages. This is a nightmare. Google is throwing up nothing on the accommodation front. It's not the sort of place people go for a chichi weekend away. There's nothing to do.'

'You'll have to make it seem fun. I mean, Alessio owns most of the Italian countryside by all accounts, and has a castle, a wine empire, a luxury family hotel with a pool. You can't book us all into Betty and Bill's B&B.'

'There isn't even Betty and Bill's B&B. I wish there was. There's nothing.'

'You must know some people there,' she said. 'You lived there for years.'

'I do know some people. A few of my school friends still live there and some are married. But they live in teeny cottages, or forest eco pods, from what I see on social media. The little hotel, the Sparrow's Nest, has closed. It's now a beauty salon. I can't think where else we could stay.'

'There has to be a farmhouse or something we could rent?'

Lara was now sitting on my desk, engrossed in the idea of a trip to the country, texting Jack what wellies to buy. (He was a style slave, of her making.) She'd already drawn up a menu for the weekend.

I scrolled down, still finding nothing. Even the neighbouring village of Annville drew a blank. I looked out of the window for inspiration.

'Wait a minute,' I said. 'Rose Hall Stables. There's a big house there. They used to rent it out for holidays. It's owned by my old riding teacher, Miss Crystal. The last time she came up to London, Aunt Belinda told me Miss Crystal's still in business. It's huge but quite homely. I could see if it's free.'

'Great idea. A big old country house. The Italians will love it. I'll tell Jack.'

'Wait a minute! See if I get it first.'

'No worries. But make sure you do. This sounds like so much fun!'

'Glad you think so.'

'It has rom-com written all over it.' She grinned.

'Aunt Belinda lives in the next village. I'll give her a call and see what she knows about Rose Hall. She might have a number for Miss Crystal.'

'Why not invite her along, too? You should see more of Belinda. She always seems lovely when she pops into the office.'

'I know. She's sweet but . . .' my voice trailed away.

'But . . . What?'

I swallowed. 'The thing is, she's so like my mother, it's hard for me. They were identical twins.'

Lara looked at me with so much love I thought I'd start sobbing. 'Oh, I understand,' she said. 'That must be tough.'

I composed myself. 'But I should stay in touch more with

Belinda. She'll know what's what with the big house. I'm going to try her now.'

'And don't forget you've mentioned horse riding to everyone. And Mr Rossini is used to horses, right?'

'He is. How did I get into this pickle? Oh yes, that's right, it's all your fault.'

She jumped off my desk as I picked up my phone. I had to call Aunt Belinda's workplace, the local doctor's surgery, as hers was one of the numbers I'd lost when I left my phone behind.

The receptionist put me through to her.

'Aunt Belinda? Is that you? It's Charlotte.'

A pause.

'Charlotte! Sweetheart! Lovely to hear from you. Are you well?'

'Yes, I'm perfectly fine. I'm coming down this weekend, with some friends, and I wondered about renting Rose Hall. Do you know if it's still a holiday house?'

'How fabulous! I'd love to see you. Yes, you can rent Rose Hall!' she said. 'I'll just give you the number now.'

'Thanks, you're a life saver,' I said.

'It's not especially luxurious,' she said. 'But I hired it for my book group's Christmas party and it's very comfortable. And it's still owned by Miss Crystal. Do you remember her?'

'Of course! I loved her.'

'She had high hopes for you with the eventing.'

'I remember.' Good development, I needed some horses for this weekend. 'Does she still have as many horses?'

'A few, from what I saw. And Jonny still works for her.'

'No way! Jonny Kent? I DO NOT believe it.'

'Yes. He's a faithful retainer. A lovely young man. I see him around town.'

'How wonderful! So, do you think I could have Miss Crystal's number? It's very short notice,' I admitted. 'I'd be delighted if the house is free, and better still if we can mooch around the stables.'

'Yes, I'm sure Miss Crystal will do her best. We could meet for afternoon tea. Maybe at the Doll's House on Main Street?'

'Oh, that place! Those Victoria sponges! Yes, that would be a treat. I'll text you once the plans are all settled.'

'Brilliant. Can't wait to see you, Charlotte. It's been too long.'

*

I called the number for Rose Hall.

A croaky-voiced lady picked up. 'Miss Crystal speaking. How can I help you?'

'Hello, Miss Crystal. This is Charlotte Alexander. Do you remember me from years ago? Sarah's daughter.'

'Oh, hello! Yes, yes. I do remember you. Of course I do! You were always such a great helper. And you rode Zebedee?'

'Yes. How I loved him!'

'Happy times. How are you?'

'I am very well, thank you. And you?'

'Ancient, but still going strong.'

'There's a reason I'm calling.'

'Well, I guessed as much . . .'

'Would it be possible to rent the house this weekend?' I asked. 'The whole house?' I have some Italian friends who would love to see Ambler.'

Eventually we established that Rose Hall was free. Which made me suspicious about its desirability. She probably doesn't advertise it, I reasoned. Aunt Belinda had suggested it was basically okay. Oh well, it would have to do. My fake weekend in the countryside was taking on its own reality now.

'Would it be possible to ride?' I asked.

'I'd be delighted if you did. The horses could do with a bit of exercise,' she chuckled.

Goodness only knew what Alessio would think of Rose Hall and Miss Crystal's horses. But I was suddenly feeling quite excited about going back to the place of my childhood.

'Jonny will be delighted, too,' said Miss Crystal, 'to have some riders.'

'Oh yes, Aunt Belinda said he still works at the stables.'

'Yes. You remember Jonny? Such a good boy – this place would go down without him.'

Indeed, I remembered Jonny very well. He'd proposed to me when I was nine years old.

42

Rose Hall

I kept waiting for the weekend plans to blow up. Alessio had said previously he didn't much like leaving his local area. Perhaps he would make it to London but then decide against this crazy last-minute trip I'd planned.

'It'll never happen,' I told Lara.

'It will. Jack's "iconic" wellies have arrived. It must.'

The message to cancel never came. On the contrary, it seemed that everyone could hardly wait. Lara had issued instructions about what everyone should bring, a list which made it seem like we were expecting Armageddon.

'Are you looking forward to seeing Alessio?' said Lara during Thursday lunchtime, as we sat out in the tiny roof garden at our offices.

'I'm nervous about the whole thing, but in a funny way, feeling nervous about staying in Ambler, and even seeing Miss Crystal, is a distraction.'

'Yeah. And did you mention a Jonny the other day after you came off the phone?'

'Yes! Jonny Kent. Incredible to think he still works at the stables.'

'He's an old friend? Boyfriend?'

'Well, if you could call him a boyfriend. We left Ambler when I was, what, thirteen? But we used to hang out together a lot. As I told you, I didn't really fit in with the girls in my year at school.'

'I was the same. But I'm interested in this Jonny. What's he like?'

'He used to be very cute. Obsessed with horses. We spent all our time at the stables. We could chat for hours. About everything and nothing. You know how it is when you're growing up.'

'Totally. Interesting to see how he's turned out then.'

'Yes. But I could never be attracted to someone who's so unadventurous. He's never left town.'

'But I thought you said Alessio doesn't like to travel?'

'I'm not really talking about travel as a geographical thing. I'm talking about progress, mindset. I can't believe Jonny's still at the stables.'

'Plus. Defending Alessio indirectly. A good sign.'

'I'm not!'

Lara ignored me and went back to checking her list. 'Now. Jack's been to get loads of wine and beer and nibbles. I'm going to collect the fresh food later,' she said.

'Thank you so much, Lara. I have twelve towels, candles, cakes, playing cards and a few waterproof jackets, as per your instructions.'

'Good. I didn't want the girls to have to bring much as they're just settling in here, but they insisted on supplying Italian rolls, coffee and cheeses.'

'And I wonder what Alessio Rossini will bring? His girlfriend?'

'Stop it! He's going to be alone. Why are you obsessing about this Bianca? They're over.'

'But you should see her! She's out-of-this-world beautiful.'

'But if it's over, it's over. Don't be so simplistic. Looks aren't everything, or even anything,' she said. 'Look at me and Jack!'

'Okay.' I couldn't help but laugh – she and Jack made a stunning couple. 'Let's see what happens. I need to apologise for running out on him like that.'

'You so do. I don't know *what* you were thinking.'

*

The nearest train station to Ambler is Laurel Bank. Lara and I, along with Jack, stood on the platform there, waiting for the arrival of the 15.45 from Paddington, on that sunny Friday afternoon in the last week of July. Not long till I'd see Alessio.

We'd arrived at Rose Hall earlier in the day. I'd driven my sporty little Fiat 500 Abarth, packed to bursting, while Lara travelled in Jack's car, with the booze and food. It had been emotional driving into Ambler after all these years, passing our perfect family cottage on Stable Road. The place where I'd picked lavender and roses to create perfume, helped Mum make apple crumble most Sundays, read the Perfect Ponies series from cover to cover a hundred times. I was glad I was alone in the car. I pulled over and sobbed quite uncontrollably for a few minutes, the sort of engulfing sobs which chase around your body in agonising lurches. But when it stopped, I felt okay. More than okay. I felt better for it, cleansed somehow.

I'd carried on through the village, seeing that nothing had changed very much, aside from the Sparrow's Nest hotel – where we'd often eaten fish and chips, with bread and butter, washed down with pots of tea, followed by iced cakes – which had been replaced by a beauty salon called Gigi's. I'd heard through social media it was owned by two of my old school friends, Georgie Black and Izzy Carling. It looked great: modern and inviting. There was a community shop too, which I loved the look of. I stopped for a closer look, parking on the street right outside. After I touched up my make-up from the weeping, I got out the car. The window display showed freshly baked bread, cakes, honey, jam, raw chocolate. I went in and bought lots of stuff, browsing posters for local events as I paid at the till. There was so much going on! Choir events, dances, book groups, dramatic performances. How odd that this place had stopped to exist for me but was more vibrant than ever. Maybe even more vibrant than the small corner of London where I lived.

As I drove out of the little high street, the car fit to burst, I saw the Doll's House teashop where I was due to meet Aunt Belinda. I'd been there so often. It was so twee and yet comforting, with its floral china plate stands, delicate cups and saucers, and chinking antique teaspoons.

When I approached Rose Hall, I noticed Lara and Jack had pulled over near the entrance gates, waiting for me. They drove in behind me as we crawled along the leafy driveway, edged to either side with clusters of wildflowers.

Miss Crystal was waiting for us at the door of the house. There she was, just as she always had been. Wearing jodhpurs and boots, silver hair brushed back, a hint of deep pink lipstick, a ready smile.

I jumped out of the car and bounded towards her.

'You haven't changed a bit,' she said.

'Nor have you!'

'You always were a pretty girl,' she said. 'And I don't think you need the make-up.'

'I'm a city girl now, Miss Crystal,' I said.

'Pffft. City girl. You're an Ambler girl. Always will be.'

'Maybe you're right.' I laughed in a swirl of emotions. 'Meet my friends, Lara and Jack,' I said.

'How do you do? How nice to have you to stay,' she said.

'Thanks for having us at the last minute,' said Lara. 'We're really looking forward to our weekend.'

'Good. Good. Come on in. I hope you'll like it.'

To our delight, the house *was* very comfortable, in an old-fashioned way, with old chintzy sofas, fine antiques, porcelain bathrooms, fluffy towels and a superb kitchen, like something from a Victorian period drama. There were many pieces of gold-rimmed china, solid silver cutlery, copper saucepans, and a large fridge freezer, filled with local milk, butter, and fresh fruit. But the Rossini it was not. I hoped the Rossini members of our party wouldn't find it on the wrong side of quaint.

'It's gorgeous. I absolutely love it,' I said.

Miss Crystal was pleased. She lived in a cottage in the grounds and after a brief chat, she decided to go back there, calling over her shoulder:

'Jonny can't wait to see you. He's gone to Cove to buy a bridle. Back in a few hours. He lives in the mews house.'

'Ah, it'll be a treat to see him again, See you later!' I called.

I texted Aunt Belinda to say how thrilled I was with the place. And we confirmed our tea appointment for the next day. After that, we unpacked the cars and made the place as welcoming as possible for the Rossinis. Following a quick coffee, it was time to collect them at the station.

As I stood on the platform at Laurel Bank, I just couldn't imagine Alessio in my out-of-the way hometown. But Lily had confirmed by text that he was in London and was looking forward to the weekend. I had no idea how I would feel when I saw him again. It was going to be bizarre to greet him on my old patch, that was for sure. It was odd enough for *me* to be on my old patch.

'Relax,' said Lara. 'This is what people do on weekends all the time'

She knew me so well. She also always said my anxious face was much less pretty than my happy face. I tried to look happy.

The train trundled into the station while my heart raced. People got off, not in droves, but in twos and threes, and at first there was no sign of our guests. I started to tell myself that they'd missed it, got off at the wrong station, changed their mind, or that an accident had befallen them. But then Lily and Lucia appeared in front of us, looking like a pair of graceful thoroughbred horses. They ran along the platform towards us, giggling, long legs on show between mini-skirts and trainers, trailing cases, fabulous hair blowing in the breeze, pink lips, perfect brows and pearly teeth.

'Hi! We made it!' said Lucia.

'Hi, hi, great to see you!' I said.

'This is going to be so much fun,' she said, sounding like an excited child, embracing me warmly. She was free of anxiety. Her face glowed with joy.

Behind them, ambling, with just one fantastic tan leather

weekender case, was an apprehensive-looking Alessio Rossini. Jeans, tan boots, a white shirt, shades. Utterly Italian. Utterly gorgeous.

The girls went to the car with Lara and Jack, chattering, laughing, leaving a trail of Si by Armani, while I waited for him.

He smiled shyly. I walked towards him. We kissed briefly, on each cheek, like acquaintances.

'I hope you don't mind me joining you?' he said politely. His English was very polished, even more so than it had been in Montecastello.

'I don't mind at all.'

'That's good.'

'My car is this way,' I said, guiding him out of the station.

'Are you glad to be back in the UK?' he asked.

'Yes and no. I've been sorting out some business things.'

'Ah. Nice little car,' he said, with a brief smile.

'I like it.'

'I do too,' he said, maybe worried that I thought he'd empha-sised 'little' – which he hadn't.

We put his things in the back and when we both got in the front, we seemed to be so near to each other, almost touching. I lowered the canvas roof to give us slightly more space to breathe.

I thought of saying sorry about abandoning him at the wedding, but it didn't seem like the right moment. We were still awkward with one another. But the amazing thing was that he'd come to Ambler. I was tingling with anticipation.

43

Jonny Returns

The Rossinis loved Rose Hall – how very English and eccentric everything was – and settled in happily. Lily and Lucia decided they would cook for everyone and they played Italian dance music in the kitchen and banished the rest of us while they prepared dinner. That left Lara and Jack, plus me and Alessio, chatting in the drawing room which overlooked a paddock. The late sun glinted through the huge bay window and dressed the faded old room in a layer of golden gossamer.

'This place is wonderful,' said Alessio, sipping on a glass of red wine.

'But don't get too comfy.' Lara laughed. 'I hope everyone's up for horse riding tomorrow?'

'Sure,' said Alessio.

'I'll give it a try,' said Jack. 'Just don't make me wear those wellies!'

'You'll look lush in them,' Lara said, giving him a gentle punch.

'We should go around to the stables and see what's on offer?' I suggested. 'Pick our horses.'

'It's a plan,' Lara agreed.

'Follow me,' I said. 'The girls should come too.'

We went out from the kitchen door to the stables. There were eight loose boxes around the square courtyard. Although it was nothing fancy, it was immaculately clean and well swept.

The scent of straw, leather and horse dander circled in the air. I caught my breath as I was transported back to being nine years old, brought here by my mother and father, dying to jump onto Zebedee, the bounciest pony in the stables, a palomino with a velvet nose. Mum taking endless photos of me on horseback, Dad smiling proudly. Mum and Dad holding hands, waiting as I came in from countryside hacks. A perfect world. Heart-breaking memories which I hadn't allowed to surface for a long time. And, although those images made tears prick my eyes, I was glad to be remembering such lovely times.

As we nosed around the stable yard, trying to decide which horse was the right size for each of us, a bashed-up Land Rover Defender tore into the courtyard. Out jumped two big glossy black Labradors, followed by a gorgeous, dark-eyed sex god.

'Oh my word,' murmured Lara. 'Behold the king of the horses.'

I cleared my throat. 'He's changed!' I replied under my breath.

Jonny Kent had grown up.

*

He was brandishing a new bridle as he strode towards us, smiling broadly.

'Charlotte!' he said. 'Charlotte Alexander? Is it really you? I don't believe it. After all these years.'

It was an automatic response when I ran towards him and fell into his arms, as if all the time that had passed was concertinaed into this moment.

'Jonny! It's wonderful to see you.'

'You're as glorious as ever, Charlotte Alexander,' he grinned.

We babbled for a few minutes, almost forgetting there were others present. I introduced him to Lara and Jack and, of course, Alessio. Then we all met the dogs, Bunty and Beau.

'Would you like me to take you out for a ride across the countryside tomorrow?' Jonny said.

'That would be perfect,' I said. 'We were just wondering if there would be suitable horses for all of us?'

'Yeah. And I have the perfect horse for you, Charlotte. Follow me.'

It was as if we were thirteen again. I trotted beside him and was soon introduced to Suki, a sweet but spirited bay mare. The others waited behind us.

'You'll love her,' said Jonny. 'She's just the sort of horse you like.'

'And what sort is that?' said Alessio.

'Charming but strong-willed,' said Jonny. 'Just like Charlotte.'

'I see,' said Alessio. 'You match the rider to the horse in that way. Anything for me?'

Jonny thought about this for a moment.

'Come this way,' he said, with a wink.

We all followed him as he led us to a the largest of the loose boxes, to an impressive russet horse. There was a sign on his door, reading: 'Be careful, Magnus is known to bite.'

*

Lily and Lucia made a delicious dinner of vegetable lasagne and rainbow salad, dressed with orange and mint, followed by strawberries topped with whipped cream and raw chocolate. Alessio was on his best behaviour, helping around the kitchen, telling funny stories and listening attentively to others.

'He's a dream,' whispered Lara.

But Alessio overheard her. 'And, crazily enough, I don't bite,' he said.

We were having a lovely time, much better than I could have hoped, and more memories were coming back to me.

'Shall we go for a walk through the woods?' I suggested, recalling how Dad often took me out with a torch after dark.

Everyone was keen, so we got our boots on and headed outside. Stars shone in the clear sky and the air was still.

'This way,' I said. I knew there was a lovely route through the woods, along the enchanting edge of the river.

Alessio and I walked together, leading the way. He took the torch, lighting up the path.

'So, this is where you walked as a child?' he asked.

'Yes. This part of the woods is known as Owl's Nest. My father used to bring me here and tell me stories about the owls.'

'What stories? What did the owls do?'

'They feuded. One family of owls thought they owned the woods, but a rival family turned up, muscling in.'

'Like the Rossinis and the Morettis?' he said.

I laughed. 'Yes, exactly like that.'

'And how did the story end?'

'There was a huge fight.'

'And were there winners and losers?'

'No. Dad said they were all losers because war has no victors.'

'Profound. And that lives with you? You don't like conflict?'

'That's right. I think it achieves nothing. I prefer to sidestep people who are bad for me, rather than fight with them.'

He paused. 'As when you left me at the wedding?'

It was inevitable that we'd discuss it.

'Yes, and I can only apologise for that. It was cowardly of me.'

'Or brave. I don't blame you. I can see it looked bad. Dancing like that with Bianca. I am sorry. There was really nothing to it. It was thoughtless of me to leave you on the side-lines.'

'Are you and she . . .?'

'No. Not at all. She's having boyfriend issues, but it's none of my concern. I left her right there on the dance floor when I noticed you'd gone. I rushed back to the hotel, but your cab was disappearing into the distance. I was gutted.'

'Really?'

'Yes. I called you immediately, repeatedly. It wasn't until I went back to the room that I found your phone.'

'I did think of turning back,' I admitted. 'Everything would have been so different if I had.'

'Well, I'm here now,' he said softly, moving closer to me. We stopped walking in a patch of forest where the moonlight shone through the trees. I turned to see what the others were doing, but there was no sign of them.

'They must have taken another route,' he said, smiling.

'You asked them to?'

'Yes.'

'I hope they'll be okay. What if they get lost?'

'They have torches and phones. Stop worrying.'

I looked up, tilting my chin towards him.

I knew he was going to kiss me. I took in the moment. Moonshine on the river, an owl hoot in the distance, the smell of his cologne. Alessio bent his head towards me. Our lips were so close, they were tantalisingly close to touching.

I placed my hand gently on the back of his neck . . .

Then we were startled by the sound of paws pounding along the forest floor.

I saw a black outline, moving through the trees.

'Oh my God,' I breathed, looking over my shoulder. 'I think it's one of those big black cats! There are a few of them here in the countryside.'

He pulled me towards him. 'Are you sure? Can you see it?'

'Yes, it's in the trees over there.'

'Stay close.' He wrapped his arms around me and I fell into him. We were frozen like that for a few moments, thinking we might be eaten alive by a rogue black panther.

'I will protect you,' he said, chuckling. 'I will fight it while you hide.'

'How heroic you are!' I couldn't help but smile. 'You're always looking after me.'

'If you let me, I always will.' His tone was suddenly serious.

I could feel my body melting into his, but then we glimpsed the silhouette of another black beast ahead,

'God, there are two of them!' I whispered. 'We're doomed.'

'I didn't expect to come to rural England and find this . . . it's like we're on safari.'

This one padded closer.

I clung to Alessio; both of us holding our breath.

We dared to look at the beast.

And that's when we realised.

It was less of a panther ... and more of a Labrador!

Yes, the two deadly big cats were in fact Bunty and Beau. Which meant that Jonny Kent was also nearby.

'It's the dogs!' I said, so relieved that I broke away from Alessio with a laugh and went to greet them.

I heard him sigh and grumble something in Italian. The romantic moment had passed. When Jonny emerged from the trees, he looked delighted to see me. 'Well, well well! I didn't expect to see you guys out here,' he said.

'Oh really,' mumbled Alessio. 'Must have been a total surprise.'

We walked back together, with Jonny and I reminiscing. We said goodbye at Rose Hall, and I was pleased to see the others were safely inside, playing Cluedo in the drawing room. As Jonny sloped off down the lane with the dogs, I felt a bit guilty leaving him out ...

'Jonny,' I called out on impulse. 'Want to come in and join us for a drink and game of Cluedo?'

He spun on his heel. 'Yes, that sounds good.'

Behind me, I heard Alessio sigh again.

44

My Aunt

Saturday passed in a blissful blur. Alessio and I made pancakes for everyone about ten o'clock, served with local honey, Greek yoghurt and raspberries delivered by Miss Crystal. A horse ride across the fields followed. Even on horseback, Jonny and Alessio couldn't agree on anything, but their sparring was good-natured. Mostly. Then it was time to meet my aunt.

'Shall I come with you?' asked Alessio.

I hesitated. 'I think my aunt and I will have a lot to catch up on,' I said. 'I haven't seen her for ages. I hope that's okay?'

'Sure. I understand. I will brush down the horses and take a rest.'

'Are you having a nice time?' I asked.

'I am having the best time. I'm so relaxed.'

'I'm glad. It's so nice to see you again.'

'I didn't like you leaving like that. Diana got totally fed up with me asking what I should do.' He smiled. 'But I don't want to keep you from your aunt. Go. We'll talk later.'

*

As I was pulling out of the driveway of Rose Hall, Jonny and the dogs were coming towards me. I stopped and rolled down the window.

'Hey.'

'Where you off to?' said Jonny.

'Heading into the village. I'm going to have tea with Aunt Belinda.'

'Nice. She's so like your...'

'Mum. I know. I find it hard.'

'I'll come with you if you like?' said Jonny.

'Oh, that's okay. Really, there's really no need –'

'But I'd love to say hello to Belinda – I haven't seen her for ages.'

'Okay. Sure, why don't you come with me then?'

'I'll just put the dogs back in the house. I'll run back to the mews with them; you follow with the car. I'll be ready in two minutes.'

They jogged down the lane while I turned and headed towards Jonny's house by the stables. A few minutes later, just as Jonny was getting in the car, Alessio walked by to get on with grooming Magnus. I waved but he barely nodded his head. *Oh God*. In my mind, Jonny coming into town with me was totally different from Alessio coming. Jonny belonged to this part of my life. We were familiar together; we had history. I didn't feel as if I had to justify myself to Alessio.

'Your Italian chap looks like he's in a mood,' Jonny observed.

'Maybe.'

'But you don't care?'

'No, I do care. I just don't want to fuss about it right now. I'm looking forward to seeing my aunt for the first time in a while.'

'Understood. Parking tip. Try behind the camping shop, they have a few spaces.'

'Will do. Let's go.'

We found a space easily and cut through an alley to the teashop.

She was waiting. I realised it was over a year since we'd last met in London. Yes, Aunt Belinda was so like my mother. And yet, different from how my mother had looked. Delicate fine lines around my aunt's eyes and mouth and across her forehead made her look older, as indeed she was. And, as I'd never seen my mother with such lines, it made a point of difference between my recollections of my mother's face and the face in front of me now. And that was a good thing. As I gazed at my aunt I reflected on how hard it must have been for Belinda to lose her sister. I'd been so self-absorbed and felt so sorry for myself I'd barely considered it before. Selfish of me.

Jonny popped into the café with me. And, as we drank Earl Grey from vintage teapots, we all ended up reminiscing about old times.

'Charlotte, I'd love to hear more from you,' said Aunt Belinda, holding my hand across the table.

It was true that she often tried to contact me, and so often I'd ignored her texts or replied hastily to say I was too busy to meet.

'I'm sorry.' I knew I needed to apologise to my aunt. 'I've coped by distracting myself. But this summer, I've had a little bit of time to reflect. I've been so busy these last few years. It's terrible that I've hardly seen you and barely been in touch. Please forgive me.'

My time with Diana had made me see what I was missing.

'Of course, there's no forgiveness needed. I'm just so happy to see you, you really are your mother's daughter ...'

'Oh, Aunty, and you are her sister.' I squeezed her hand. 'I've missed you.'

'Gosh, I've missed you too. You've done so well. I've read about you in the newspapers this year. We're all so proud of you.'

'I've just been a work machine. A robot, really. I should take more time out. Why don't you come and visit me in New York? I'm going to have a lovely house there. And lots of down time when I sign Damselle over to Florinda.'

'I'd love to. Never been to New York. Closest I got was my *Friends* obsession.'

We kept the conversation light. There were things I wanted to ask about my mother, but I wanted to build my relationship with Belinda slowly. And Jonny's presence meant we didn't go too deep. After a delicious tea, Jonny and I set off back to Rose Hall.

It was fun to spend time with Jonny, just the two of us, and we giggled all the way back in the car. When we pulled up at Rose Hall, there was an awkward silence. I was about to say what a lovely afternoon it had been when Jonny spoke.

'Are you in love with that Italian guy?' he said, bluntly.

I hesitated. 'No. Maybe. I don't know. But I'm going to New York next month. For a couple of years. I'm not the settling down type, Jonny.'

'You know, I sort of always hoped you'd come back,' he said, with a half-smile. 'And then you do. But you bring this guy with you. This snazzy Italian guy I can never compete with.'

'I'm sorry. But, believe me, he's not competition. I'm going to New York alone. I like being alone.'

I blushed though, as I thought about the near kiss in the woods with Alessio. I wanted to be close to Alessio. I did have feelings for him. But would they last? Did those feelings of yearning ever last?

As for Jonny. He was as adorable as ever. But I'd been through such changes and he'd stayed much the same – familiar but also surprisingly hot. But that was it. I'd been altered by tragedy, success, adventure. Some might say it had toughened me. I'd prefer to say it had made me robust.

'But we can stay in touch?' said Jonny.

'Yes. I'd like that.'

We hugged, clumsily, across the middle of the car and then I went into the house, looking forward to seeing everyone. They were in the snug, drinking coffee. But he wasn't there.

'Is Alessio still at the stables?' I asked.

'No. He came back from there. But he went out again,' said Lara. 'Seemed a bit distracted.'

'Probably because you drove off with Jonny.' Lily smirked at me. 'Jonny the stable lad is one sexy dude.'

'Oh, that was just a last-minute thing, Jonny wanted to go into town ... But I'm happy to confirm – he is single!'

'Good to know,' said Lily, her eyes sparkling.

But I wasn't really in the mood for joking. I felt a horrible surge of panic, as my eyes darted around the room, desperately looking for some of Alessio's belongings. I couldn't bear it if he'd left. Then I saw his cashmere sweater across a chair, which made me breathe a little easier.

45

Back into the Woods

'Do you know where he went?' I asked.

'He put on some walking boots he found in the porch, and said he'd be gone for a while,' Lara told me. 'I think he said something about the river path?'

I followed the route we'd taken the night before. I was running, panting, fretting. I wanted to find him and reassure him. Now I looked back on it, I knew it must have looked bad, seeing Jonny in the car when I'd said I wanted to go on my own into town. I didn't owe Alessio any explanation. But still, I didn't want any more misunderstandings.

I wasn't convinced I was on the right track. He could be anywhere. I stumbled, breathless, desperate now to find him.

I got to the Owl's Nest, but there was no sign of him.

'Damn!' I said. I was sure he'd be there.

I heard a hoot from a tree on the riverbank. Was it a human hoot? I spun around.

Relief!

He was sitting under the tree, as if waiting for me.

I didn't say anything, but I went and sat right next to him, so close that we were touching.

'I hoped you'd come looking for me.'

I smiled. 'I had to tell you – Jonny is just an old friend.'

He turned to me, and I to him, and we looked into one another's eyes, and then we kissed, slowly and deeply, and everything was right with the world.

'You will come back to Montecastello, won't you?' he said.

'Maybe someday,' I said. 'But I can't at the moment. I have to go to New York. I have to take that opportunity or I'll never forgive myself.'

'I suppose I should understand the business spirit,' he said. 'And admire it.'

'We're alike in that.'

He nodded. 'How long will you stay there?'

'At least two years. It's a long time.' I looked away, a little awkward. 'You'll probably forget all about me.'

'Why would I do that?'

I didn't have an answer to that.

'I know this is more than a fleeting thing for me,' he said.

'That's lovely of you to say. But people say a lot of crazy things when they first –'

'I mean it. I've never said it before.' He kissed me again, sweetly, intensely. A kiss that felt so binding. 'There's something else I want to raise before you go . . .'

'Yes?'

'About Lavandula.'

I sighed. I wasn't sure I wanted to talk about it.

'Did you know that Cosimo left? When he found out Gabriella didn't really own the farm?'

This was news to me. 'No. No, I didn't hear that.'

'Gabriella has finally admitted it isn't her property.'

'Progress, I guess. For you. I'm glad some good came out of the sale that never was.'

'Yes. It means I could rent it to you. Commercial rates. If you're still interested? Or even sell it to Florinda?'

I thought about this. It was tempting. But there was no way Florinda would go back to that scenario now. And I didn't want to get tied up with business matters in Montecastello. At least not until Alessio and I had explored the strength of our feelings.

'Thank you,' I said. 'It's a generous offer. But, really, it's too late.'

'Seriously?'

'Yes. The New York company have written off that option. We've moved on, no turning back.'

'I'm sorry.' I was surprised at how genuinely devastated he sounded. 'You know, I'd do anything for you.'

'Come and live in New York?'

He smiled, ruefully. 'I'm not sure that I could do that. Business stuff...'

'I understand.' And I did.

He was quiet for a while, then: 'My friends really liked you; you were the perfect wedding guest.'

I blushed. 'I'm so sorry I left you in that situation.'

'I said you had a flight to catch after all. An emergency in London.'

'Phew, thank you. Not quite so embarrassing. I'd like to see them all again without seeming like a crazy English girl. Did you stay in that cute little hotel?'

'Yes, I'd had a glass too many of champagne, so I slept for a few hours then drove home. I was hoping against hope you'd gone back to the Rossini.'

I sighed and took his hands in mine. I realised that all of my wild imaginings about him getting back with Bianca were nothing more than my own insecurities playing through my mind. Or, maybe, a contrived narrative I designed to protect my heart from this man who had made me feel more alive – more excited and free – than I'd ever felt before.

'Jealousy is a terrible thing,' I admitted to myself as much as to him.

'It is,' he replied. 'But sometimes it confirms to you that your feelings are real.'

'True. Very true.' I turned and gazed into his eyes. 'What are we going to do?'

We looked out at the river for our answer; it coursed along over boulders and stones, smoothing them as it carried on its journey.

And we kissed again. A kiss I would never forget.

46

Lavandula Once More

I was glad Alessio and I were both too experienced and ambitious to change course for one another. That was nonsense in old-fashioned rom-coms. Stories which were set in days when women didn't follow their business dreams. Days when people – well, women – allowed their heart to rule their head.

Over the next few weeks, Lara and I made plans for the new Lily & Lucia fragrance, and the Rossini cousins were brimming with ideas for that. They enjoyed coming by the office. The whole London team was delighted that, even though they were losing Damselle, they had a new project, equally promising and exciting. And to add to the joy, I was leaving town too! It was great to see Lara in her rightful place as overall boss of that office. I had no worries about leaving her in charge.

I dithered about what to do on the twenty-eighth of August. The day of the lavender festival and, more importantly, the day that Diana and Umberto were due to be married. I didn't want to let them down. But I didn't think it was wise to see Alessio so soon after we'd parted. News came through from

New York which helped form my decision. They wanted me there by the last day of August, which allowed me no time to stay in Montecastello at the end of the month. After a lot of thought, I decided to make a day trip to Italy. I found an early morning flight which would get me to Lavandula by noon, if I got a cab from the airport, then a return flight at nine in the evening.

The London gang all flew separately into Italy at the end of the month. Lara and Jack were invited too, and they planned to stay for a few days so arrived well before I did. Lucia was excited to see her father, and she decided to fly to Pisa with Lily, and travel north by train, because she couldn't bear to be in Venice again.

*

It was midday when my airport cab arrived in Montecastello on the day of the wedding. I checked my face in a compact mirror in the back seat. My heart pounded as we drove along the main street, scene of my first arrival in the beloved little town. I pushed away thoughts, thoughts that I had come back home. Those were fanciful notions; demons trying to derail me from my route to New York. But it was harder than I'd imagined. A fleeting visit I told myself, no problem. Don't engage with the place or people too much. Just do the right thing for Diana and Umberto. Easy. Only it wasn't.

I applied some coral lipstick, hoping my floral dress was okay. My hair was lying pleasingly well. Something to be thankful about.

'You look lovely,' said the driver.

'Ah, thank you. I'm not feeling it. Got ready in a rush at the airport.'

It was tricky to look smart enough for a wedding and relaxed enough for a lavender festival.

'Don't worry. *Perfetto.*'

As we approached Lavandula, I noticed that the fields were powdery, the lavender a softer grey-purple than before. It was the end of the season and that helped me think of this event as a full stop at the end of a magical summer.

I was astounded at how much of a carnival atmosphere was underway when I arrived. The courtyard was brimming with bars and food stalls, a band played by the barn, children played games in the meadow, old men threw bowls, people danced, while others lazed in the sun, chatting, laughing, gossiping.

I held back shyly, my eyes dancing around for Alessio. I recognised a lot of Rossini family members from Alessio's birthday party. So many of them approached, greeting me warmly, asking how I was, how was life, what was I doing now? I felt incredibly welcome.

Diana and Umberto were mingling too. The ceremony was going to be in the top field at two o'clock. Diana saw me and came across immediately.

'Charlotte. You made it! I am so pleased and so touched. Come and see Umberto.'

I followed her and the loveliest sight awaited me. Umberto, with his arm around Lucia. She was laughing, teasing him, kissing his head. 'Papa!' she scolded him, as he told her to eat more. 'I'm a grown-up now. I decide.'

'Okay, darling.' He kissed her nose.

My eyes filled. Diana's too. 'This is the greatest gift. We

have her back,' said Diana. 'Thank you for all you have done.'

'My pleasure,' I assured her. 'And has Umberto been well?'

'He's been great. We feel as if everything changed when you came into town that Wednesday with your delicate ankle all puffed up, and your kind heart...'

'Oh, please, no. I had nothing to do with it.'

'But the girls feel you helped them get to London. And your Lara has been so helpful. Lucia is out of all that now, and that's made the world of difference.'

'Well, I'm delighted to hear that. Happy days indeed.'

'If only you and –'

'Stop!' I said, laughing. 'That's all resolved.'

'And did you hear that he can't make it today?'

My heart stopped. I gulped. 'No. no, I didn't. Why is that?'

'Poor Alessio. He has to appear in court. A tiresome situation. A journalist made some terrible allegations about him in a Venetian newspaper, and he has challenged them. Today is the preliminary hearing.'

'He's in Venice?'

'Yes, that's right. He was distraught about missing the day. But we said he must go. He's the finest of men. He can't allow people to ruin his reputation through jealousy and spite.'

'Exactly,' I said, my stomach churning at the thought of what might have been written about him. 'I admire his courage.'

'He has plenty of that,' said Diana.

I was impatient to read the story. God forbid that Allegra mentioned me! But that would have to wait.

'Now, let's mingle,' said Diana. 'You know a lot of people in the family, but there are some other folks here from Montecastello you should meet.'

I had a lovely time, chatting to local people; bakers, teachers, carpenters. It was great to see Rosa from the hotel – they had closed it for the day – Ed and Antonio, and crazy Aunt Maria. Like the recurring characters from a favourite novel, they did not disappoint. But I was heartbroken that Alessio wasn't there. I kept thinking that I could sense his cologne floating on the breeze, but I was let down every time.

Two o'clock came, and the band struck up with 'Tupelo Honey'. Umberto and Diana walked together with Lucia as flower girl, along with some little maids, to a modest altar of lavender, where they were married by the local priest, Raphael.

There was much whooping and cheering. The band then played 'When I'm Sixty-Four' and everyone danced and toasted the happy couple. There were no speeches, but the bliss on their faces spoke of a love deep, tender and sincere.

I knew that Calandra had been adopted by Jasmine Pirelli, and was being well cared for, but I couldn't be so near without going to see her. An hour before my cab was due, I set off for the stables at the Rossini. I loved that route between the farm and the hotel, passing by Alessio's business, this time with pride and affection for him instead of that terrible loathing I'd felt before.

And there she was, looking splendid. Her mane was pleated with ribbons, and she came to the stall to see me with her usual nosy cute expression. It was as if I'd only been away for a day. I found it hard to leave her, but the cab arrived and I had no choice but to kiss her velvet nose for the last time. She broke my heart when she went to stand at the back of the stall, refusing to look at me as I left.

*

As I sat in the departure lounge at Venice airport, I searched for the article about Alessio. It came up straight away. It was vile, full of lies and hearsay about his relationships, his business, his character. I was filled with indignation on his behalf. As I sat there fuming, a text arrived.

From Alessio!

'Just arrived at the wedding party. Can't believe I missed you. Have you left the country? Please don't go.'

47

A New Life

Touching down at JFK two days later, I stared out of the window in disbelief. I'd done it. I had arrived in New York for a two-year stay. There was something about New York City that really gripped me. Excited wasn't the word. It thrilled me. I felt like I was appearing in a movie as I sashayed out of the airport to my waiting car. Yeah, this was the life.

Hello, New York City. Goodbye, London.

I'd come to terms at last with the lavender issue. The pragmatist in me had triumphed. The farming and travel costs we were saving had some impact on our carbon footprint. It was admirable, environmentally, to use manufactured oil! By far the best outcome! Thank goodness Gabriella had let me down. It now seemed outrageously complex to farm lavender in rural Italy. It might not even save money when you added on the extraction and travel costs. And, now that I'd seen the flowers turning to powder already at Lavandula, I considered how short the season was. Everything was going to be great in New

York. I was rich, successful, a determined businesswoman, so what else mattered?

The car took me to my new home on the Upper West Side, about a forty-minute ride from the airport.

'You're British?' said the driver.

'Yes. But I'm going to be here for a couple of years.'

'All right! So you got a green card okay?'

'Yes. My company organised all that.'

'Nice. Well, welcome to the Big Apple.'

'Thank you. Got any tips?'

'Sure. Watch you don't get your dreams broken,' he said. 'People can play nasty in this city.'

'Okay, understood. Thank you.'

I got out of the car on Beechwood Avenue, and the driver helped me up the front steps with my bags.

There was a plaque by the bell of my new front door which I stopped to read. 'Ernestina Jacobs lived here between 1889 and 1907.' Incredible! My favourite American author had actually lived in my new house. I trembled. This whole experience was going to be unreal. I felt thrilled with my decision to press on with the Florinda deal. A whole new world was before me.

The keys to the house were in a secure box, and my hand shook as I tapped in the code. I got the keys and checked that I could open the door.

'Thanks for looking out for me,' I called back to the driver.

He turned to face me, standing squarely on the path. 'Remember, lady. Keep your wits about you.'

I saluted him. 'Yes, sir.'

'You're the boss,' he said, with a grin and a wave.

Once inside the house, I was mesmerised. It was so elegant.

White walls, high windows revealing the leafy green street, grey sofas, teal curtains, vintage fireplaces, deep architraves and cornices. I loved it. The light was exquisite, not bright, or even warm, but deeply atmospheric. It made me think of all that had happened in this house before I arrived. It had soul.

The kitchen was functional but fabulous. Wooden butcher worktops, white units, black floors. And the flowers! Bryony and the team had sent flowers, lots of them. White roses and lily of the valley; the smell was divine. Ah, the Florinda folks weren't so bad.

I took a few days to settle in, unpack, work out the appliances, find the local food store, sort out my banking and my medical care. I met the neighbours. Then the weirdest thing happened to me. The house next door was occupied by a young couple with their baby, Nula. The first time I saw them, I was looking down from my bedroom window and they were on their path, making the baby more comfortable in her pram. Smoothing her blankets, plumping her pillow, patting her chubby little arm. She smiled out at them and they looked at one another with such pride and love and contentment, it was palpable. It was in that precise moment that I started to obsess about having a baby. From a starting point of absolutely no interest. I chastised myself. I'd come to New York to live the single, professional life, not dream of motherhood.

Why didn't I become obsessed with awesome Libby at number 28, who jogged every day, ran her own investment house and had Ben Fyfe suits in every colour? She was very far from motherhood. She had the perfect New York life. I bought some trainers and a decent sports bra and started running too.

One day during that first week, I met Libby on the bridge.

'Are you living in Kirstie's house?' she asked.

'I guess I am. I've seen mail for Kirstie Copeland.'

'Yes. She's a good friend,' said Libby. 'She moved to California.'

'Cool.'

'And, oh my goodness, have you met baby Nula in the house next to you? Isn't she adorable?'

And we spoke about little Nula all the way home.

Turns out Libby was dreaming of babies as well.

*

Bryony was in constant touch those first few days and couldn't have been more helpful. After about a week and a half, I finally went into the Florinda offices. I was going to be given my own room, learn how the place worked, hear about what I would be doing. I had a proper NYC manicure and blow-dry, wore a sober navy-blue business dress and nude pumps, what else?

They didn't let me down on the office. I loved my new space, overlooking the city. On the first morning, Bryony's assistant, Amy Corniche, informed me that I should go to the board room at eleven o'clock.

The team I met back in April were all there. Warm hugs all round, and Cooper Dean looked as handsome as ever. Kind of.

'So, Charlotte,' Bryony announced. 'We have some surprises for you.'

'Great!' I said, although what I actually wanted to say was that I totally hate surprises.

'We have a presentation for you and you're gonna LOVE it.'

'Exciting!' I smiled. (Very much doubting I would love it.)

'Tabitha is going to lead the revelation,' continued Bryony, who I noticed actually looked a little nervous.

So now it was a revelation, as well as a surprise and a presentation. Hat-trick of horrors.

The lights were dimmed on that warm September day, and I settled down for the show. A huge screen dropped down.

'This,' said Tabitha, 'is our new fragrance. Behold ...'

I held my breath. What had they been up to? No doubt they had tweaked the brand a little.

An elegant bottle emerged on the screen, and to its side, a lovely, crisp white box, with the letters P-L-U-M written across the side.

'Yes, our delightful new artisan fragrance, PLUM!' said Tabitha. 'P-lum,' she added.

I gulped. Then giggled nervously. 'P-LUM?'

'Yes,' said Bryony, stepping in, 'P-LUM. In focus groups, we found this name was more popular across all territories. We like to think *globally* here at Florinda.'

'Ah, I see.'

'But you like it, right?' said Tabitha.

'Wrong!'

Nervous laughter rolled around the table.

'But you see why we have to do this. Let me explain.'

'Please do.'

'We love the scent you've created. But now we have to give it our holistic branding treatment to bring it in-house,' said Tabitha.

'Okay. And the bottle ... the box ... the whole look? That had to change too?'

Tabitha had prepared a speech. 'To you, as creator, we fully appreciate that this looks a lot different. But we've actually made very minor changes. Please trust us. Building brands is what we do.'

I relaxed a bit. What was the point of fighting now? 'It does look modern and chic,' I said. Then, not wanting Tabitha to suffer, I added: 'Yes, it's actually very fresh and sleek.'

'Phew!' said Tabitha with a nervy smile. 'Shall I carry on with the presentation?'

'Yes, please do.'

I swallowed hard. I'd have to deal with my feelings of disappointment later; this was about gathering facts. Tabitha explained their global strategy to make PLUM the best-selling perfume within three years from launch. She explained the markets they would target, price points, and outlets they had already sold the new look into. Amazing, I thought, that they've done so much already. But, as they went on to explain, there would be a dedicated team ensuring the brand's success. That was a level of commitment I could never have offered with my artisan operation.

At the end of the presentation, I thanked them sincerely. I'd just have to accept that part of what I'd given up by selling the intellectual property, was an element of control as well. Or to put it another way, I'd sold my soul.

As I walked through Manhattan that lunchtime, I still felt excited to be there. I tried not to obsess about business stuff. I wanted to sign up for a hot yoga class, find a book group, and go jogging in Central Park. But there was a nagging voice at the back of my head, saying:

What are you going to do at the office, Charlotte? There are people all over the brand. Why do they even want you to be involved? If they can change the name and packaging of your fragrance without your say-so, surely it's clear that you're just here as a gesture?

Until they want rid of you ...

But I pushed those thoughts out of my mind. There was more to living in New York than work. I decided, on a whim, to go to the Frick Collection at 1 East 70th Street. I browsed around, admiring the works of Goya, Veronese, Manet. And then I came to the Titian. His portrait of his friend, Pietro Aretino: 'A well-connected author, playwright, satirist, blackmailer and libertine.' I smiled; it sounded so Venetian.

I fought hard against it, but it was no good, I had to admit that the painting naturally made me think of the Rossinis. The Titian Umberto had allowed Gabriella to keep, simply to avoid hurting Lily. Alessio had gone along with this for the sake of his cousin. He was so honourable, in his tough but tender way. I hated the idea of that gossipy journalist Allegra dragging him over hot coals for spite.

As I gazed at the texture of the fur and brown silk cloak, and at the gold chain worn by the sitter, I thought of the need some men had for outer signs of greatness. Military uniforms, expensive shirts, well-cut suits. But Alessio had no need to display his wealth or greatness. It was in his behaviour not his props. Driving around in a tractor, in jeans and T-shirt, in touch with the land, eschewing city sophistication. Okay, admittedly he drove a Ferrari too, but he had no need to be flashy.

I must have gazed at the painting for ten minutes or more, recalling every detail of my first encounter with Alessio in Montecastello, as I marvelled at the brushstrokes on the satin sleeves of Pietro Aretino. Why had I fought Alessio so much when he'd been so kind to me? That was a mystery. But I was being disingenuous, even with myself. I had liked him from the very start and that had alarmed me. There. I had confessed it to myself in the Frick in front of this masterful portrait of Pietro Aretino.

I sat for a moment on one of the gallery's plush benches, my head filling with thoughts of our kiss in the woods in Ambler. But I couldn't afford to think about Alessio. *This* was my dream come true. New York. I needed to make sure it was a wonderful dream.

48

The Cocktail Party

The Thursday of week three saw me slipping into a black cocktail dress, bought from Percy's on Fifth. Bryony said she had organised a welcome party. I don't mean a group of people to welcome me. No. An actual party in a venue near Central Park, called the Riversdale, for seven hundred people.

'Seven hundred?' I'd said.

'Yes, and all for you arriving in town. It's your evening.'

'No! That's crazy.'

'Well, it's also to celebrate the fragrance, you know.'

Turned out it was actually a launch party. *Phew.* Thank goodness; it sounded like a huge expense simply to welcome me to town.

It was by now coming towards the end of September and the humid summer air had burned out, replaced by a fresher feel as the coolness of the fall set in. The turning trees, the elegant streets, the bewitching shops and extraordinary people, were all staged in an orange autumnal light. I hadn't had that long-promised dinner with Cooper Dean yet, but I knew he was going to be at the party.

I was ready well before the car was due to arrive – when I think of it now, I had so much time on my hands – and I sat by the window, looking out at the burnished leaves, which I could have touched, had the window been open. My attention was piqued by activity next door. The neighbours had brought Nula back in their car. Her father undid a strap and lifted her out of the car. She looked irresistibly cute in her car seat, wearing a green knitted hat with a white flower to one side. She was just too sweet. She smiled as her father effortlessly carried her inside, like a basket of love. It looked as if she was pointing her toes, in white cotton tights which were the tiniest bit too big for her perfect feet.

I was reminded that Aunt Belinda had sent me a few baby photos of myself, some of which I'd never seen before. I glanced at them as I waited for the car. My mother and father looked adoringly at me in each one. I was dressed prettily in little Liberty print dresses with gentle knitted cardigans. It was odd to think that was me, and this was me too. My thoughts drifted back to Ambler. I'd had such a lovely time there. Seeing our old cottage, meeting Miss Crystal, Jonny and Aunt Belinda, and, of course, connecting with Alessio in a new way. Even though we weren't able to try out being a couple, I felt grateful that we'd had those moments. As I waited to go to one of those events I'd come to New York for, I found myself looking back on that country weekend just a few weeks earlier.

On the Sunday in Ambler, the day after the kiss, we'd gone out for a roast dinner, to a country hotel in Laurel Bank. The type of place that had its own spaniels in residence and served food that you would eat at home, if only you could cook so well. Alessio and I chatted casually, acting as if we'd never kissed the night before, or asked the river to answer the question of our future. At times I caught him looking at me; gazing, in fact. And at other moments, he caught me looking longingly at him. I wanted to throw my arms around him. But I didn't. And he didn't. Only an hour or two later, they left on the train from Laurel Bank, and it trundled out of town, almost mournfully, leaving me feeling as if I had dreamed the whole experience.

The day I spent in Lavandula hadn't altered things because of how Alessio had been delayed at the courts. And I was glad of it. The next phase of my life was what I had to concentrate on. And that involved living here in this amazing city and embracing all the opportunities it had to offer.

Out on the street, the car had arrived and I pulled myself together. This was the life. I grabbed my Kate Spade bag and was soon being whisked over to the Riversdale venue. There were huge banners for PLUM above the entrance and, as we drew up outside, there was a lot of publicity going on; press, photographers, models and media types gathered in the street. I felt almost paralysed by anxiety.

I stepped onto the pavement, shaking like a willow in a storm. There was no one I knew on the street and it seemed no one knew me either. Nervously, I went inside, passing the beautiful people. They didn't notice me either. I found it amusing that no one would have cared if I hadn't gone. I'd made the fragrance after years of trial and error. But here it was, going global, made by other people, called by a new name and being celebrated by complete strangers. But what had I expected? And did I mind? No, I didn't. I minded that

Bryony had pretended this corporate launch was a party in my honour, that was all.

My eyes darted around inside, hoping for a familiar face or, failing that, a sign to the powder rooms. At last I saw someone I recognised.

'Hi Charlotte!' he said, making his way over. 'You look amazing. How are you?'

'Hi! I'm great, thanks. Loving New York so far.'

'That makes you the only one.' Another guy, handsome and warm, came over to join us. Cooper Dean smiled proudly.

'Charlotte,' he said. 'I'd like to introduce you to my partner, Baillie.'

They looked gorgeous together. 'Fabulous to meet you, Baillie,' I said. 'Do you work at Florinda as well?'

'No, I have a heart,' he said. 'So that excludes me.' Which made me laugh.

'I'm a teacher,' he explained. 'One of us has to have a conscience.'

We chatted for a bit. Then they caught the eye of some friends and moved along. I smiled at my own stupidity. I'd built towering stories – pure fantasies – on the flimsiest of foundations. Me and Cooper Dean rocking round NYC, yeah right!

I spun around and found myself behind Bryony who was talking to a guy who was holding a microphone in front of her.

'Are you wearing PLUM?' said the guy, inhaling deeply. 'Smells divine.'

'Thank you. Yes, I am, of course!'

'How did you hit on the idea? It's a really unusual combination,' he said.

'It is unusual,' she purred. 'But so perfect. We've been

planning PLUM for a while,' she went on. 'We started playing around with combinations, with base notes of lavender and basil . . . it takes a while to get the balance right. But we have an outstanding team. So inventive.'

So the real reason for the name change was to claim ownership? Everything was making sense now. I sloped away, feeling so tense and uncomfortable I thought I might snap. I craved fresh air.

I went out onto a balcony overlooking the Manhattan skyline. This wasn't working out as I hoped. But I had to give it a chance. Charlotte Alexander wasn't a quitter.

49

Decisions

I went to my desk in the Florinda offices Monday to Friday and tried to get involved in the launch. I made sure I was in group emails and made some small suggestions to Tabitha about how the marketing could pan out. Out of the office, I joined a hot yoga class and a book group. Of course, Lara kept me informed as to Lily & Lucia progress.

In the coming weeks, I went for brunches and suppers with acquaintances from my groups, then ran in Central Park for the fresh air and greenery. Aunt Belinda flew over and we had a wonderful time, shopping, mooching happily around the art galleries and going to the ballet. We chatted, we ate, we went to the top of the Empire State building.

As we sat in the elegant restaurant in the concourse of the Empire State, eating the best Caesar salad we'd ever tasted, she brought up the subject of romance.

'Is there anyone in your life, Charlotte?' she said, adding: 'I hope you don't mind me asking.'

'I don't mind at all. And no. Nobody in my life. But I'm hoping that will change.'

'There was nothing between you and Jonny, meeting up again after all that time?'

'No. Definitely not.' I smiled. 'He's got to be a great catch for someone, though.'

'For sure. No one else? Maybe in the new office? It's always fun to work in a big office.'

'I did think there was someone I liked. I hardly knew him before I arrived. But it turns out we're not a match. And I'm not upset about it.'

'Hm. So back to square one then.'

'Kind of. But there was someone I really liked when I was in Italy in the summer. He was with me in Ambler that weekend.'

'An Italian, then? Lovely.' She smiled. 'And?'

'I don't know. He's complicated. Successful. Doesn't want to leave Italy.'

'You're complicated and successful and a bit of a commit-ment-phobe yourself, so I think you'd know how to handle that,' she said, knowing me better than I knew myself. 'But are you prepared to spend more time in Italy? Maybe all your time in Italy?'

'Good question. I really want to live in New York for a while.'

'More than you want to be with him?'

'I don't know the answer to that.'

'Listen to your heart,' she said, taking my hand. 'Your head has brought you success in terms of material things. See if your heart can do the same for your emotional needs.'

I smiled. It was lovely to talk to her as I used to talk to my mother.

'Good advice. You think that's what Mum would say?'

She nodded. 'I do. Definitely.'

'Okay. I'll keep busy for a few weeks and see if my heart still aches for him.'

'It's a plan. Because, remember, while you're dithering, he might be giving up and meeting someone else. Don't leave it later than you need to, Charlotte.'

She was right. I already knew from the wedding party how much I hated the thought of him with someone else.

It was painful to say goodbye to Aunt Belinda. I felt foolish and a little shamed for shutting her out for so long. It felt so comforting to talk to her. Someone with my interests at heart, someone who knew me so well and who loved and missed my mum too.

And, after I'd waved her off at the airport, I had to admit that I was lonely.

I loved the energy and drama of New York just as much as I thought I would. But I didn't feel right there. I felt disconnected, lost and detached from myself. I was texting Diana a lot, and of course, in regular touch with Lara and the Rossini cousins. They all sounded like they were loving life. Diana and Umberto were blissed out, while the Londoners were building the Lily & Lucia brand, and loving every minute.

It was freezing by early November, with some flakes of early snow in the air, and Christmas decorations started appearing on the streets; strung lights, garlands, baubles and stars. After dark, shop windows dazzled with jewels, glittering gifts and exquisite toys. Christmas. Don't think about it, Charlotte, I told myself. But it was all I thought about. My usual Christmas over the previous five years had been to eat dinner with Lara and her family then come home at night to watch a film. I usually spent Boxing Day longing for the office to re-open. But what about this year? Would I fly back to London? Would the neighbours invite me in for eggnog?

Admittedly, I liked the family next door more and more. Katerina and Nathan, with their baby Nula. They were lecturers in English Literature at Colombia university. I had invited them in for coffee one Sunday, and we started to discuss Edith Wharton's novels, and Ernestina Jacobs' too. My brain was crammed full of business deals, numbers, percentages, figures – and I felt so refreshed by talking to them about fiction, characters, language, psychology. For them, money was not a goal. They lived for books – and for the insights into human nature they derived from reading.

Perhaps I connected with them so strongly because I'd had this recurring thought since I arrived in New York. That I would write that book I'd made notes for by the pool at the Rossini. I hadn't decided yet how I would tell the story, or if it would be happy or sad, or factual or fanciful.

'Do you write?' I asked Katerina, after Nathan had gone off to do some marking.

'I try. Some poetry. A few short stories published. Are you a writer?'

'No. Not so far,' I said. 'But, who knows?'

'I suppose,' said Katerina, 'everyone is a storyteller, but we do it in our different ways.'

'Yes, I see what you mean. It doesn't always have to be written down. What is your own story? How did you meet Nathan?'

'That's a long one. We met at college. Broke up, got back, broke up ...'

'Really? You seem so sorted.'

'Now we are. We took our risks.' She beamed at her daughter. 'And now we have Nula.'

'But how did you know that Nathan was the one?'

'Because I was always thinking about him, even when we weren't together, even when we didn't get on and I was making lists of all his faults.'

I was holding little Nula on my knee and her mother's words struck me with a swooping clarity. I had to take that same risk. To find out if Alessio and I were a perfect, harmonious match. Was it possible we could become as settled, loving and easy with each other as Katerina and Nathan?

I went for a long walk that night, passing age-old brownstones with a thousand stories to tell, past, present, future tales of families, love, drama, intrigue. I'd pinned all my hopes on my stay in New York; that it would fix the broken Charlotte, cure my emotional self. But somehow, unknown to me at the time, that repair job had started in Montecastello in the summer.

I stopped under a snow-covered chestnut tree and, without considering my words too closely, I texted Alessio:

'How are you? I miss you. Maybe we could spend some time together?'

50

Christmas

Alessio's response was slow to come. I could hardly look at the text when it arrived:

'Charlotte, it was lovely to get your message. I miss you too. But I have realised I am not suited to a relationship. I've been so sad since you left, and I'm just getting over it. It's taken a lot out of me. I wish you well.'

I was devastated. I read it over and over, trying to unpick a different meaning. I understood. I related. I agreed. But I was never surer that I truly wanted to be with him. I began to feel that for the rest of my life I would think of the kiss at Owl's Nest in Ambler woods and realise I'd missed out on the most important opportunity of my life.

I had no words to reply to him.

After two days of solid moping, eating chocolate and lying in bed, I had no choice but to throw myself back into my New York life. I needed to get myself sorted. Lara and Jack had booked flights to come and stay for New Year – and they wouldn't be expecting a self-indulgent misery fest. Plus,

Katerina had asked me to join her and Nathan for Christmas dinner. I accepted, gladly.

'That's so kind,' I said. 'But I insist on bringing some dishes, Katerina. Just tell me what I should make.'

I surprised myself by starting on a serious catering mission about two weeks before Christmas, freezing the soups and pies and cakes I cooked up. I then set about making the house look beautiful. I invited some people from the office over for drinks on the twenty-seventh of December, just to motivate myself to make it look good. Katerina and her sisters made decorations and gifts one evening each week, and I started to join them, learning new felting crafts. They were all domestic goddesses with an array of beautiful cherubic children. I loved hanging out with them, but felt destined to be the mad, fake aunty forever.

The week before Christmas, I took delivery of a perfect fairy-tale tree, bushy and fresh. Once it was decorated with magical silver and felt creations from my crafting sessions, it was time to start on cards and gifts. Of course, I still went into the office; they had a Christmas party, and I tried to be jolly there. The truth was that I was desperate for Christmas to be over. Perhaps the start of a new year would help me to forget Alessio. Surely I'd meet the perfect man at some point during the following few months? I covered my ears when Katerina said that New York was the toughest city in the world in which to meet a man – and keep him.

*

The hardest part of the festive season, if you're sad, is that gooey feeling in the build-up, before people get tipsy and squabble. Before the batteries are put in the kids' annoying toys, before there's a mountain of dishes to wash and your throat aches as you're run down and have made small talk at too many parties.

I woke on the morning of Christmas Eve and pictured everyone in the whole wide world with family members, cosying up in front of fires as they prepared food and wrapped the odd-shaped presents always left until the end, which should really be done at the start.

I carefully wrapped the gifts I'd bought for Nula. I was so in love with them. I'd gone crazy; a hand-smocked dress from Liberty, a set of baby books, a soft toy and an antique silver hairbrush.

I tried my best, but was morose, lethargic and very lonely. I had a shower about midday, put on the fairy lights, activated the playlist on my phone and got busy in the kitchen, finalising the dishes for next day at the neighbours. Lara called about two o'clock, sweetly making out she wasn't having a nice time at Jack's parents' place at all, but I could tell that she was.

'I can't wait for you and Jack to get here,' I told her.

I kept thinking about what was happening at the Rossini. Diana had sent gifts to me and also messaged pictures, and it looked amazing. Like a winter wonderland, totally unlike how I had seen it. I imagined how much fun they'd have in that perfect dining room, sparkling with baubles, flickering with candles. They were a joyful family, the Rossinis. I missed them. The teasing, the laughter, the endless dramas that go with belonging to a large family.

But most of all, I missed Alessio.

The doorbell rang about four o'clock. I wasn't expecting

anyone. I went to see who was there, and was greeted by a flurry of snow, but saw no one. Odd.

I turned to go inside, but an owl hoot drew me back to the door. I looked down this time, to see a hand-tied posy of lavender on my mat, with a note attached. All too mysterious. I picked it up. Did I have a secret admirer?

'Come to the gate,' it said. My heart skipped a beat. *Probably Lara's idea, something to cheer me up.*

I was too impatient to find a coat. I was so intrigued. I ran down the path and onto the street. There was no one to be seen. But a familiar scent was in the air. Another hoot. My heart danced. I hardly dared to hope. I looked away for a second and when I looked back, he was there, before me. Smiling, a very large case at his feet.

'I hope you don't mind,' he said. 'I've come for Christmas.'

I ran towards him and he wrapped me in his arms.

I breathed in his scent and swooned. 'What took you so long?'

51

Back Home

It snowed all through that Christmas, hushing us in our private frosted paradise.

We went for dinner next door on Christmas Day. Their house was brimming with friends and family and gleaming with lights and vanilla candles. It was so relaxed, with a help-yourself-to-food policy – roasts and pies, salads and breads, cheeses and puddings galore – and music from *The Nutcracker* playing very low. Katerina approved whole-heartedly of Alessio and didn't bat an eyelid at how far our blossoming romance had progressed in such a short space of time. Obviously, baby Nula beamed her adoration of him from the get-go.

'Babies instinctively recognise good people,' said Katerina, rosy cheeked from stirring pots at the stove.

Then we hosted the office party on the twenty-seventh – Bryony seemed almost as smitten as Nula with Alessio. *Dream on, sweetheart, he's mine!* I couldn't help but think, a thought almost too delicious to be true. And then we looked forward to the arrival of Lara and Jack. Otherwise, apart from an outing to Browne & Co to buy a cashmere scarf for Alessio, we made the bed our sanctuary for whole days, with the curtains not quite drawn, watching silent snowflakes flutter, secure in our togetherness.

'I wanted to kiss you since the first time I saw you,' he murmured gently one afternoon.

'That's a nice line,' I said, refusing to believe it.

'It's not a line,' he huffed. 'It's true.' He paused. 'But, oh no, you preferred to kiss a bad-boy artist you'd only just met ...'

I laughed. 'I was confused – and more than a little tipsy.' Then I looked at him. 'Were you jealous?'

'Pah! Me? Jealous? I don't get jealous. It's a futile emotion for the unsophisticated.'

I raised an eyebrow.

'Well, maybe a touch.' He smirked, lying back on his pillow, his eyes searching the ceiling. 'My biggest fear was that you would leave town without warning. And my second biggest fear was that you were going to hate me, over the whole Lavandula fiasco.'

'So it was rather lucky that I simply hated you in general?'

He rolled over towards me, pulling me into his arms, those beautiful bronzed arms I'd noticed as he drove the tractor through town that first day.

'You never hated me,' he teased. 'You fancied me all along. It was clear as day.'

'Ha! You're obviously a mind-reader, along with your many other skills.'

'Ah! So that WAS what was on your mind!'

'That's not what I meant –'

'But when you looked down at me from your balcony after

the party . . . I nearly came up and kissed you there and then. I could tell you'd be happy to kiss me back –'

Gosh, who knew I was so very transparent. But really. In the dark, from a hundred paces?

'Really?'

'Yes, really.' He touched my face, tenderly. 'So, we could have been kissing way back then. So much lost time to make up for.'

And we did.

Thoroughly.

*

We had so much fun with Lara and Jack, all of us in beanie hats and snow boots, walking the highline, arm-in-arm, like extras in a gloriously festive film.

'You two are perfect together,' said Lara one day, as we walked along behind Jack and Alessio on Lexington.

'You think?'

'I do. Definitely. Don't lose him.'

'Yes, boss.'

'I mean it,' she said. 'He changes you. In a good way. Anyone can see it. He gets you.'

'You're right.' I nodded. 'Spot on, as always.'

The strength of my feelings for Alessio was becoming evident to me. This wasn't a holiday crush. Far from it.And, as much as New York was heady, iconic, buzzing, the clear calm of Montecastello away from the urban frenzy tugged at my heart strings too.

Still, after a perfect farewell dinner for four in Alfredo's, we had to say goodbye to Lara and Jack. That was a wrench enough, but only a blink later, it was Alessio's turn to go.

'I don't want to leave,' he said as I watched him pack, my heart like a heavy weight in my chest.

'Really?'

'No, that's not true,' he said, reconsidering.

My heart stopped thudding for a moment.

'I do want to get back to Montecastello,' he clarified. 'But I want you to come with me.'

'How lovely.' I paused. 'It sounds lovely. But, reality check? I've taken on a new home here and made plans . . .' I said. 'Long-term plans.'

'I know. I understand.' He sounded disappointed, solemn for a moment. 'I don't want to spoil those plans. But what if . . .'

'Yes?'

'If I were to . . .' We locked gazes for a moment. 'Nothing. I'm getting carried away. We've had such a beautiful time.'

'It's been blissful,' I said, wondering what he'd been about to say. 'Truly. This place is going to seem so big and unbearable without you.'

It felt that there was more to say, but I didn't want to push it and the cab for the airport was due.

Impossible that our time together was over.

The cab arrived and we sat in the back, silently moving through the blanketed streets of snowy New York, then onto the highway to JFK. My hand was clasped in his.

'Come into the airport with me?' he said as we pulled up.

'Of course.'

After he'd checked in his bags, we made our way to a soulless coffee lounge.

Conversation was limited. After many days of constant chatter, we seemed shy again with one another.

We knew he'd have to go through security soon. There didn't seem time to embark on any big topics, and small talk felt wrong too.

'Take this,' he said, offering me the soft scarf we'd bought from Browne & Co when he first arrived. 'I'd like you to have it.'

I leaned into him and he draped the scarf around my shoulders.

And then, with nothing more than a fleeting kiss and an inadequate 'speak to you soon,' Alessio disappeared through the sliding doors.

The feeling of loneliness was so acute it actually hurt. I felt utterly bereft, hollowed out without him. I snuggled into his scarf, for comfort, a sense of his warmth.

Slowly, I started to walk in the opposite direction, telling myself we'd meet again soon, that my life in New York would gradually become my new normal – no man would ever be my whole world.

*

Before Alessio's plane even took off, he'd sent me a text, inviting me to come stay at his house. I was making my way back home when I replied, agreeing to visit. That took away some of the pain. It would be wonderful to see him in his own place. Find out even more about him. Be back in Montecastello, amid the olive trees.

I floated on air for a few days, recalling our time together and dreaming of more to come. I couldn't believe how in love I felt.

My Italian trip hadn't turned out anything like I'd imagined. Sure, I'd wanted a boyfriend, but ...

It was tough to realign my plans, but it seemed pointless to fight against my feelings. They were so resounding I could not ignore them – nor did I want to. It made perfect sense to book a trip to stay with Alessio for a few weeks and see if our magic continued. We confirmed a date for a month ahead and I spent my days thinking of nothing else.

I went to stay with him in the middle of February – flying out on Valentine's Day, aptly enough. I was so nervous. What if there had simply been a little too much festive sentiment? Would we get along, living together, eating together? Would we run out of chat or start to irritate each other? What if he scattered his dirty socks across the floor or liked to leave the TV on all night? Maybe he would slurp soup in a way I hadn't noticed before, or even his laugh would start to grate. If so, I told myself firmly, I'd be on the next plane back to New York, where I'd launch into my life there with gusto.

Alessio picked me up at the airport and, after greeting each other with a polite rather than passionate double-cheek kiss, we chatted about this and that on the way to his house. He was as charming as ever, but still I felt a little trepidation.

But, oh, the pleasure of being in Italy again! I gazed out at the peach trees, vineyards and soft-hued rustic houses, feeling as if I'd come home.

Then, Alessio's house broke the ice between us. It took me totally by surprise. Not at all huge or grandiose, his home was a very contemporary glass and timber eco-lodge tucked into a quiet corner of the estate.

'I love it,' I said. 'It's perfect, a slice of paradise.'

'I'm glad. Of course, you can change things around,' he told me. 'That wouldn't be a problem.'

I looked at him askance. 'I highly doubt that.' I've never met anyone who lives alone who appreciates someone coming into their home, switching everything about.

'Well, let's see how it goes,' he said with a slightly sheepish smile, linking his arm in mine. 'Who knows? Some of your ideas might be better than mine.'

I laughed.

I suppose I should have guessed that he was a down-to-earth person from the fact that he drove his own tractor around town. But I loved how, despite his wealth, he did everything himself and had very little help in his house.

'It's my home,' he said. 'I don't expect others to pick up my dirty socks.'

Had he actually read my mind?

It was all so casual and comfortable. A large kitchen table made from reclaimed wood, calm grey sofas, lots of books. People dropped by on a regular basis. People connected with the Rossini business, family and friends. Alessio was warm and welcoming to everyone. How could I have read him so wrongly at first? I loved to look at his photographs, the paintings on his walls, the books on his shelves. In some ways he became more real, more ordinary and straightforward. Yet, in other ways, he became more complex and mysterious. I had the feeling that I'd never understand everything about him. And that intrigued me all the more.

*

During my second week there, Alessio was preparing one of his delicious dinners. And it began like any other evening. A glass of fizz each on the terrace, overlooking the herb garden, chit-chat about what we'd been doing that day. I was huddled in a blanket – February in Italy isn't all sunshine! Then the tone changed and his dark eyes became serious, even anxious.

'Is everything okay?' I asked.

'Yes, fine,' he said. 'There's something I wanted to say...'

He came right over beside me, bending low by my chair.

'Charlotte,' he said, clearing his throat nervously.

'Yes?' For some reason my own throat felt very dry.

'I would be so honoured...' And, at this, he reached into his pocket, producing a little antique box. 'If you'd wear this. It belonged to my mother – and her grandmothers before her – and I promised her I'd give it to the woman I truly want to spend my life with.'

I was taken aback. Really, I was. And delighted.

'Oh, Alessio!' I said, gulping back a sob of pure happiness. 'Of course I'll wear it. It's exquisite!'

I fell into his arms and we kissed until we heard the saucepans bubbling over in the kitchen. It was so beautifully ordinary and extraordinary at once.

And then he gently insisted that I take the ring from its velvet box. I was quite overcome, touched that it had been in his family for hundreds of years.

'I took Lara's advice on size,' he admitted when I showed him how well it fitted.

'It's perfect,' I said. 'Thank you with all my heart.'

'My mother would have loved you,' he said. 'I can still picture her with that ring on her beautiful hand.'

*

I went back to New York to clear my desk at Florinda. I spent a few weeks saying my goodbyes and sorting out the re-let of the house. I didn't look back. I could think of nothing but Montecastello. My heart was in northern Italy – with the love of my life.

I returned to paradise in April. For real this time. We moved Calandra to Alessio's stables, next to Bruno. I set up an office in the stable block – happy that I could be so close to Calandra – and there I embarked on working out how best to drive Lara and the team back in London completely crazy. By which I mean, helping them develop the Lily & Lucia brand.

That July, we held a celebratory summer party. The perfume of the lavender was in the air. We invited a hundred guests – including Alessio's friends from the summer wedding we gate-crashed, David and Leonora. Unexpectedly, joyfully returning the party favour!

We feasted in the gardens of the Rossini, and danced and cavorted round the pool. That is until the blue of the water proved too enticing and we all jumped in as the finale to a riotous Macarena.

When we finally fell into bed, Alessio wrapped his arms around me. I felt cherished, adored, blissful.

I still insist I didn't love him from the start. Alessio obviously disagrees.

Okay, I'm going to let him have that one.

Acknowledgements

With thanks to Emma Hargrave and Janne Moller who helped bring this book to life in so many ways.

With thanks also to Kirsty Neilson Kyle, for invaluable help with all things Italian, especially Venetian. To Marc Anderson, for help with the perfume world. And to Jack Vettriano and Carolyn Osborne.

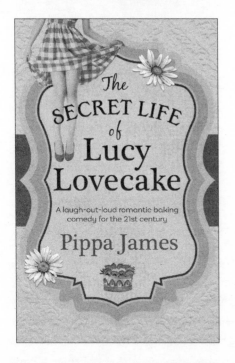

JANEY JONES is a full-time writer with a love for food, fashion and all things French and Italian. She is the author of the fantastically successful Princess Poppy series, with global sales of over 7 million copies. Before Princess Poppy took over her life, Janey had always intended to write contemporary fiction, and *Perfume Paradiso* is her second novel after the very popular *Secret Life of Lucy Lovecake* (written as Pippa James).